RAVE REVIEWS FOR CINDY HOLBY!

WIND OF THE WOLF

“A wonderful story! It captured my attention, pulled me in and made me feel like I was there with the characters.”

—*Old Book Barn Gazette*

“Cindy Holby displays her talent with an insightful look at tragedy.”

—*Midwest Book Review*

CHASE THE WIND

“Cindy Holby takes us on an incredible journey of love, betrayal, and the will to survive. Ms. Holby is definitely a star on the rise!”

—*The Best Reviews*

“*Chase the Wind* is like no other book you'll read, and you owe it to yourself to experience it.”

—EscapetoRomance.com

“Cindy Holby proves she is quite talented with an enjoyable saga that fans will relish.”

—*Midwest Book Review*

“A novel filled with warmth and love.”

—*Old Book Barn Gazette*

“An enthral[...] book.”

—*[...]ll About Romance*

ETERNAL EMBRACE

"I think that as long as I have you by my side, anything is possible." His lips lowered to hers and once again she felt the familiar thrill of being swept away on the tide of his love for her. Their bodies molded together in the dance that was as much a part of them as breathing, but yet still felt new, exciting, and perfect. Each touch, each sigh became an extension of each other as they melded into one being with one spirit and one purpose. The big bed in the small cabin was the center of their universe, and they were the moon and stars all coming together in one special moment that would last for all eternity.

Other *Leisure* books by Cindy Holby:

WIND OF THE WOLF
CHASE THE WIND

Crosswinds

CINDY HOLBY

LEISURE BOOKS  NEW YORK CITY

For Uncle Bob and Aunt Shirley

A LEISURE BOOK®

February 2004

Published by

Dorchester Publishing Co., Inc.
200 Madison Avenue
New York, NY 10016

ISBN 0-8439-5279-2

Printed in the United States of America.

ACKNOWLEDGMENTS

Thanks to the 2003 Viking Baseball Team who fought a good fight and showed us the meaning of teamwork. And to my girlfriends, who keep me humble: Brenda, Debbie, Katrina, Lori, Mary Kay, Robin and Susan.

Crosswinds

Chapter One

Catherine Lynch Kincaid could not believe how warm it was for late fall, but then again she was accustomed to spending her falls in the foothills of Wyoming. By this time of year the ground would be frozen solid and there would be the promise of heavy snow in the stiff winter wind swirling down from the majestic mountain peaks that lay beyond the gentle valley where she had spent her childhood. Instead of wrapping up in a heavy coat and stomping down to Grace's cozy cabin to enjoy a meal with her friends who lived and worked on the ranch, she was now dreading the prospect of another dinner in the stiffly formal dining room of the big plantation house that had been home to her husband's family for several generations.

Cat stopped by the trough stationed before the cluster of buildings that housed the working area of the plantation and dipped her kerchief in. Gratefully, she wiped away the sweat that had gathered around her collar as she had ridden around the land that her husband, Tyler Kincaid called home. Several of the slaves working nearby smiled at her as she sighed in relief when the cool water trickled down her neck. One of several children ran up with a half-full dipper of water and she drank deeply of the pure sweet well water and returned the vessel to the helpful little girl with a smile. Cat watched her go and then smoothed back the golden-brown curls that had escaped from the piece of rawhide holding it away from her heart-shaped face. She knew without a doubt that there would be frowns all around at her state of dishevelment. Cat's slanted green-gold eyes crinkled with a smile as she thought of carrying on her masquerade. She enjoyed acting the uncultured hoodlum for Ty's always proper family. Ty would frown at her escapades if he were there, but he wasn't and tormenting his brother and sister-in-law was her only relief from the boredom that consumed her days. Ty was off having wartime adventures with Jake and Caleb, friends and coworkers from her father's ranch who had enlisted along with him to fight in the War Between the States. The fact that Ty knew the surrounding land like the back of his hand after years of hunting and boyish exploration had kept him from being mustered into the general army. Instead he had been given a small command of his own and was involved in scouting the Blue Ridge for enemy activity and getting supplies to the troops.

Cat surveyed the well-manicured lawns and gardens that surrounded the many buildings making up the business end of the plantation. It was like a village with its orderly rows of white-washed slave cabins and neatly painted outbuildings. It was certainly different from what she was used to. She had traveled widely in her young life, spending many a season in New York with her aunt, and going abroad to Europe. But now she knew that she preferred the wide open spaces of the rolling prairie to the dense foliage and fields of crops that comprised the North Carolina countryside.

She wondered briefly where Zeb was. The huge slave usually met her in the yard to take care of her horse when she got back from her daily rides, but today he was nowhere to be found, and she had unsaddled the fine chestnut mare herself. Not that it was any great task for her since she had grown up on a ranch and was used to caring for horses, but she didn't want to get Zeb into trouble. She had come across Thompson, the plantation overseer, administering punishment in the fields a few times, and it had made her very uncomfortable. She had never thought about slavery much before since it had not been a part of her life, but now that she had seen it in action, she realized that she hated it. She also hated the fact that since she had married Ty last winter, she now owned slaves. She wished again that her father was close so she could talk to him about it, but Jason Lynch was back in Wyoming with his newfound granddaughter Jenny and his great-grandson Chance.

Cat felt the familiar ache go through her again at the thought of the baby boy who'd been born to Jenny and her husband Chase. She had hoped and prayed after Ty's last trip home that she would become pregnant, but once again she had been denied. *I'll make sure it happens the next time he's home, even if I have to keep him in bed the entire time.* Cat laughed out loud as she made her way to the big house. Actually that wouldn't be any chore at all, she decided as she pictured her handsome husband in her mind. The look of shock that would land on her prudish sister-in-law's face would make it twice as enjoyable, if that was possible. Parker, Ty's older brother by seven years, would disapprove and Ty's widowed mother Penelope would just ignore it, as she did everything that was unpleasant. Cat decided that the project was worth considering and became so engrossed in her musings that she ran right into the huge wall that was Zeb.

"Excuse me, Miz Catherine," the tall, broad slave mumbled with his head down.

"It's alright, Zeb. It was my fault. I wasn't paying any attention to where I was going." Cat looked up with a smile but all she could see was the close-cropped tight curls on top of his head and the wide flare of his nose as he kept his head bent in submission. She reached out to lay her hand on his arm as a gentle assurance and was amazed when he flinched from her touch. Cat quickly withdrew her hand. "Would you mind checking on Scarlet for me? She was favoring her left foreleg when we came in. I checked to make sure she hadn't picked up a stone, but she might have strained something on that last jump we made."

A brief glimpse of a smile flashed around his cheeks as he nodded. "I'll be sure to do that, Miz Catherine." Her uninhibited style of riding had become popular talk for the slaves on the plantation.

"Thank you, Zeb." Cat turned to watch him as he went off to the barn.

Every time she saw him she thought of Jamie, Jenny's twin brother. They were of much the same height but Zeb was even broader than Jamie had been. Her heart still grieved whenever Jamie entered her mind and she thought of his tragic death on his wedding day as he sacrificed his life to save his sister and the man she had married, his blood brother Chase the Wind. Jamie had filled his part of the world with joy and Cat was still angry that he had been taken from them so soon. He had been her nephew and she hadn't even known it, none of them had until the birth of baby Chance this past July and the discovery of Jamie and Jenny's mother's parentage in the Bible that Jenny kept on her nightstand.

Cat dashed away the tears that had gathered at the corners of her eyes. She wished again that the anger and frustration they had all felt at Jamie's death would go away, but it hadn't. It was something they just had to live with. Good people died needlessly every day, probably more so now with war consuming the country.

"God, please spare us from more death," Cat prayed. She looked up at the big house that lay before her and decided she wasn't ready yet for the stifling heat and formality inside. She turned left and made her way into the tall hedged formal garden that lay off to the side.

As she entered the arched gate between the hedges, Cat was once again impressed by the neat beds that had been placed within the boundaries. A few summer flowers remained, most of them leggy but still colorful with the late growing season. Cat wandered the neat gravel paths as she prayed for a wall of protection around Ty, Caleb and Jake. A flash of color amid the rich hues of green caught her eye, and she spotted the swish of Lucy Ann's skirt as she came out of the small secluded arbor in the corner of the hedges and made her way to the house. Cat was grateful that Lucy Ann hadn't noticed her; the last thing she wanted right now was to engage in addle-brained conversation with her self-absorbed sister-in-law.

"Ty . . ." Cat sighed when Lucy Ann was gone. Was there a more proud, stubborn, idealistic, caring, handsome man on this earth? From the first time she had laid eyes on Tyler Kincaid, she had wanted him. The day he had walked into her father's office at their house in Wyoming and asked for a job had been the day her young and previously frivolous life changed. Ty's grandfather and Jason Lynch had been best friends in law school. Ty had planned on going to law school himself, but nearly killing his brother in a fight over the treatment of slaves had quickly changed his plans. He had left home and gone west to seek his own destiny, but the threat of war had brought him home again. Now he was back fighting for the land that legally belonged to his brother. And when you got down to it, he wasn't even fighting for the land; he was fighting for the principle of being allowed to live his life as he saw fit, without the interference of government. Cat's mind began to chase the never-ending circles of the dilemma of her life. She was living a way of life of which she didn't approve, under the roof of a brother that her husband had almost killed while that same husband was off fighting a war so the brother could stay home and take care of business. It didn't make sense at all, but at least their friend Zane would get a good laugh out of it, if he hadn't already. Cat could almost see the hazel eyes of the ranch hand dancing with joy as he teased Ty without mercy while they sat around the scarred wooden table in Grace's cabin.

The warm breeze carried the mouthwatering scents of another opulent dinner, and the responding growl of her stomach brought Cat's wandering mind back to the present. Should she dress up for dinner in one of the beautiful gowns she owned, or make an appearance in her "awful ranch-wear," as Lucy Ann called it? Cat dusted the sides of her well-worn pants. They should still be clean enough to grace the delicately upholstered chairs in the dining room. Her green-gold cat's eyes crinkled into a grin as she made her way into the house.

Chapter Two

Tyler Kincaid shielded his blue eyes against the bright sunlight of midday as he came out of the natural cave buried deep in the mountains of western Virginia. Funny how his present circumstances didn't fit the image he had held in his mind when he had decided to come back and fight in this war. Of course they all had their roles to fill, but he had hoped for something a bit more satisfying than sneaking around the Blue Ridge with a small troop of men. They had a purpose, watching for enemy movement, making sure the gunpowder that was made and stored in the caves remained safe, and helping to safeguard the shipments of gunpowder as they traveled down the mountains toward the coast. But so far his experience as an officer in the Confederate army had been pretty boring. Jake had taken special care to point that out many times.

Ty shook the dust off his hat and shoved back the locks of sandy-brown hair that hung in waves to his shoulders. An image of Jamie flashed through his mind as his fingers ran through hair that was in sore need of a washing. Jamie's hair had always fallen into his eyes whenever he took his hat off. But Jamie was dead now. Ty placed his hat firmly on his head and after taking a firm hold on the sword that hung in a scabbard at his side, made his way through the throng of soldiers and miners to where his small troop was waiting. He still wasn't used to the trappings of an officer but had decided that the sword might possibly come in handy at some time or another and had kept it.

Jake was leaning casually against a tree, polishing one of the pearl-handled revolvers that he wore on each hip. His light blue eyes took on a dangerous glint as he sighted down the barrel. "Boom," he said with a mischievous wink to Willie, who just happened to be in his line of fire. Ty watched as the scrawny farm boy moved out of the way. The boy was terrified of Jake, who hadn't done anything to deserve it, other than show off his prowess with his guns a few times. Caleb managed to suppress a grin but ruffled the boy's stringy hair as he walked by.

"We've got to get that boy a decent coat before winter sets in," Ty said as he joined Caleb.

Caleb's warm dark brown eyes followed Willie as he made his way toward the horses. "Better find him a pair of boots, too. The ones he's wearing don't look like they'll make it through the week, much less the winter."

"Best put in an order with Mr. Bishop then."

"Mr. Bishop?"

"The trader. We're taking him down the mountain.

Apparently he wanted to see our little operation up here and make sure that we really could supply the gunpowder. He'll be making the run between Wilmington and New Orleans and has agreed to bring us back any incidentals that we can think of."

"By that do you mean the necessities not provided by enlistment in the army of the Confederate States of America?"

"Something along those lines." Ty flashed a rare smile. "Why don't you make an outline of Willie's foot and then add a few inches. As gangly as he looks, he's bound to grow some more."

"Yes sir." Caleb threw up a mock salute along with a cheeky grin and took off after Willie. Ty's eyes wandered over the rest of his troop. His mind raced as he took careful inventory of the twenty men who were his responsibility. What else did they need to make it through the winter that was yet to arrive? They were for the most part local men of various ages, who knew this part of the Blue Ridge like the back of their hands and could easily go home if and when the need arose. Willie was an orphan who had been pawned off on Ty when he had reported for duty in Raleigh and been made a captain in the Confederate army.

"What do we do now?" Jake asked as he joined Ty.

"We're to escort Mr. Bishop back down the mountain."

"Don't reckon we'll run across any Yankees on the way."

"Your guess is as good as mine, Jake."

"This is the boringest war I've ever heard of." Jake, as usual, was desperate for action of any kind.

"I'm sure the boys up at Rich Mountain and Manassas would have something to say about that." They had arrived in North Carolina too late for those victories, and Ty was getting tired of Jake's constant complaining.

"Probably so, but at least they got something to write home about." Jake stalked off.

"Jake!" Jake stopped and turned, waiting for his commander to speak. "Get them together. We're moving out in ten minutes."

"Yes, sir." Jake whistled and swung his arm over his head in a small circle. The men started to gather around the horses. They might not be much to look at, but they were ready. Ty went off to collect Mr. Bishop.

There was a letter waiting for her on the silver tray that graced the fine mahogany table in the foyer. Cat snatched it up and recognized the fine swooping handwriting of her father. The elderly butler, Silas, smiled behind his white-gloved hand as Cat let out a whoop and stomped up the stairs to Ty's bedroom. The loud slamming of the door finalized her assault on the elegant curving staircase and then the only sounds that marred the silence were the ticking of the huge grandfather clock and the clink of the fine silver as the table was set. Silas resumed his dusting and hoped the letter contained good news for Miss Catherine.

Cat bounced across the mattress as she hastily tore open the envelope. Would it be too much to hope that it would contain a likeness of baby Chance? She wished again that Caleb, as dearly as she loved having him close, had stayed in Wyoming just so he could send her a drawing of the baby.

Her eyes quickly scanned the opening paragraphs of the letter. Jason was amazed at how quickly Zane had settled down and taken over the day-to-day running of the ranch. Before he had been such a cutup but he had stepped up when needed and taken over when Ty had left. Cole was a big help, too, and the romance between the former Texas Ranger and Grace was deepening. Cat was happy for Grace, the elegant woman with the scarred face who had gently guided her into womanhood, but wondered if her father perhaps might be a bit jealous. "You had your chance, Daddy. You should have taken it."

The new hands, Dan and Randy, were getting along fine, although they had a tendency to waste time picking on each other and bragging about how good they were instead of getting any actual work done. Cat laughed as memories of Zane picking on Jamie and Ty washed over her. Nothing had changed at home except for the cast of characters.

Chase was back to his old self, but there were times when it scared Jason to look into his eyes. They still didn't know what had happened between him and Logan, the man who had murdered Jamie, and probably never would. The letter went on to talk about Jenny and how baby Chance had helped to heal her broken heart. She was laughing again and working with the horses, but taking care of two babies was wearing her out.

"Wait a minute, *two* babies?" Cat scanned the last paragraph to see what she had missed.

Yes, daughter, I said two babies. Chase and Jenny now have another son, James Ian Duncan Junior, whom Chase calls Fox. He is the image of his father. We were all surprised when Sarah's father showed up with the newborn child in his arms and handed him to Jenny. The child was half starved and dripping wet but otherwise healthy with a good appetite, just like his father. Sarah died right after he was born, but not before asking her father to take the babe to Jenny. So now I spend my evenings sitting before the fire with a baby in each arm. The only dilemma I have is how I can hold three, for I know it won't be long before you present me with a grandchild also.

Cat held the letter to her breast as a sob caught in her throat. Jamie had a son. The sudden miracle that had come into their lives took her breath away, and there was no one with whom to share it. She walked to the window that overlooked the west. It would be cause for a celebration when Ty, Caleb and Jake came home. But when would that be?

Chapter Three

"It sure is hot."

Ty looked back at the soldier who had made the comment. The small band had just forded the New River and would begin the last part of the mountain descent that would bring them out of Virginia and into North Carolina. The men who traveled with him would peel off, one by one, making their way to their own homes which were buried deep within the safety of the foothills. By mutual agreement one of them would take Willie and take care of him until they met again a few days hence with new orders. Ty, Caleb and Jake, along with Mr. Bishop, would ride on to Ty's home, located on the Yadkin River in northwestern North Carolina.

It was hot. Ty took the time to wipe the sweat from his forehead before he replaced his hat. At least it would be good for the tobacco harvest. Lots of time for the leaves to cure. Of course, that wouldn't do the planters much good if they couldn't get the tobacco to market. The South had relied too long on foreign buyers. Parker seemed confident that they would continue to do business as usual. Ty wasn't so sure. At least the long growing season would give the family plenty of time to put up stores for the winter. Ty had a feeling that when the season arrived, it was going to be a long one, although not as harsh as the winters in the wilds of Wyoming.

Nothing like last winter . . . Ty's horse picked its way up the river trail toward the rolling valleys that made up this part of Virginia. He felt more exposed here. All it would take was one well-placed cannon and whoever rode through this valley would be dead in an instant. Ty rode on, his eyes constantly scanning the gently sloping hillsides while his mind wandered to last winter.

They had all been in Wyoming then, buried hip-deep in snow and wind that never stopped; all of them watching and waiting for Chase, who had taken off in pursuit of Jamie's killer. When he thought about it, there wasn't much difference between this winter and last. Even though he had committed himself to fighting in this war, he was still in a state of limbo, doing nothing more than watching and waiting. And to make matters worse, he had dragged Cat, Caleb and Jake across the country with him.

Ty rolled his shoulders back to relieve some of the tension that always seemed to gather there. He felt as if someone was watching him, waiting for him to make a mistake, waiting for him to fail. Just as his father had watched and waited. He couldn't allow that to happen. Failure meant death to those that rode with him; failure meant Cat would go home a widow with nothing but misery to show for her love and belief in him. He could not fail.

The trail widened out a bit and Caleb and Jake pulled up alongside Ty. "That thing sure does make a lot of noise." Jake inclined his head toward the cavalry sword that hung from Ty's saddle. "You take that thing back home with you, and it will spook every cow for miles around."

"Yeah, but it has some other benefits that make it worth keeping." Ty was glad for the distraction. At times the responsibility of other lives tied his insides into knots. "I can lop Zane's head off whenever he gets mouthy."

Caleb laughed. "It's been so long since I've heard his mouth that I'm beginning to think I miss him."

"You must be suffering from battle fatigue, son," Jake said, snorting. They rode for a while in silence, each caught up in memories of home. "Going to be dark soon," Jake added after a while.

"I was hoping we'd make it home by tonight," Caleb added.

"Not enough daylight this time of year." Ty had hoped for the same thing.

"How long is this Mr. Bishop going to be hanging around?"

"Just one night, Jake. He's going on to Raleigh and then to the coast."

"I don't like him," Jake began.

"You don't like anyone, Jake," Caleb interrupted.

"That's not true, Caleb. I like you. After all, you're pretty enough to be a girl and the pickin's have been kind of slim lately."

Ty looked at the shaggy length of dark hair that surrounded Caleb's handsome face and gentle eyes. "Remind me to sleep with one eye open from now on," Caleb said to Ty who laughed at the bantering as Jake continued.

"There's something sneaky about him. And I don't like his eyes." Jake glanced back the few paces where Mr. Bishop rode and noticed their new companion taking careful note of the territory. "It's almost as if he's looking for something or someone."

"And we did show him one of our best-kept secrets," Caleb added.

"No, he *thinks* we showed him one of our best-kept secrets. He has no way of knowing that we use that cave for storage only," Ty said as he considered their remarks. "We will keep an eye on him." Jake smiled grimly from his saddle. "But that doesn't mean you can go around breathing down his neck."

"Yes, sir. He won't even know I'm around." The pale blue eyes were as cold as a frozen lake as Jake pulled his horse up and fell back to ride alongside Mr. Bishop.

"He's just itching to kill someone," Caleb commented. "Or get himself killed." Ty and Caleb rode on in companionable silence, accustomed to each other's company after working together for several years. Behind them the troop began to peel off, some alone, others in pairs, making their way to their own small farms planted in the foothills along the border between the two states. The remaining four made their way down a long sloping curve and suddenly a valley opened up to their left, looking south and east into the Piedmont of North Carolina. In the distance a strange rounded peak shot up from the landscape, rocky on the sides but covered on top with trees. Beyond that was another set of mountains, silent sentinels left from a time before memory.

"There's the Pilot." Caleb pointed out the strange geological formation to Mr. Bishop.

"*Jomeokee.*" Ty added the Saura Tribe word for the mountain. "And beyond that is home." Only now would he let himself think of Cat waiting there for him. He hoped she hadn't caused too much trouble while he was gone.

"Miz Catrin, Miz Catrin, Mister Ty done come home!" Cat stuck her head out the window of her room to see a gang of children from the slave quarters jumping about and pointing at a cloud of dust that was quickly making its way up the long drive.

"Lord, we need some rain," Cat commented to the mirror as she quickly checked her appearance. No time to change into a dress. If she had her way, she'd not be wearing anything very soon anyway. She flew out of her room and straight into the back of Lucy Ann's wide skirts as her sister-in-law made an appearance on the staircase.

"It's Mister Ty, Miss Penelope," Silas said to Ty's mother as he stood in the open doorway with a wide smile on his dark face. "Mister Caleb and Mister Jake, too, and somebody else—I don'ts know who."

Cat took one look at the elegantly curving staircase, which was blocked from banister to wallboard with hoops. Cat had no use for hoops and refused to wear them. There was no way she was going to mince quietly along behind Lucy Ann, who loved to make an appearance each time she entered a room. She hopped on the polished banister rail and proceeded to slide down backward, picking up speed as she came through the curve. She saw Lucy Ann's mouth open in shock as she sped by, the sky-blue eyes wide between the huge sausage curls that were artfully arranged on either side of her porcelain-fine face. The banister ended in a graceful downward swoop, but not her descent.

Cat felt herself flying through the air and then the impact as she tumbled against Parker, who had the misfortune to enter the foyer from his study at the exact same moment that Cat ran out of banister. She managed to untangle herself from his flailing limbs before Lucy Ann had a chance to smother her with her skirts and propelled herself as if shot from a cannon through the still-open door, which was shaking slightly with the effort Silas was exerting to control his laughter. She hit Ty's chest at the exact moment that his foot hit the ground and only the sturdy weight of his horse behind him kept them both from landing in the dust.

"You're so thin." Those were the only words she could think of as she buried her head under the scruffy growth of beard.

"Hopefully some of Portia's good cooking will take care of that." Ty placed a slightly grimy finger under Cat's chin and lifted her face for a kiss. She smoothed the unkempt locks of his sandy-brown hair back and cursed the world again for bringing her wonderful husband to this sad state of affairs. At least he was home, for the moment.

"Hello, Cat." Jake, still in his saddle, grinned through his pale blond beard. "Glad to see you, too." Caleb chuckled in agreement and scratched several days' worth of growth on his chin.

"Baths for everyone, Silas. We're not fit company for anyone until then." Ty swung his arm around Cat's shoulder and waved toward the stranger with his other one. "This is Mr. Bishop. He'll be spending the night."

Ty and Cat managed to make it through the front door together, which was no easy feat since Cat had both of her arms wrapped tightly around his waist. Parker was sitting on the floor, both legs spread out in a less than elegant pose as he leaned his back against the wall. Lucy Ann was alternating between fanning him with her embroidered linen hankie and blotting the trickle of blood that oozed from a small cut on his forehead.

"Gee, Parker, what happened to you?" Ty asked as he surveyed the disgruntled face of his older brother.

"Your wife practically killed him." Lucy Ann's deep southern drawl drew out every syllable of her tirade. "She slid down the banister like an unwashed heathen."

Jake and Caleb punched each other as they swallowed back the laughter that was threatening to overcome them. Silas managed to keep a polite smile on his face as the stranger, Mr. Bishop, blinked in disbelief.

"Right now the only unwashed are the four of us.

Bishop, this is my brother, Parker, and his wife, Lucy Ann. Oh and my mother, Mrs. Penelope Kincaid." Ty completed the introductions as Penelope came sweeping into the foyer, carrying a tray full of remedies for Parker.

"Wade Bishop. Charmed to meet all of you." Mr. Bishop's accent rivaled Lucy Ann's as he bowed and nodded with a dazzling smile beneath a clipped mustache. Penelope had knelt to blot Parker's cut with a towel dipped in water but politely stood and let Mr. Bishop take her hand in greeting.

"Sorry about that, Parker. I guess I was just so excited to see Ty that I just wasn't thinking," Cat apologized from the safety of Ty's side as Parker managed to stand with the help of Lucy Ann and Silas.

"I've had baths sent up to each of your rooms." Penelope was always the perfect hostess, even to the point that she set aside her own excitement at the safe homecoming of her younger son. "Dinner will be ready at the usual time."

"Thank you, Mother. A bath and dinner are just what we all need." Jake and Caleb voiced their agreement as they headed for the stairs.

The ever-suffering Lucy Ann covered her nose with her blood-stained linen hankie as the dusty and travel-worn group made its way up the stairs. The stranger, Mr. Bishop, followed along with his dark eyes taking careful consideration of Cat, who had eyes only for her husband.

Finally. Cat shut the door firmly behind the last slave carrying away the last emptied bucket of hot water.

Ty was chest deep, soaking in a huge porcelain tub that had been carried up from below. His razor, strop and mirror lay on a small table next to the tub, along with a bar of lightly scented soap.

Cat frowned as she saw how tightly his muscles lay across the shoulders of his golden-tanned skin. Was it her imagination, or were the blades protruding more? She had noticed the definition of his ribs behind the firm muscles of his abdomen as he had gratefully sunk into the tub. Cat took the bar of soap into her hands and began to lather his back, starting with his neck and working her way down his spine. Ty sighed and leaned forward to give her better access to the lower muscles of his back as she worked away some of the tension of leadership and responsibility.

"Who is this Mr. Bishop?" she asked, mostly to make conversation.

"He's a trader, or a smuggler, depends on what side of the line you're standing on."

"Oh, so he's helping with the supply lines."

"Helping himself mostly, but he does have his sources, and we need what he can provide."

"Such as?" Cat had finished with his back and moved the soap around to the crisp golden hair on his chest.

"Weapons, hmmm, shot, oh that feels good." The soap trailed across his stomach as Ty leaned back. "Shoes . . ."

"Shoes?" The soap slipped out of her grasp and plopped into the tub.

"Yes, shoes. Some of these boys barely have enough clothes to cover their backs, and winter will be here, sooner or later, especially in the mountains of Virginia." Cat made a mental note to ask her father to send new pairs of boots for Ty, Caleb and Jake.

"Oh, my goodness, I almost forgot, I got a letter from Daddy. You won't believe what's happened."

Ty had found the soap and was lathering his face and hair. He managed to get one steel-blue eye open to see Cat's face as she knelt beside the tub.

"Grace and Cole got married?"

Cat grinned with her secret. "Nope. Better than that."

Ty picked up the razor and mirror and raised an eyebrow at Cat. "Are you going to tell me now, or wait until I'm shaving and risk cutting my throat?"

"Jamie has a son."

"What?" Cat went to get the letter while Ty looked at her with his mouth hanging open.

"Sarah was pregnant when they got married. She died giving birth and her father brought the baby to Jenny. His name is James Ian Duncan Junior but they're calling him Fox," she explained all in one breath as she handed the letter to Ty.

"Chase always said Jamie grinned like a fox." Ty skimmed the letter as he spoke, knowing he'd take time to read it later. "It's wonderful, especially for Jenny. But can you imagine having two babies to take care of?"

"It's not any more than what her parents did." Cat was suddenly quiet. She couldn't believe how much it hurt sometimes to think about her own childless state.

"Just wait until the boys hear about this." Ty resumed his shaving.

"Don't tell them in front of everyone else. I don't want to have to explain about Jamie."

Ty stopped again and looked at the sweet heart-shaped face of his wife. So much had happened to all of them and still here she was, clear across the country from everyone she knew and loved. Her own family had more than doubled since she had left Wyoming, and yet she had stayed, patiently waiting for the few days he could give her every few months. And it would only get worse. The Southern cause had experienced some great victories, but Ty knew they were in for a long haul. Winter would soon be upon them and though the South had plenty of grit, the North had many more resources and many more men to send into battle. He didn't know what the future held for any of them; all he could do was appreciate the day that was before him.

She had to be lonely. "Don't worry; we'll make time, just the four of us."

Cat smiled at her handsome husband. The line of his jaw had reappeared, his sensuous lips were apparent again. "Are you about done?" A delicate finger trailed a lock of hair behind his ear.

Ty hastily lathered the soap. "Just about." He reached for a foot and began scrubbing. Thank God Cat had quit helping him or the upcoming physical reunion would be short lived.

A dense fog cluttered his mind as Cat turned from the tub and began unbuttoning her shirt. *Nope, that wasn't helping at all.* She moved away from him toward the bed at a slow pace, humming a tune as the shirt slipped from her shoulders and down her arms. The soap slipped from his grasp again, and he groaned when her pants began a slow, sensual descent over the gentle curve of her hips. If she was trying to arouse him, then she had definitely succeeded. The proof of it was very obvious, not that he needed any help getting that way. Just being in her presence after their long separation was enough to have him sniffing after her as if he were a stud and she a fine mare. A few misses as he searched beneath the water and the soap was finally back in place. He quickly slid it over his calves and up his thighs, bringing a sharp gasp to his lips as he touched a sensitive spot with the bar.

"Did you say something?" Cat asked innocently, shaking her golden-brown curls loose from the rawhide thong that had held the heavy mass neatly in place.

Ty swallowed and ground his teeth together. The late-afternoon sun shone behind her through the wide double window that was open to catch whatever breeze was available in the still-warm day. The light linen camisole and petticoat she wore turned translucent in the light, catching her curves and shadows and a slight darkening at the top of her legs as she turned to pick up her brush.

Cat heard a sudden rush of water behind her as Ty stood in the tub. She turned with brush in hand and gasped as the sunlight on his lean frame turned his body golden and glistening with the fine sheen of water that still covered his skin. His desire for her was obvious, and his gaze intense as the steel blue of his eyes settled on her, burning into her with a purpose, making her legs feel weak beneath her.

Ty reached for the towel that had been placed on a chair and blotted it across his chest as he stepped from the tub. He rubbed it down his hips, swiped it across his back and dropped it on the floor as Cat moved toward him, her heart beating hard in her chest, the blood pounding in her ears. She was in his arms, her skin soaking up his dampness, her fingers twining in the sandy-brown of his hair that now trailed in waves down to his shoulders.

"Ty, give me a baby, please."

His mouth trailed down her temple, tracing the delicate line of her jaw, capturing her full mouth as he lifted her into his arms. "I will, I will . . . Cat." She felt herself falling gently, slowly, onto the mattress. His face hovered over hers while the strength of his arms twined around her, capturing her hair, her back, her hips. His mouth was on hers, on her breasts, and she felt a burning urgency consuming her, and then the joining, filling her to the brim as the world exploded around her, and everything was gone except Cat and Ty and the fulfillment of being his wife.

Chapter Four

Ty and Cat had hoped to share the news from home with Caleb and Jake before dinner, but ended up making a late appearance in the elegantly appointed dining room. Cat had asked Ty to help her with the line of pearl buttons that ran up the back of her pale green satin dress, but he was more of a hindrance than a help, with hands that continually strayed from their assigned task. They finally made it down the stairs with Cat tying her curls up with a perky bow as they breathlessly rushed into the room. Lucy Ann sniffed her disapproval at their tardiness and frowned over Cat's fashion rebellion. Cat wondered, and not for the first time, if there was ever any intimacy between Parker and his wife. Probably not since they had been married for several years and still had not produced a child.

Not that she would be tempted by Parker. The well-lit room showed the thinning of his hair, which was even more obvious when compared to Ty's thick and lustrous crown. There was a resemblance between the two brothers, especially around the nose and eyes, but there was also a hint of shallow selfishness in Parker. Where Ty's eyes were strong and steady, Parker's blue eyes never settled on anyone; they were always shifting around. And his mouth always seemed to be held in a thin line, as if in disapproval. By contrast, the sensuous tilt of Ty's full lower lip constantly fascinated her. Her own lips felt swollen and bruised from the attention he had just given them.

Lucy Ann, on the other hand, was a complete enigma to Cat. Prim and proper, always immaculately groomed, not a hair out of place, she seemed the model of the perfect plantation mistress. Just the sight of her was enough to give Cat the urge to shove her in a puddle of mud. Her attention was drawn to Jake as he heaped a great helping of peas onto his plate, and Cat had a sudden flash of memory of her own dunking in a mud puddle, which had taken place just more than a year ago, thanks to the lean man with long blond hair who had followed her husband across the country.

"What are you laughing at?" Jake asked as he caught the sudden flash of her smile and the mischievous glint in her slanted green-gold eyes.

"Oh, I was just remembering the day that you threw Jenny and me in the mud."

Jake's pale blue eyes crinkled with a grin and Caleb laughed. "That was pretty funny."

"Oh, please tell us the story." Penelope, always the perfect hostess, showed great interest in the personalities that graced her table.

"It was raining, actually pouring, and we were all

down in Grace's cabin." The stranger, Mr. Bishop looked up from his plate with interest as Cat went on. "Jenny and I were baking cookies, and Jamie was trying to eat the dough . . ."

"Eating dough? That sounds positively disgusting," Lucy Ann commented.

"And who was Jamie?" Penelope asked.

"Jenny's brother. You remember, Mother," Ty quietly interjected.

"The one who was murdered on his wedding day?" Parker was not known for his tact.

Three of the four who had known and loved Jamie looked at their plates as they gathered their composure. Jake gave Parker one of his icy stares as Cat resumed her story.

"Anyway, we were playing around, and throwing the dough—"

"I wanted some, too," Ty explained.

"And Jake wound up with some on the back of his head." Jake sat back and crossed his arms, looking as if he was still annoyed at the memory of the sticky mess that had stuck in his hair. "Jenny and I decided to get out of his way—"

"Jake's not known for his tolerance or patience," Caleb volunteered.

"And I caught them and threw them in the mud."

"After we tripped you and you landed face first in the puddle."

"Just be glad it's not raining right now," Jake growled teasingly. Lucy Ann looked aghast at the conversation while Penelope politely tittered into her linen napkin.

"So Mr. Bishop, what part of our new country do you call home?" Penelope asked.

The dinner guest turned from his careful perusal of Cat's glowing face to look at his hostess. "New Orleans, ma'am. I'll be heading that way as soon as I can get to the coast," Mr. Bishop replied in his soft drawl.

"Oh, how lovely, I've always wanted to visit there." The conversation was now civil enough for Parker's wife.

"Mr. Kincaid and I went there, many years ago, of course. It's a beautiful city," Penelope added.

Cat's attention quickly went from the charms of New Orleans to the flush that was slowly creeping up Ty's neck, due most likely to the attention her satin slipper was giving his calf. They still had to sit through the rest of dinner, and then there would be an elaborate dessert, followed by brandy, cigars and talk of the war. Parker thought himself an authority on the politics of the war; after all, he had been one of the first in western North Carolina to rally for secession.

It would all be terribly boring and a waste of time as far as Cat was concerned. There were more important things to talk about, like having babies. Not that she planned on doing much talking, actually. Ty suddenly had a coughing fit as her now shoeless foot found its way to his thigh. Cat smiled sweetly and rubbed his back as Caleb hastily reached for his own drink.

"My goodness, Tyler. Has living in the wilds made you unaccustomed to fine dining already?" Lucy Ann felt it was her mission in life to educate people on their manners.

"A lot of the soldiers are already going hungry, Lucy Ann. Most of them have never even seen a table set with such excess." Ty waved his hand toward the sideboard, where a quiet servant waited to refill their plates.

"Tyler." Penelope cast a glance toward Mr. Bishop in distress. Now was not the time to air their family's dirty laundry.

"Most of them are going hungry because they can't stand Jake's cooking." Caleb, always watching, gracefully saved the conversation.

"Well, I'm sure dear Mr. Bishop will bring plenty of supplies for our brave soldiers when he returns. Isn't that right, Mr. Bishop?" Lucy Ann batted her pale eyelashes at their guest and graced him with a smile. Cat decided if she heard any more of Lucy Ann's simpering drawl, she would slap her.

Penelope rose from the table, signaling the end of dinner. She took Mr. Bishop's arm and departed, followed by Parker and Lucy Ann as they made their way to the parlor. A look from Ty held Jake and Caleb back and they both smiled when Ty handed Caleb the letter from home. Caleb began reading while Jake, whom Jamie had taught to read just last year, looked over his shoulder. "Dang," Caleb said with a huge grin.

"What?" Jake asked.

"Keep reading." The grins of the others were infectious. Jake shook his head and went back to the paper, taking it from Caleb's hands. The three of them watched as his eyes widened in disbelief and he reread the paragraph about Jamie's baby.

"Dang." Jake looked up with his own watery smile. "Getting kind of crowded back home."

"Probably noisy, too," Caleb added and dashed at the corner of his eye.

"Eats just like Jamie, it says."

"Wish I could see that." Ty squeezed Cat against his side as Jake and Caleb continued talking about Jamie's baby. It was bittersweet for her. Cat was thrilled that a part of Jamie would live on in his son, but also sad that she had yet to become pregnant. Penelope stepped into the hallway, summoning them to the parlor in her own gentle way.

"Let's go to bed early tonight," Ty whispered against Cat's forehead as they made their way to the parlor. "I suddenly feel very tired."

Late morning found Cat still lingering in the four poster bed that had been Ty's since early childhood. She lazily stretched as the bright rays of sunlight tiptoed through the open window and danced across the rumpled sheets. Cat sighed in contentment as she remembered the night just spent. Their loving had left her breathless and she had bit Ty's shoulder to keep from screaming as he brought her again and again to the heights of passion. Surely after last night she would be with child. Her hands caressed the flat planes of her smooth abdomen as she imagined it swelling with a healthy baby and envisioned a birth sometime next summer. The urge to relieve herself soon overcame her fantasy and she regretfully made her way to the chamber pot just as Ty came bursting through the door.

"I thought you were going to sleep all day."

"I could be persuaded to go back to bed if I had some company," she tossed over the privacy screen as she went about her business.

"Tempting, but I've got a better idea." Cat looked at him as if he had lost his mind. What could possibly be better than what she had just offered? "Portia's packed us a picnic."

"I thought you had to take Mr. Bishop into Salem."

"Jake and Caleb are going to do it. As a matter of fact, they've already left. Parker and I went over the books while you were sleeping and you, dear wife, will have my undivided attention for the next twenty-four hours."

Cat threw herself in his arms with a squeal of delight, her hastily donned robe falling open as she did so. Ty took advantage of the situation and ran his hands down the curve of her back as she giddily swung against him. "Hurry up and get dressed," he said against her ear. "Or we won't make it out of this room today." He planted a kiss that left her breathless and then was gone before she had a chance to protest.

She caught up with Ty in the stable some ten minutes later, finding him deep in conversation with Zeb. It amazed her to hear the steady cadence of words coming from the slave as the dark head bent next to the golden one. She had barely heard more than three words at a time come out of his mouth. The flow ceased, however, when she came into the cool dimness of the neat interior and Zeb went back to saddling her horse.

"What were you and Zeb talking about?" Cat asked when they were on their way.

"Everyday things mostly. I just wanted to see how he was doing."

"He's pretty quiet around me."

"He didn't used to be that way. That's why I was talking to him; I was trying to figure out what was wrong with him."

"You mean besides the fact that he's a slave?"

"Cat, it's just the way things are. If he wasn't our slave, he would be someone else's. At least he's been able to stay on the place where he was born and he is still with his family. Zeb and I were raised together. Portia was more of a mother to me when I was little than my own mother. She was the one who took care of my skinned knees and wiped my nose."

"It sounds like you're closer to Zeb than you are to Parker."

Images from his childhood flashed through his mind: running through the fields, climbing trees, swimming in the Yadkin, stealing cookies from the kitchen, all of it done with Zeb at his side until the young slave have been deemed old enough to earn his keep and was put to work in the stables. "In a lot of ways I am." His father had not approved of his relationship with Zeb or anything else in his life for that matter.

"But would you let someone make a slave out of Parker?"

Ty sighed. "What do you suggest I do? Free all our

slaves? Then what would they do? It would break Portia's heart if I told her she had to go. Silas, too."

"You could free them and pay them wages."

"They are paid, in a way. They have a home, they get doctoring when they need it and they have food." He had explained it to her many times, but it was as if she didn't understand.

"They also get beaten with a whip when they don't work fast enough to suit Thompson."

"You've seen that?" Ty had hoped that she would be spared that aspect of plantation life.

"Yes, out in the fields. I was out riding and came across him administering punishment as he called it. It was horrible."

"I'm sorry you had to see that, Cat."

"Why can't you stop it?"

They were now in the deep woods that led to the river. The air was cooler here, the setting close and private among the tall scrappy pines and hardwoods of oak, poplar and maple. Leaves crunched under the horses' hooves as they progressed and the squirrels and chipmunks that had been disturbed in their work of autumn gathering scurried up tree trunks or into the dense growth of the mountain laurel. Ty didn't see any of it; his mind was focused on an incident that had happened several years earlier.

He had only been home a few weeks from his tour of Europe when Thompson accused one of the slaves of stealing a piece of Lucy Ann's jewelry. The man was one of the field hands, bought while Ty was away. He had no history of the man, no knowledge of his honesty and integrity as he did of Zeb or the others who had spent their lives on the Kincaid Plantation. He would never forget the sight of the strongly built man stretched between two posts, his muscular arms strung so tight that his toes barely touched the ground. The other slaves had been herded into the yard to watch, and the air was full of muffled sobs and groans as the first whiplash was landed.

The memory that would never leave him, however, was the look on Parker's face. It was the overseer's job to administer punishment, but Parker had decided to do it. He couldn't conceal his glee as he drew back the whip again and again. Lucy Ann was watching also, and Ty could have sworn that she was smiling behind the dainty white hankie that she held over her nose and mouth during the proceedings.

Something inside of him had snapped, and the next thing he knew the whip had gone sailing into the yard and he had Parker down on the ground and was pounding him with his fists. It had taken three men to pull him off and a bucket of water thrown into his face to bring him back to his senses. In the end it hadn't made a bit of a difference. Thompson had continued the lashing and Penelope had sent Ty away from his home in disgrace.

"Ty?" He hadn't even realized that he had stopped his horse until Cat placed her hand on his arm and looked up at him with eyes that reflected the deep green of the pines.

"I can't stop it, Cat. Don't you see? I tried and nothing came of it."

"Well, that's not exactly true." Ty looked at her quizzically. "Our marriage came of it." Cat smiled sweetly at the serious look that had settled on his handsome face. "Something good came out of the bad."

Ty took her hand in his and brought it to his lips. "Isn't it funny how fate steps in without our even knowing it?"

"It was meant to be. I knew it the first time I saw you."

"I guess it would have saved everyone a lot of trouble if I had known it, too."

"Oooh, you're asking for it now." Cat pulled her hand away and kicked her horse into a gallop. "You will pay for that," she threw over her shoulder as she disappeared down the trail.

Ty shook his head as he heard the hoofbeats fading away into the deep carpet of the woods. He'd better catch her before she got into trouble . . . again.

The lunch Portia had packed had been filling, a quick dip in the shallows of the Yadkin River had been refreshing and what followed had been most satisfying. Cat stretched and ran her toes up the bare calf that lay beside her. Ty was lying on his back with one arm crooked behind his head and the other around the petite form of his wife. His steel-blue eyes were squinting against the afternoon sun, giving him a stern look. Cat tickled the golden hairs on his chest with a blade of grass.

"You can beg me for forgiveness now," she said.

"I thought you were the one doing the begging." His skin jumped as the blade touched a sensitive area on his chest.

"No, no, that was you. I distinctly recall . . . oof." Her breath came out in a rush as Ty rolled over on top of her and pinned her arms over her head with one hand.

"You were saying?"

"You have to beg for forgiveness for that remark you made back in the woods." She was at his mercy now, and yet she expected him to beg.

"I do?" His fingers wound through her golden-brown curls.

"Yes."

"What if I don't want to?" Ty decided the side of her neck needed his immediate attention.

"Quit trying to distract me." Cat wiggled out from under him with the help of a well-placed knee. "You have to say you're sorry." Ty reached for her and she rolled off the blanket and to her feet. "Nope, you're not having your way with me until you apologize."

Ty lunged after her, and she danced away, leaving him grinning as he leered at her naked bottom. "We'll see," he promised, rising to his feet. Cat shrieked and ran to take cover behind a huge oak that grew on the bank of the river. Ty gave pursuit but pulled up suddenly when he noticed the vine growing up the side and the sets of three leaves that were still holding summer's green hue. *Leaves of three, let them be.*

"What?" Cat peered around the trunk of the tree. The front of her body was pressed against the trunk and a red-veined leaf tickled her cheek.

"I said we'd better get back. It looks like it might rain." Ty pointed off toward the west where dark clouds were starting to gather on the horizon. Cat followed his glance and decided he was right.

"Okay, but you still have to say you're sorry."

He took her hand and led her over to the pile of clothes. "I have a feeling you're going to be sorrier."

"And what exactly do you mean by that?"

"You'll see." Ty hid the grin that kept threatening to erupt by pulling his shirt on over his head. For once he was glad he was leaving, and the sooner the better, as far as he was concerned. Best warn Portia as soon as he got back. Life was sure to be miserable around the Kincaid plantation for the next few weeks.

Rain came that night and with it colder air and the promise that winter would indeed come. Ty rose with the dawn and gently kissed the tip of Cat's nose, which was the only place that had not broken out in angry red blisters. He considered himself a brave man, most of the time, but this was one situation in which it was better to run. Her sleep was restless; the itching had already set in and her hand went constantly to her face as she slumbered, oblivious to the sudden change in her appearance that exposure to the plant had brought on.

Jake and Caleb were mounted and waiting with rain running off their hat brims and down the backs of their long coats. "You sure you want to leave in this?" Jake asked as Ty swung up on his horse. "We don't have to meet the boys until day after tomorrow."

"Under the circumstances, it's best we move on out."

"What circumstances are you talking about?"

A wail sailed above the wind and rain, hanging in

the air for a moment before dying into a shriek of frustration. Jake and Caleb looked at Ty with eyes wide and curious.

"Cat met up with some poison ivy yesterday afternoon." Ty took off, his horse flinging muddy water behind him as he rode.

Caleb laughed. "We'd best make tracks while we can."

"That man's a born leader. He knows when to advance and when to retreat," Jake added as they took off down the drive.

Portia had everything ready and waiting and advanced when the first scream sailed down through the house.

"What is wrong with me?" Cat cried as the tall, slim woman came into the room carrying a tray.

"Mister Ty said you done got in the poison ivy," Portia explained in her deep, rich voice.

"Why didn't he tell me that?"

"By the time he realized it, it was too late. You done been exposed to it and there weren't nothin' he could do for you." Portia patted a chair encouragingly with her large hand. "Now come on over here and let me put this poultice on you."

Cat angrily flounced into the chair. "Where is Ty?"

"Mister Ty done left along with Mister Jake and Mister Caleb."

"He left? Without saying good-bye?"

"Sit back down now, he done gone and there ain't nothin' you can do about it. He said you wouldn't want him lookin' at you no how with your face all red and swollen." Portia smeared a salve down the side of Cat's face with a surprisingly gentle touch.

"Ow, what is that? It burns."

"It's supposed to, got to burn out that poison. It's lye and some other stuff that my mammy told me about a long time ago. It's goin' burn and it's goin' dry up all that ooze and then it will all peel off and you'll be your pretty little self again before Mister Ty gets back."

"How long will that take?"

"A week or two."

"Two weeks?" Cat settled back in a huff and let Portia finish doctoring her face.

"All done; now don't you go scratchin' it or it will just spread all over the place."

"It already has," Cat cried miserably.

"What?"

Cat stood and opened her robe, showing Portia the angry red blisters that covered the entire front of her torso.

"Lordy me, chile, I'm gonna have to make some more poultice."

Misery loves company was something her father had said on many occasions, but this was one time when it wasn't true. There was no way that Cat wanted any company. She just wanted the misery to end. One eye was completely swollen shut and her face, along with her chest and legs, was covered with angry red blisters that itched and oozed disgusting yellow pus. The fingers on her right hand were webbed with blisters, making it impossible for her to write letters, and with her eye swollen shut, reading was difficult also. On top of everything else, her monthly courses, which had never been reliable, had shown up, so once again her dreams of having Ty's baby had to be postponed. There was nothing to do but sit in her room, try not to scratch and watch the cold gray rain that had settled in over the countryside. A tear slid from beneath her dark lashes and took a wandering course down her blistered cheek. "Oh, Daddy, I wish I was home." The only response was the pounding of the rain.

Chapter Five

How different this Christmas is from the last, Jenny thought as she watched Jason roll a brightly painted ball toward Chance, who immediately picked it up with chubby hands and tried to stuff it in his mouth. He was teething and the pearl tip of a bottom tooth had just started to break through his lower gums.

Jenny sat on the thick softness of the Oriental rug that graced the floor of the parlor of the big house, her deep blue velvet dress pooled around her, creating an ocean of vivid color against the more subtle hues of the carpet. Chance sat in front of her, still a little unsure of himself in this position, prone to falling over in a heap if he moved suddenly. Jenny lowered the ball from his mouth, along with a thread of baby drool that created a bridge between the ball and Chance's full lower lip.

With work-hardened hands wrapped around his baby-soft fingers, she rolled the ball back toward Jason, who waited with his own hands open and a giant smile on his kind face. Fox grunted as he raised his head off the blue wedding ring quilt to follow the ball's progress between the two. Chase saw his struggles from the doorway and came to the rescue, joining the game with Fox safely tucked into the well that his crossed legs made on the floor.

So many faces missing, yet there are new ones here now that are just as dear. Where would she be now if not for these precious babies that God had given her? A year ago Jamie and Sarah had both been alive and on the threshold of starting their lives together. A year ago tonight she had sat with Jamie in front of a fire in her cabin and talked about their lives and how far they had come since the tragic loss of their own parents so many years ago. Her heart still ached for her twin brother. There was an empty space inside that would forever be hollow. Close to a year after his death, she still had to remind herself that he wasn't here. There would no longer be a brother tugging on her golden braid or sharing a wide grin with her as he had done when he knew they were thinking the same thing. He had been violently taken from her in a single moment, then restored to her in the gift of his son.

Fox giggled as Chase helped him hold the ball with little fingers that were better suited to holding on to the engraved silver rattle his doting great-grandfather had given him. Hands that were capable of unspeakable violence were gentle as they held the innocence of Jamie's son. The hands that had ruthlessly sought Jamie's killer now caressed a swirl of copper hair as the ball went rolling toward Chance, who was now concentrating on his own silver rattle. The startling blue eyes beneath dark lashes widened in surprise as the ball landed against his feet and his face twisted in concentration as he pondered the dilemma of holding both the ball and the rattle. Chase laughed as he watched his son work on the problem before him and Jenny felt her heart swell with the sound of it.

Thank you, God, for bringing back my husband, Jenny thought again. The season had made her more sentimental than usual and she had made use of the time to count her blessings. Chase had returned to her physically after the months he had been gone chasing Jamie's killer. The birth of their son and the surprising arrival of Fox had returned him to her spiritually, bringing healing to the damage done to his soul by his ruthless desire for revenge. He had made peace with himself and his demons, but there were still times when his dark, piercing eyes would turn inward and she knew that he was still haunted by his time out in the wilderness.

That was what scared her the most, the fleeting moments when the sins of his past would catch up with him and his eyes became shadowed and secretive. She would go to him then, wordlessly holding on to him, willing to share the demons that taunted his soul because of his love for her and her brother. He had gone after Logan because Logan had killed Jamie, but he had also gone after him to make sure that he would never again hurt Jenny. When the demons were upon him he would hang on to her with quiet desperation, sometimes making love to her fiercely as if he was afraid she would disappear and he would never see her again. And always, Jenny rose to meet him with her own passion. She had learned the hard way how precious life was and she was determined to make each minute count.

Chance decided that a few tears would solve his dilemma and screwed his face up to let loose a wail of frustration. Jenny promptly turned him around to distract him and caught the warm regard of her husband as she quickly turned the baby's tears into smiles.

"Let me take him for a while." Jason eagerly stretched out his arms for his great-grandson. "Both of them," he said when he had settled in to a chair before the fire with Chance on his knee. Chase handed Fox to him and then extended his hand to help Jenny up from the carpet.

They stood for a moment, Chase's strong arm wrapped protectively around Jenny's shoulders as they watched Jason juggle babies and a colorfully illustrated picture book that had also been among the too numerous Christmas gifts that Jason had showered on his newfound family. The fire popped and hissed in strong contrast to the snow that swirled outside. It was a peaceful evening, a fine ending to a beautiful day that would have been perfect if those who were missing had been present.

They had prayed for blessings on the missing at dinner: Cat, whose last letter had been full of tales about her mishap with the poison ivy and sliding down banisters; and Ty, Caleb and Jake, who were off fighting in the war. And of course they had prayed for Jamie, not because they doubted for his soul, but because they missed him still. A white picket fence now surrounded his grave on the ridge, leaving plenty of room for others to join him there when their time came. It helped somewhat to have him close, to be able to go and talk to him as if he were still there listening with his broad grin and wide blue eyes that seemed to hold the depths of the sea.

Jenny watched while another pair of blue eyes blinked and then a rosebud mouth yawned as the soft litany of Jason's voice lulled Fox to sleep. Chance wasn't far behind his cousin and soon their great-grandfather was able to lay the book aside and just hold the two precious babes against his body as he considered the fire before him. Chase tilted his handsome dark head toward the dining room, where the soft conversation of Grace, Cole and Zane could still be heard as they lingered over dinner.

"Jenny, would you get a letter off my desk for Cole?" Jason whispered as they made their way from the parlor. "With all the festivities, I forgot to give it to him."

Jenny's responding nod and smile assured her grandfather that she would take care of it, and she soon deposited the letter in the former Texas Ranger's hand as she and Chase joined the group who were still lingering over coffee and cake at the table.

"What's this?" Cole asked as he examined the writing on the envelope.

"Jason said it came in the mail and he forgot to give it to you."

Cole nodded as he opened the envelope, which contained a letter and another envelope. "This letter was addressed to my sister."

"How strange," Grace commented. "She died several months ago," she added in explanation to the others at the table.

"Apparently it was delivered some time after she died and now the postmaster in town has forwarded it to me." Cole quickly scanned the note added by the Texas postmaster before he opened his sister's letter. Suddenly the weathered face of the former Texas Ranger turned pale as he read Chloe's letter. "It's from Amanda . . ." Cole's dog and constant companion, Justice, looked up from his place on the floor.

"Amanda?" Grace asked in amazement.

"Who is Amanda?" Zane asked, his hazel eyes sparkling with curiosity.

"Cole's niece. She was kidnapped off the streets, and Cole was never able to find her," Grace explained to Zane. "He traced her to a ship that was in port in Galveston and then she just disappeared into thin air."

"She's in New Orleans, or she was." Cole jumped up from the table. "This letter is more than a year old."

Chase squeezed Jenny's hand as they watched the frustration mount in Cole. Jenny had just barely managed to escape the clutches of the same man who had taken Amanda. Wade Bishop had come across Jenny after she had been taken away from the orphanage and her brother all those years ago and had carried her down to Texas. Jenny had escaped by climbing out a third-story window and then making her way across the rooftops of the town where Bishop's sister ran a whorehouse. She had then cut off her long, golden hair and disguised herself as a boy, spending the next five years hiding her identity as she searched for her brother.

When she had finally shared her story with Grace, they had discovered that the same man who had kidnapped Jenny had also scarred Grace's beautiful face with his knife, cutting her from temple to mouth. Cole had overheard them talking and shared his own hatred for the man who had taken his niece off the streets of her hometown and sold her into prostitution.

The trail had ended in Galveston; Amanda had been taken onto a ship that had sailed off for an unknown destination. Cole had left Texas soon after, unable to remain there after he had failed his sister and his niece. Chloe had died of grief soon after he left. Only the four of them knew the entire story, leaving Zane to ask several questions as Cole tried to control the sudden outpouring of anger and frustration that threatened to consume him.

Grace picked up the letter, her voice breaking as she read it aloud:

"Momma, I'm being held prisoner by a man named Wade Bishop. I'm in New Orleans. I am in a yellow house with green shutters. It has a courtyard with a black iron gate. I can see a brick house from my window and there is a church nearby with a bell that rings the hours. I am hoping that I can get this letter smuggled out by one of the men. That's all I know to do. Bishop says he's taking me somewhere else soon so please tell Uncle Cole to come for me. I love you and miss you so much. I want to come home. Love, Amanda."

"Do you think she could still be there?" Zane asked

Cole, who was pacing the confines of the dining room.

"There's only one way to find out."

"You're going to New Orleans?" Grace's brown eyes widened with fear for the man who had just recently come into her life, offering her a love that she thought she would never have.

"I have to go, Grace. You lived in New Orleans; do you have any idea where this house could be?"

Grace had lived in New Orleans for many years after her father had left her orphaned and penniless. She had been born on a plantation on the Mississippi river and raised by her grandparents. At their deaths, her father had returned and lost everything gambling. He had then taught his beautiful teenage daughter how to deal and play cards, leaving her with a way to support herself when he was killed after cheating in a card game.

She had done well for herself until she met Wade Bishop. She had thought herself in love with the man until he stole all her money and left her scarred for life. Jason Lynch had found her working as a maid in a hotel and saw something in the still elegantly beautiful young woman. He had brought her to Wyoming to care for the troubled young men he was always taking in to work on his ranch. He had never asked for anything in return except for an occasional game of chess.

"It could be anywhere." Grace shook her head in sadness at this sudden turn of events. "I should go with you."

"No!" Cole grabbed her arms and pulled her to

him. "I don't want you anywhere near that man." Justice jumped to his feet, and Grace tried to stop the trembling that threatened to overcome her in the wake of Cole's sudden fury.

"Cole, the chances of her still being there are slim at best." Chase had his own experiences from which to draw. He had followed a fresh trail and it had still taken him several months to catch up with Jamie's killer.

"I know, but I still have to go. It's a chance to find her, and it's all I've got. I can't just ignore this letter." The dog watched his master with expectant eyes. He sensed the battle raging within the man and was ready to follow him.

"We don't expect you to," Chase assured him. "Do you want some company?"

Jenny couldn't hide the fear that came into her wide blue eyes as she saw the firm resolve on her husband's regally handsome face.

"No, this is something I have to do myself." Chase understood, he had felt the same just a year ago. "Besides, you have a family to take care of."

Jenny had not realized she had been holding her breath until she heard Cole's words.

"I'll go with you," Zane volunteered. He was tired of letting everyone else go off to have adventures while he stayed on the ranch doing their share of the work.

"You can't, Zane. Someone has to stay here and take care of the ranch. We're shorthanded as it is and who knows when I'll be back."

"I'm beginning to think I should have gone off and fought in the war," Zane grumbled.

The cry of a baby took Jenny from the table and brought an end to the discussion. Chase took a moment to speak with Cole before he left to help Jenny with the babies. They were probably hungry and ready for their own beds down in the cabin.

"Why don't you just stay up here?" Jason suggested again as he had several times before while Chase and Jenny bundled the babies into their blankets for the march down the hill. "There's plenty of room."

Jenny gently kissed the still-handsome cheek of her grandfather. "We like the cabin, Jason. It's our home. Besides, when Cat and Ty get back, this house will fill up soon enough." She arranged Fox in her arms and wiped a trail of drool from Chance, who was sucking on his fingers. Chase laid his son over his shoulder, taking care to cover Chance with the quilt. "We've got to get these two to bed. They've had a big day."

Cole and Grace were waiting to talk to Jason so Zane left with Jenny and Chase, volunteering to carry Fox down. The snow was deep and Jenny had skirts to contend with.

"Looks like it will be a clear day tomorrow." The night sky was bright with more stars than they could count, and the crisp cold air made it seem as if the stars were close enough to touch. Chase stopped and pointed the bright glow in the heavens out to Chance who was more interested in his fingers and the coming meal than the beauty of the night sky.

"He can't even see that far." Zane laughed at Chase as he continued to point out the stars that sparkled and glowed above.

"Of course he can. He has the eyes of a hawk."

Zane waggled the fingers of one hand in front of Chance's wide blue eyes. "Yeah, right." The baby stared at him solemnly and continued sucking on his own fingers.

"Will you two quit arguing and come on? It's cold out here." Jenny stomped the snow off her boots on the small stoop outside their cabin and took Fox from Zane.

"Don't worry about me; I'll just go back to that cold lonely bunkhouse by myself . . ." Zane waited expectantly beside the stoop. With his single friends off fighting and Chase and Cole now committed to their women, he was feeling a bit lonely lately. The other hands, Dan and Randy, had taken time off to visit their own families, which left Zane feeling a bit out of place among the couples. For years he had enjoyed the single life and having lots of women instead of one, but lately he had been thinking that marriage, especially to a fine woman like Jenny, wouldn't be so bad.

"Oh good, you can help me change diapers." Jenny smiled sweetly at Zane, who suddenly decided it was time to go. Marriage was one thing, being a father was something else entirely. Perhaps he would take a ride into town instead and see if he could offer the whores at Maybelle's some Christmas cheer. It was, after all, a bright night and he knew the road into town well enough. Jenny's soft laughter followed him as he made his way across the valley toward the stable.

She hadn't realized how close the fear was until she had heard Chase volunteer to join Cole in his search for Amanda. Jenny tried not to dwell on it as she sat in the wing-back chair before the fire, nursing Chance. She could hear Chase moving around behind her as he dealt with the nightly ritual of preparing the babies for bed. She listened to his gentle voice and Fox's soft cooing along with the fast gulps of Chance as he tugged on her breast. His wide blue eyes rolled back as he tried to look around her arm to see what was going on with his father and cousin.

"Hey, I'm right here," Jenny said to him softly, bringing his eyes back toward her. "Ouch!"

"What's wrong?"

"He bit me." A wide grin split the chubby baby face as he released her nipple. "That has got to stop, young man, or it will be solid food for you from now on."

"Don't you dare hurt your mother." Chase wagged a long finger under Chance's mischievous grin.

"I can just imagine what it will feel like when he actually has teeth." Jenny rubbed her wounded breast as Chase lifted Chance from her lap. "And besides, I have enough scars without him adding to them."

"I love your scars. They're a sign of your courage." Chase dropped a kiss on the top of her head and then started talking to his son. "Your mother is a very brave woman and you're a very lucky boy. She doesn't let me do that anymore since you came along . . ."

Jenny laughed at his remark; her breasts were usually sore from the demands the two babies put on her. She followed her handsome husband with her eyes as he continued chastising their son for his small indiscretion. What would she do if he left again?

The thought hadn't occurred to her before that night, but it could happen. Something could come up requiring him to leave the safety of the ranch. She had been so happy to have him back after the long months that he had been gone; it never occurred to her that he might leave again. But he was an honorable man and his honor might require it of him. He had offered to help Cole in his search; he would offer to do the same for any of his other friends. He had said on more that one occasion that Ty had saved his life when he found him burning up with a fever in the snow the previous spring. What would his response be if Ty sent for him and asked for his help?

A log split in the fireplace, showering sparks out on the rug. Jenny stamped them out with her bare feet and quickly swept the ashes back toward the hearth. Chase had both babies settled in their beds before long. He joined her in front of the mantel, where she had remained, staring down into the fire.

"It was a nice Christmas," he said against her neck as his arms came around her from behind.

"Yes, it was." Jenny leaned against his solid frame.

"Jason went a little overboard."

"Just making up for lost time." She looked at the drawing of Jamie, Chase and herself that graced the mantelpiece. Caleb's fine hand had captured Jamie's personality and the camaraderie they all had felt. "For all of us."

His hand crept inside the open front of her gown and gently caressed the flat planes of her stomach. Jenny turned in his arms, pressing her full breasts against the crispness of his fine white dress shirt, nudging his hips with her own.

"Stay with me, Chase."

The fear in her voice surprised him, but then again, she had reason to be afraid. Hadn't fate shown her several times that nothing and no one was permanent in her life? The time when he had been away from her had been the worst of his life. And yet he had consciously chosen to leave her, his hatred and desire for revenge temporarily stronger than his love and desire for Jenny. But she had taken him back with open arms and healed him with her love. Suddenly Chase recalled what he had said to Cole, and his arms closed around her tightly, assuring her with his strength, his strong presence that he wasn't going anywhere.

"I'm here." He had learned not to make promises anymore. Life had a funny way of making a liar out of you, no matter what your intentions. Soft, pliant lips sought his; hands that tended babies and horses along with dozens of daily chores worked the buttons on his shirt. One of his hands ran through thick golden waves of hair that flowed over her shoulders while the other splayed across her lower back, pressing her flesh against his, feeling the heat of her body through the thin fabric of her gown. It was a barrier and he tugged the gown down around shoulders, capturing her arms as he urgently yanked at the material. Jenny sighed as it ripped. It didn't really matter when Chase's mouth was caressing her neck and the heat of his passion was pressing against her. Her hands freed him as he bent her back toward the fire and then they both sank to the rug in one fluid motion, his hands supporting her as she melted beneath him and he melted into her.

Chapter Six

"How much longer are we just going to sit here?" Jake flung his tin plate against the side of the tent as he cursed the meal of beans and corn bread that had become the staple of their diets since they'd been sent to serve with General Thomas Jonathan "Stonewall" Jackson last fall. Caleb calmly dusted crumbs off his sleeve and then flicked a bean in Jake's direction. Jake's angry outbursts had become just as monotonous as everything else on this assignment. Christmas had come and gone along with the new year and the only difference was that Jake's fits were coming closer together, while the days were dragging out longer.

Willie picked up Jake's plate, which had landed face up and still contained a fair portion of the meal. "Are you done with this, Jake?" Six months ago he wouldn't have dared to speak to the lean gunfighter, especially when he was in one of his surly moods. Now he worshiped the ground Jake walked on. At the present, Willie was in the middle of a growth spurt and couldn't find enough food to fill his belly, or clothes to cover his long and lanky limbs. Jake snorted and stomped away, his long blond hair flying out behind him as Willie scraped the abandoned food onto his own plate.

"Might as well clean that up for him, too, and save yourself some trouble later on," pointed out Pope, one of the Ridge Riders, as Willie tossed Jake's plate aside.

The moniker of Ridge Riders had been hung on the band upon their arrival with the troop. They wore the title proudly even though they had seen little action. They had done their part to protect the gaps along the Blue Ridge from an invasion by the Union Army and were anxious to do more, even though that meant giving up the convenience of having home close at hand. They, along with ten thousand other men, most of them militia, had been sent into the Shenandoah Valley to defend against the Union troops that would surely be coming that way. There had been word that General Kelly had taken Romney, a town about thirty-five miles northwest of Winchester, with five thousand men, and the boys were all itching for a fight. Now they were just waiting for their orders and patience was wearing thin.

"I guess Jake's in one of his moods again," Ty said as he joined his small group of men. He handed Willie a worn coat that looked long enough to cover his skinny arms.

"No news there. Where'd you find that?" Caleb had finished his meal and was sketching on a small pad of paper that he kept in his coat.

"At the field hospital." Caleb's eyes widened as he looked up at Ty. Everyone knew that being sent to the camp hospital was almost the same as a death sentence. The conditions in the field were horrible and if a soldier's wounds did not kill him, disease or infection would. Most men relied on the kindness and care of their comrades when they were wounded. "We can't have that boy freezing to death before he dies on the battlefield." Ty poured himself a cup of coffee.

"We'll all probably die of boredom before that happens," Caleb muttered.

"Not unless you're planning on dying tonight." Caleb looked up from his drawing at Ty's words. "We're riding to Romney tomorrow." The men around the fire perked up at the news. "And since we're mounted, we're riding point."

"Point?" Willie asked.

"Scouting," Caleb explained, drawing a huge grin from Willie along with the rest of the Ridge Riders.

"Why don't you go find Jake before he gets into trouble and misses out on all the fun," Ty told Willie. The boy took off, anxious to see the look on Jake's face when he heard the good news. "I sure hope that boy don't get himself killed following along after Jake."

"I'll keep an eye out for him," Caleb volunteered.

"As long as you don't get killed doing it." Ty smiled casually but he could not hide from himself the fear he felt for his friends.

"Hey Jake, wait up." Willie fought his way through the small groups of men who stood between him and his hero.

Jake heard him but kept on walking. The kid had gotten to be downright annoying, hanging around all the time, watching him like he was some kind of hero or something. Jake shoved a butternut-clad soldier out of his way as he stalked through the crowd, itching for a fight, daring someone to challenge him so he could get rid of all the anger that was coiling up inside him. If only Willie hadn't seen the scars on his back. . . .

It had happened the past autumn after their last visit to Ty's home. The three of them had ridden for two days through a cold rain to their rendezvous with the rest of the riders. The following morning had been clear but cold and they had decided to dry their clothes while they had a chance. They were camped by one of the hot springs that were to be found all over the area. Even though the air smelled of rotten eggs, a soak in one of the springs felt pretty good on a cold day. Jake had known Ty and Caleb long enough to feel relaxed and comfortable in their presence, but that was where he drew the line. He didn't need anyone else involved in his business, especially some snot-nosed kid coming up and asking him about the scars that crisscrossed his back. Did it matter that the kid had his own scars from his own beatings? What should he care? He had survived and apparently Willie had, too. Was that supposed to make them brothers or something? Worse, did Willie expect him to be some sort of guardian angel over his scrawny hide? Why should he worry around the kid? There hadn't been anybody to worry about him, not even his mother or sisters had taken his side.

Even now, years after the scars had been inflicted, he would wake up trembling in the night, his mouth open in a silent scream as he begged his father to stop the beatings. He was evil, his father would say, possessed by demons, and they needed to be exorcised. When he was small his father used his belt, which hurt but only left a few bruises. As he grew, however, so did the demons, and something stronger was required. That was when his father started using the whip, tying him facedown to a scarred table behind their cabin in Minnesota and beating him until he was bloody while his mother and sisters watched in horror.

Shortly before his sixteenth birthday, Jake decided he was better off on his own than living with the beatings. Either way he would be dead soon enough, and he'd rather meet death on his own terms rather than someone else's.

And here he was, nearly ten years later, still very much alive with a scrawny kid that a stiff breeze would blow away hard on his heels. If he wasn't in such a bad mood, he'd have a good laugh about it.

"Jake!" Willie might be scrawny, but he was quick. Jake swatted away the hand on his arm and whirled to face his stalker.

Willie ignored the scowl that twisted the pale blond goatee Jake was now wearing. "We got orders. Capt'n Kincaid says we're gonna go fight tomorrow."

The ice-blue eyes lit up as they looked back toward Ty and the others. "Orders? They don't have to order me to fight." Jake turned on his heel and headed back to his friends.

"Yeah." Willie shook a fist toward the north. "Me, too." He swiped at his nose with the back of his hand and followed, his eyes riveted on the scarred back of his idol.

Chapter Seven

Cole Larrimore could not remember being more frustrated in his whole life. Never once in all the years that he had spent as a Texas Ranger had he come up against so many dead ends in his pursuit of a criminal. Wade Bishop had learned to cover his tracks well.

The first thing Cole had done on his arrival in New Orleans was search for the house that Amanda had described in her letter. He had started with the churches; Amanda had mentioned that she could hear a bell tolling the hours. There were several. From each church he would take off in an ever-widening circle, searching for a yellow house with green shutters that had a courtyard with an iron gate. He never knew that yellow was such a popular color for a house. Or that most of the houses in New Orleans had courtyards. Each time he found what might be the house he met with a dead end when he knocked on the door and presented himself. There were no answers to his questions, no leads to take him anywhere else, no hope of finding his niece. She might as well have been a grain of sand in the desert that had been blown away with the wind.

Cole decided to change tactics after weeks of disappointment. He started to haunt the bars and taverns along the waterfront. Surely someone would have some word of Wade Bishop and his dealings. He soon realized, however, that his physical presence was enough to alert the underworld that he was not someone to whom they should be talking. He wore his years as a Texas Ranger as if they were a badge. His reputation from the dime novels that had been written about him was greater than he had originally thought. But Cole also knew that money could buy answers so he picked a well-placed tavern that Grace had mentioned as one of Bishop's former haunts from the time she had known him and sat down to wait. Eventually someone desperate enough and hungry enough would come. Surely there was someone else out there whom Bishop had crossed at some point in time. Someone would want revenge. All he had to do was wait.

Cat had stopped counting the days and moved into weeks. She hadn't seen Ty since late October and it was now the end of March. She had received one letter from him in that time telling her that he was stationed with the main army in Virginia. Since then she had gathered her news from the local gossip after church on Sunday and a weekly newspaper. Penelope pinned her hopes on the fact that no news was good news. She insisted that Ty was alive and well, but that didn't help Cat when she climbed into bed at night and cried herself to sleep. She felt worn and thin, like a dress that had been made over too many times and was weak at the seams.

Cat's life had settled into a routine and in that routine she found comfort. She rode each morning, her jaunts on the back of her chestnut mare as commonplace as the rising of the sun. She knew the trails around the plantation as well as she knew the ones around the ranch where she'd been raised. She became familiar with all of the slaves and came to know and love the smaller children. Parker disapproved of the candy she gave them and forbade her to teach them to read. When she found out the punishment for any slave caught reading, she agreed that he was right in forbidding her. She spent her afternoons with Penelope, whom she had come to love after familiarity broke down the walls of formality. On the outside, Penelope was the model of a genteel plantation mistress, but Cat soon found her to be a strong-willed woman, who realized that she had made some mistakes, especially with her sons.

"I never should have sent Ty away," Penelope admitted to Cat. They were taking tea in the garden on an uncommonly warm spring day. The bright pinks and reds of azaleas in bloom set the air ablaze with color. A fat bumblebee worked the blossoms with his loud buzz while robins and cardinals pecked at the soft dirt beneath in their search for food.

"I have to admit that I'm glad you did." Cat added sugar to her tea and wondered how long their dwindling supply would last. With the blockades that covered the coastline, it was almost impossible to count on the little things to which they had once been accustomed. Things that they had once taken for granted cost dearly as the blockade runners risked life and limb to bring luxuries into port.

"I am most happy the way things turned out for him." Penelope laid a carefully manicured hand on Cat's arm. "You are good for him, my dear. It's just that I now realize that perhaps he could have done a better job of managing our affairs than Parker."

"If you mean stockpiling for the future instead of pretending that the South has already won the war, I have to agree with you wholeheartedly."

"Parker is a great patriot." Cat let out an unladylike snort at that remark, which Penelope politely ignored. "I just wish he had planned for the future better."

Parker, along with most of the other planters in the South were counting on England and France's need for cotton to propel those nations into taking sides in the conflict. Instead of selling last year's crops and having the money to see them through the winter, they had withheld shipment, hoping to force the two countries into action. They had not counted on both England and France having their own stockpile of cotton, which would see them through a few years. Now the South's bounty was rotting in warehouses while Federal ships patrolled the waters beyond.

"I do wish we would hear something from Ty." Cat took a sip of tea to cover her despair. "It's so hard not knowing."

"But you do know, my dear."

"What do you mean?"

"Did I ever tell you about Ty's father and how he died?"

"No. I was told he died while Ty was in Europe on his tour. It was some sort of accident, wasn't it?"

"Yes. He was thrown from his horse and his neck broke. I remember exactly when it happened. I was sorting the silver for a dinner party we were giving. I was in the dining room with Portia and suddenly my heart just stopped. I recall looking at the grandfather clock out in the hall and noting the time for some strange reason. When the men carried him in, I discovered that his watch had broken in the fall. George set his watch by the clock in the hall every morning. It had stopped at the exact same time that I had felt my heart stop for that brief moment. So you see, I felt it when he died. When you truly love someone, when you're truly connected to them as I feel you and Ty are, then you know if something happens to them." Penelope's smile was reassuring.

"George was always harder on Ty than Parker," Penelope continued. "I can see that now. I think it was because Ty had this special spark that seemed to be lacking in Parker. So George demanded nothing but the best from him. Parker always knew that as the oldest he would inherit everything, so he never had to put forth much effort. Ty, on the other hand, always had to prove himself to his father. I know George was hard on him because he wanted Tyler to succeed and knew he would have to succeed without the benefit of the land, but there were times when I wondered if perhaps he was too hard on him. George always had a difficult time showing his affection for the boys."

As Penelope spoke, Cat recalled the little things that made up Ty's personality and realized that he was a product of his father's stern upbringing. Ty always gave his very best in everything that he did. Could she expect him to do otherwise in this war? Would he sacrifice his very life because of it, knowing that it was the most he had to offer? What price had the young Ty paid continually trying to please a father who couldn't be pleased?

"That's strange; I thought Lucy Ann said she was going to take a nap." Cat turned to see what had caught her mother-in-law's attention. Through the hedge she saw the pale yellow of Lucy Ann's dress as she hurried in the direction of the stable.

"Maybe she's looking for Parker."

"Parker went into Salem and won't be back until tomorrow evening."

"That is strange." Cat mused on the secretive life of her sister-in-law. She had never seen her astride a horse, or even touch one for that matter. If she needed to go someplace, she would have sent one of the slave children down to the stable to summon a buggy and Zeb to drive her. "What does she do with her days?"

"She's helping the war effort. She meets once a week with the other ladies of the county to discuss what they can do to help our fighting men."

Cat knew a sorry excuse when she heard one but she also knew that Penelope would never say anything negative about any member of her family. What did Lucy Ann do with her time besides nap and primp and fawn over Parker? Maybe it was time she found out.

* * *

Jenny sat straight up in the bed sucking in great gulps of air. She had dreamed she was drowning. She had dreamed of drowning before, as a girl in the orphanage. When she awoke she found the mission priest standing over her bed. Jenny glanced around the cabin to see if that ghost had come back to haunt her, but all was quiet. The space beside her was empty and she noticed the cabin door was open a crack, letting in the first pink light of dawn. She threw the quilt over her shoulders and stopped to check on the babies.

Chance lay in his cradle on his back with both arms flung wide over his head. His blanket had been kicked down around his ankles and Jenny took a moment to pull it up and tuck it in around his waist. Another month and they would have to find him a bigger bed. Fox's cradle was empty and the soft sound of singing from the stoop led her to her husband and nephew.

Chase had Fox lying across his knees and was bouncing him up and down while chanting softly in Kiowa. Fox sucked greedily on his fist but looked up and grinned at Jenny as she settled beside them on the stoop.

"Hey, what are you up to?" Jenny asked the smiling baby.

"He was fussy and I knew you needed some sleep." Chase changed the bouncing to swaying.

"Fussy? Are you sure you got the right baby?" Fox had shown himself to be exceptionally good natured, even when he was teething as he was now. Chance, on the other hand, was very demanding and not afraid to let the world know what he wanted. Sometimes his angry cries would fill the valley, and Zane swore that they were loud enough to sour the milk from the dairy cow.

Chase laughed. "Yes, I'm sure. Chance was snoring when I checked on him. I didn't want this guy to wake him up so we decided to come out here and keep Justice company." The dog lifted his dark shaggy head and thumped his tail in the dirt at the mention of his name.

"Poor fellow. He misses Cole." Jenny slid under Chase's welcoming arm.

"We all do." Chase pulled her close against his side. "Spring's a busy time around here, and Dan and Randy just aren't good enough to take up the slack."

"If we're lucky, Cole will be back soon, with Amanda." The thought of Wade Bishop sent a chill down her spine.

Chase looked at Jenny with dark eyes that saw everything. "Why do you not sound sure of that?"

"I had a dream, just now."

They had learned through the years that her dreams were usually a portent of something momentous happening in their lives. "Tell me about it."

"There wasn't much to it really. I was on a ship with Cat and several other women. I know one of them was Amanda. I just sensed that it was she. Wade Bishop was on it, too. He locked all of us below the decks and then the ship started sinking. The water just kept pouring in, and we were all trying to stop it with our hands but it just kept on pouring in."

Chase kissed her forehead. "You know Wade Bishop doesn't have a clue as to where you are."

"I know." Jenny laid her hand against the copper swirl of Fox's hair. His eyes had grown heavy and he blinked against the coming sleep. "He's just about gone." Chase shifted the baby into his arms to cradle him. Fox fought the motion with one last smile and settled into sleep.

"Jason is talking about building another barn for Storm and the mares."

Jenny settled in against his side. "Yes, he mentioned that." She wrapped her arms around his waist.

"I think I'll just add some to his lumber order and start on another room for us." She could feel his lips move against her hair.

"That's a good idea."

"Not all dreams are bad, you know."

"I know, I had good dreams about you, before . . . I just didn't know they were about you." Her voice sounded far away against the solid wall of his chest.

"Do you ever dream about Jamie?"

Jenny raised herself from his side and looked at Chase with wide blue eyes that were so much like her brother's. "No, I haven't. Not at all. At least not that I can remember."

"I saw him, Jenny." Chase looked off toward the north as he spoke. The mountains beyond were still deep purple shadows in the soft glow of the sunrise.

"When?" Jenny pulled away and wrapped the quilt around her shoulders.

"The day that Ty found me in the north pasture. Jamie was there. He led Ty to me." Jenny looked at him questioningly. "His scars were gone and he was laughing. He said you needed me and I'd better get home. When I couldn't get up, he said he'd find someone to help me. Ty said he saw a red fox in the field and it led him to me."

Jenny looked at the ridge where a single headstone stood as sentinel over their small valley. "He's watching over us?"

"Yes, he is."

Jenny settled back against Chase contentedly. It was silly to be worried about a dream. She had her wonderful husband beside her and her beloved brother as a guardian angel to watch over her. She saw the sunrise through half-closed lids as she sought her last few moments of lost slumber.

Cole had lingered long enough. The approach to New Orleans had been under bombardment by Federal ships for most of the week. Cole knew he couldn't afford to be trapped in the city once it was taken, but he also didn't want to leave until he was sure that he had left no stone unturned in his search for Wade Bishop. How could such a notorious man, who had his fingers in so many pots, disappear into thin air? Cole knew the man was profiteering so somebody had to have some dealings with him, but so far no one had come forward. The threat that Wade Bishop held must be great indeed to offset the reward Cole was offering.

His bags were packed and his horse was ready. Instead of turning north he decided to make one last pass along the waterfront. His passage was difficult due to the steady flow of traffic heading in the opposite direction. Cole shook his head at the amount of baggage that had been abandoned on doorsteps and in the street as the townspeople hastily left their homes and headed for a safer refuge in the surrounding countryside. Where could they hope to go? Union forces were coming from the north down the Mississippi and from the south and the gulf. Cole planned on going west, away from this war. He had his own battles to fight, and this wasn't one of them.

"I figured you had done skedaddled back to Texas," the bartender greeted him as he came through the door.

"I'm on my way. Just thought I'd give you a chance to tell me how much you're going to miss me." The tavern was empty except for a lone man at a corner table.

"I won't miss you a bit. You're bad for business. But at least you'll be happy to know you haven't wasted your time." Suddenly, after many weeks, the bartender was a font of information.

"What are you talking about?"

The man pointed to the corner table. "Someone's been waiting for you."

Even though the tavern was empty, the stranger at the corner table looked furtively around as if someone might be listening.

"Are you looking for me?" Cole decided the man needed firm tactics. He looked a bit shifty around the eyes and he was definitely nervous.

"Depends. Are you the man looking for Wade Bishop?"

"I am." Cole sat down, making sure he could see both entrances as he did so.

"He ain't here. He was here about a month ago. Bastard was supposed to take me with him. He's off sipping planter's punch in Nassau, and I'm stuck here for the duration."

"Nassau?"

"That's where the blockade runners call home. He's been running supplies in and out of here. Charging an arm and a leg, too."

"What about the women?"

"What women?"

"Bishop deals in women, too. Where does he take them?"

"Could be anywhere after they leave here. It's hard to say." The man jumped in his seat as an explosion echoed across the waterfront. "Shouldn't be long before those Yankees are breathing down our necks."

Cole opened his watch, revealing a picture of Amanda. "Did you ever see this girl with Bishop?"

"Going to be hard for a man like me to survive with Yankees all over the place." The man scratched his beard as he nervously watched Cole's reaction.

A small pouch hit the table with a clink. "Did you ever see this girl with Bishop?"

The man tentatively reached for the pouch and took its measure. "She looks like one he took out of here last spring. There was two of them, this one and a yellow-haired gal."

"Do you know where he took them?"

"He took them to Nassau—that's all I know. Where they go after that, you'd have to ask the man himself." The stranger left, taking the pouch with him.

Cole sighed. He should have known better than to

get his hopes up. His chances of finding Amanda were as slim now as when she was first taken. If only he could get his hands on Wade Bishop, he'd choke the information out of him and then enjoy watching him die. Perhaps he'd give him a few slices with his knife as the man had done to Grace.

Grace. Cole found himself longing for the peace that being in her company provided. He wondered how Justice was faring without him, how much the babies had grown, and how much trouble Zane had gotten himself into while he was gone.

"A Yankee ship is coming up the harbor!" The boy who hastily stuck his head through the tavern door to make the announcement went on with his mission.

It was time to go home.

Chapter Eight

August in North Carolina had to be a preview of hell, Cat decided as she kicked the sheets away in her never-ending quest for relief from the oppressive heat that had settled over the plantation. Even now, in the wee hours of the morning, there was no relief. If only she could sleep . . . but the heat combined with her worry over Ty and her growing concern for Penelope's health conspired against her. She had received one brief letter from Ty since spring. She knew he was still with Jackson and the newspaper said they were winning their battles, but battles meant the risk of injury or death. She wrote to him faithfully in hopes that the letters would somehow reach him. She also wrote to Caleb and Jake in hopes that somehow among the three of them she would receive some word of reassurance.

Cat gave up on her struggle for sleep and went to the window, hoping beyond hope that there would be a breath of air, or better yet, a thunderstorm. They had gone too long without rain. Her room at the back corner of the house faced west on one side, and she went to that window to see if perhaps there was a darkening of the sky over the mountains that would indicate an approaching storm. The sky was clear and full of stars on a moonless night. She plucked at her gown, pulling it away from her breasts and lifting the tail of it up around her hips.

If only she could get Penelope to see the doctor. The woman kept insisting that she was fine, but she had not been able to hide the blood that stained the fine linen of her handkerchief during her coughing spells. Cat had not mentioned that to Ty in her letters. He had enough to worry about. Staying alive should be his number one priority. He did not need any distractions.

Once again, she debated telling Parker about Penelope. There was something about him that kept a wall of formality between them. They shared none of the easy banter that had been so much a part of her life on the ranch. And there was no way she was going to tell Lucy Ann. She would either faint or make such a fuss over Penelope that the poor woman would be ill just from the commotion. Cat decided she would just keep an eye on her, a decision she had already made a hundred times over, though she continued to debate the question in her mind. She felt so alone without her father, Grace or Jenny with whom to talk things over.

How could it be so hot? She had to do something; she couldn't stand being so miserable. She ripped the gown from over her head and searched the small writing desk by the window. She knew she had seen some scissors there earlier in the week. Her hand roamed across the surface and came up empty. She stood with gown in hand and surveyed the dark room. It was too hot even to think about lighting a lamp. A glance toward the window on the back side of the room jogged her memory and she found the scissors on the washstand where she had left them the day before. She held the gown up to her chest for measurement and then cut it so the bottom would fall around her thighs. The sleeves were the next to go, followed by the collar. Satisfied with her alterations, she slipped what was left of the gown back on and paused to look out over the grounds behind the house.

That was strange. It looked as if a lantern was burning in the stable. Zeb would surely be in trouble if Parker or Thompson saw the light. After a month without rain, the stable would go up in flames in a heartbeat, along with everything else in its vicinity. Cat found her robe and quietly tiptoed downstairs.

She prayed that the dogs wouldn't be roused by her prowling about the grounds. Surely they were used to her scent. Cat was surprised to find the main entrance to the stable barred from the inside. What was going on? The windows to the stalls were open and she noticed that the horses within seemed a bit restless as she walked around to the smaller side door.

It took only a second for her brain to register what her ears were hearing. Someone was having a tryst in the stables. Cat turned to leave. It had to be Zeb, and the last thing she wanted to do was embarrass him. The sound of a slap and a protest froze her in her tracks. There was no doubt in her mind that the voice she heard belonged to Lucy Ann.

The ladder to the loft was right in front of her. Cat couldn't resist. She hiked up her robe and climbed up the ladder, cautiously making her way across the hayloft toward the end stall from which the noise and light were emanating.

"I said to keep your hands off me, darkie." Cat's eyes grew huge as she peered over the side of the loft. The sight below her made her stomach lurch. Zeb was flat on his back in the straw with his eyes closed and Lucy Ann astride him. The words coming from her were so obscene that they would make a cowhand blush and the sounds she was making revealed how close she was to her climax. Cat told herself not to look but she couldn't tear her eyes away. Then she saw the knife in Lucy Ann's hand as it flashed near Zeb's throat. Cat watched in amazement as Lucy Ann shuddered and gasped and wondered how she managed not to cut Zeb with the knife.

"You tell anyone about this, and I'll make sure it's the last time you ever do it." Lucy Ann trailed the knife down Zeb's chest as she dismounted and arranged her skirts back in their proper place. Cat couldn't believe the venom in the words.

"Yes, ma'am, I won't tell nobody. I ain't tole nobody yet."

"Just see to it that you don't." Lucy Ann flounced out of the stall with a swish of her skirts. Cat turned away when she realized that Zeb had been left wanting, and the sight of him as he curled on his side with a sob was more than she could bear. She didn't dare move until he was gone.

What should she do? Her mind raced around the problem as she lay in the straw and listened to the broken groans and sobs of Zeb. No one would believe her. Zeb was surely in fear of his life. The penalty for touching a white woman was death, and Thompson would make him pray for it before he was done with him. Surely he hadn't agreed to this. But how could a woman force a man to have sex with her? *That's easy, Cat, just get him aroused.*

Lucy Ann used her knife, threats and her position to get what she wanted. Zeb had to cooperate or he would die at her word.

Suddenly Ty's revelation about his fight with Parker flashed through her mind. The slave Parker had been beating had been caught with a piece of Lucy Ann's jewelry. She must have planted it on him when he had turned her down. The woman was pure evil. But how did she get away with it? Surely Parker had to know.

Parker and Lucy Ann had been married for years and had no children. Cat had thought after spending time with them that it was because there was no intimacy between them, but now she believed Lucy Ann must not be able to have children. But why, oh why, would she take a slave as a lover? She must have been doing it for years with whichever one caught her fancy.

Finally she heard Zeb get up. What should she do? How could she look at either of them? *Oh, Ty, I need you to come home . . .*

* * *

Willie's eyes were wide as Jake settled against the tree with the precious piece of paper. "Somebody sent you a letter?"

"Yes, not that it's any of your business."

Willie saw through his bluff. "What does it say?"

"Just stuff, personal stuff."

"Who's it from?"

"None of your business." Jake reread the short note from Cat. It contained some news from Wyoming, mostly about Chance and Fox, and a few tidbits concerning life on the Kincaid Plantation. The rest was a plea for news of their well-being. It was the first letter he had ever received in his life. He folded it carefully and placed it in his shirt pocket.

"It was probably somebody else's letter anyway." Willie scuffed a bare toe in the dirt and hitched up his pants.

"What happened to your boots?"

"They was hurting my feet."

"Outgrew another pair?"

"Yep." The boy flopped down in the dirt, close enough to worship his idol while still keeping a safe distance in case Jake's volatile temper erupted.

Jake looked the boy over. Short rations had made Willie scrawnier than usual but he was still growing taller. It would be a sight to see him putting the food away at Grace's table. It suddenly occurred to him that he didn't know a thing about Willie's past. "Where you going after the war?"

A pair of bony shoulders shrugged in response. "I don't know."

"How about home?"

"Don't have one. Don't have no paw. My maw died and I didn't have nowhere to go so I enlisted."

"How are you around cattle?"

The boy's bright eyes turned on Jake with curiosity. "I know how to milk, if that's what you mean."

Jake threw his head back and let out a laugh from deep in his belly. "We got one that needs milking. I'm sure Grace would love to turn that job over to you." His perfect white teeth flashed behind the pale blond of his goatee as he looked at Willie's shocked face.

"Who's Grace? What are you talking about?"

"I'm talking about you going home to Wyoming with us when this is all over."

"Really?" It was more than the poor orphan had ever hoped for.

Jake ruffled the stringy hair. "Really. Go get your boots. Let's see if we can do some trading."

Ty watched as Jake and Willie took off, then slowly and carefully opened the letter from Cat. He really should have written to her a long time ago, but he didn't know what to say. He couldn't begin to tell her about the death and destruction that he had seen. They had been in more battles than he could count and were constantly on the move with Jackson and his cavalry. He was sure they had ridden around the state of Virginia at least three times in their pursuit of Federal forces. He had lost some men, some good men. Men he had come to know and depend on as they fought side by side. That was something he wasn't ready to talk about. Nor could he tell Cat about the doubts he was experiencing. Doubts that had filled his mind the first time he looked into the eyes of a Union soldier before killing him on the battlefield. Why were they fighting each other? When the two armies came together on the field, it was kill or be killed, that much he understood, but the big picture, the overall reason had vanished from his mind like the smoke from the cannons. Didn't they all have the right to live life as they saw fit? Did one man have the right to tell another what he could and could not do with his life? Where was the logic of it all? Were they all being used as pawns for some larger purpose? Would his death, or Caleb's or Jake's or Willie's, make one bit of difference in how it all ended?

It had been a mistake to come here. He saw that as clearly now as he saw Caleb's dark head bent over his sketchbook. But he wasn't ready to admit that to his wife, who waited patiently with his family at home. His honor wouldn't let him. He had committed himself and his friends to this battle and he had to see it through. Right or wrong, there was nowhere else for him to go but onward. There was nothing else for him to do but pray and hope that they came through it all right. There was nothing left for him to put in a letter, but he owed it to her. She had asked for nothing else.

"Hey, Caleb, you got a piece of paper?"

Had she changed so much or was it just the things around her? When had she become this sedate person who was content to sit and read, who had learned to knit after spending weeks on end at Penelope's side?

If only her father could see her, Cat thought as she lifted her eyes from the bright blue yarn and gazed out the window toward the west. Thoughts of her father, Wyoming and the family that was still there tumbled about in her mind. They seemed strange and disjointed, however, as if she had read a marvelous book and planted herself in the story. The memories belonged to another Cat in another lifetime. Even her memories of Ty didn't belong to her anymore. They were all a part of a wonderful dream that still had not faded in the year since she had seen him. The real Cat's life consisted of nothing more than worrying and waiting. Worry over Ty, Caleb and Jake. Worry over Penelope and her ever worsening health. Worry over Zeb and Lucy Ann's constant harassment of him. Worry over the thought that the best part of her life was over and she had been found lacking in what she had done. Worry that the punishment for her sins would be a lifetime of worrying and waiting. It was all part of the never-ending circles of her mind. Learning to knit had been something to occupy her time, but the simple task still left her mind open to chase the worries. If only she could go home and leave all this behind, but she couldn't. Penelope depended on her more and more each day and she had to be here when Ty came back. *Ty . . .*

Where was he? Was he safe? Had he forgotten about her and what they had shared? She knew the mail was slow because of the war but surely he had gotten her letters. Surely he had written to her to let her know he was safe. Was he safe? She flung the knitting away in frustration and watched as the ball of yarn bounced across the room. She stepped over the spiderweb it weaved in its escape on her way to the window, rubbing her arms against the damp chill of a rainy fall afternoon. The buggy was coming up the drive. Zeb, wrapped in a heavy coat and hat with water dripping off the brim, was handling the reins while Parker stayed warm and dry inside. At least Parker's foray into town had kept Zeb out of Lucy Ann's clutches for a day. She was still upstairs pouting in her room after pretending that she was upset because she wanted to spend the day with her husband. Maybe Parker would have some news of the war.

"Where is everyone?" Parker came into the house, stomping and dripping from his short dash up the steps.

Cat met Parker in the hall and helped him with his overcoat. "Penelope and Lucy Ann are taking naps and Silas is helping Portia with some canning."

Parker patted the pockets of his suit coat absent-mindedly. "You have a letter here somewhere . . ." He pulled a thick packet of correspondence out and handed her an envelope. "It looks like Ty's handwriting."

Cat examined the handwriting through eyes that suddenly filled with tears and impetuously kissed Parker on the cheek. "Thank you, Parker." She held the precious missive to her breast as she went back into the parlor to read it. It was dated in September. As of a month ago, he was still alive. Still riding with Jackson, now serving under General Lee. Caleb and Jake were fine; Willie was still growing like a weed.

He missed her, he loved her, and he hoped the war would be over soon. Cat read it again. It was news, but there was nothing in it of Ty, nothing of his spirit, his soul. It was words, nothing more. Had he changed? What had he seen? What had he been through? What had he done to survive?

An image of Chase after he had returned from his months in the wilds chasing after Jamie's killer came to her mind. His eyes had been haunted as he fought against the demons inside that threatened to take his spirit. Were those same demons now haunting her husband? Would she have the same strength and patience that Jenny had had as she waited for Chase's spirit to return to her? Would Ty come back to her, and if he did, would he be the same man she had married? A tear slid down her cheek as she carefully folded the letter. He was alive. *Was he safe?*

Chapter Nine

"Where are we headed again?" Jake had shown repeatedly in the past year that he could smell a battle from miles away.

"Somewhere in Virginia," Caleb responded with a cheeky grin.

Jake scowled at the sarcasm.

"Chancellorsville," Ty answered. At least Caleb still had his sense of humor.

"I suppose there will be some Yankees there." Jake had become jaded after so many battles.

"About seventy thousand of them according to the scouts," Ty informed him.

Jake looked back at the long line of infantry that was following Jackson's cavalry. Lee had split his troops and assigned twenty-six thousand men to Jackson. The force was quickly moving around to attack the Union's General Hooker on his exposed right flank.

"I bet we can take 'em." Jake liked it better when the odds were against him.

At dusk they attacked with such force that the line was shattered and the Yankees were routed from their positions. Fighting ensued in brush and dense undergrowth and across small clearings. As darkness fell, it was hard to identify friend from foe. The flash of the cannon and smoke added to the confusion. Ty watched in frustration as Jake took off, with Willie on his heels, after a small group of infantrymen who had set up a line behind a fallen tree. He saw Caleb take a spill as his horse went down with a bullet in its chest. The animal rolled over Caleb, who came back up shaking his head and shooting at the same time. He quickly took shelter behind the animal until Ty reached him and Caleb swung up behind him in one graceful move.

"Where's Jake?" Caleb yelled as they made for the shelter of the woods.

Ty swung his revolver across the field to where Jake's horse was jumping over a fallen tree where several surprised Yankees looked up at the blond angel of death with the two blazing guns who was suddenly behind them. A horse that had lost its master fell in beside Ty's, confused and frightened without a steady hand to guide it. Caleb made the transfer in one quick motion and Ty whirled around to take inventory of his men.

"*Ty!*" Caleb bellowed. Ty turned and saw what had caught Caleb's attention. A unit of Union cavalry was just now breaking out of the dense woods and bearing down on them.

Ty pulled his sword and whistled for his men. "*Ridge Riders*!" Caleb fell in on his right, Jake on his left, with the rest of the group coming in behind. As one, they advanced, the ground of the gentle clearing shaking with the mighty pounding of the horses' hooves.

Bullets were soon spent and swords and rifle barrels were used as the opposing forces fought viciously for the narrow piece of ground. Ty's arm grew heavy as his sword flashed and maimed, spraying blood up his arm and down his side. His horse was bumped on all sides when men went down and the steeds scrambled for purchase on the churned-up earth. Jake took off with a whoop and a holler after the Yankees broke and fled into the woods.

"Jake, get back here!"

Jake quickly pulled up and came trotting back with a huge grin shining through his goatee.

"Looks like you need a bath," he commented to Ty as he pulled up beside him. Ty wiped the blood from his eyes and looked around for the rest of his men.

"Willie? Anyone see Willie?" he asked the collected group as the men checked one another for injuries. Jake's grin left his face in an instant and he whirled his horse to check among the bodies that lay along the ground.

"We lost Johnson, Captain," someone said.

"Damn," Ty muttered. He wiped away the blood again and realized that it was coming from a cut above his eye.

"Schultz is hurt!"

"I'm all right. It's just a scratch."

"Get it looked at," Ty ordered.

Jake had dismounted and had taken to lifting bodies and shaking them.

"I found him. He's back here!" Caleb shouted from the rear. He quickly slid off a glove and checked the boy's pulse. "Willie?"

Jake came running and gathered the scrawny boy in his arms. "Willie, wake up!" Caleb felt around Willie's head and found a lump on the back.

"I think he fell off his horse."

"Somebody get me some water!" Jake's face looked desperate as he tried to revive the boy. A canteen was handed to him and he splashed some water in Willie's face. Willie sputtered, blinked and then sat up.

"What happened?" he asked the concerned faces around him. Jake threw the canteen in his lap and stomped off. "Did I miss the fight?"

Caleb rolled his eyes and ruffled the stringy hair. "Go see if you can find your horse."

Ty let out a sigh of relief when he realized that Willie was all right. There would be no controlling Jake if something happened to the boy. He had only lost one man tonight. One more than he wanted to lose. Around them they could still hear the sounds of battle.

"Mount up and reload, boys. It's not over yet." *Will it ever be over? The fighting, the killing, the waste, the sacrifice. Cat . . .*

For two days and nights they fought on, miraculously surviving it all and finally routing the Union troops and forcing them to retreat north of the Rappahannock River. Jackson was mortally wounded, however, by friendly fire and Ty soon found himself reporting to General J.E.B. Stuart. His small command would be part of the invasion force that was marching toward Pennsylvania.

"What do the papers say?" Penelope asked. Cat did not know how much more bad news the woman could bear but knew she would find out anyway.

"We're losing the war."

They were enjoying breakfast in the garden before the heat of another summer day drove them to seek coolness within the interior of the house. Penelope seemed to enjoy the peace that being outdoors provided her after spending another restless night fighting her illness. She was thinner, almost frail in appearance and would, when no one was watching, use a wall or chair as a support to help her stand. Cat watched over her as best she could while Parker and Lucy Ann pretended that nothing at all was wrong with their world.

It was getting hard to hide the problems they faced. Their money had run out and there was no place to turn. Plantation owners all over the South were facing the same difficulties. Cat still guarded the funds that her father had sent with her; the money was hidden in the false bottom of a small trunk. She was saving it in case she needed it for Ty. She wouldn't let the Kincaids starve, but she also wouldn't let Parker get his hands on it. He had squandered enough as far as she was concerned.

Parker alternated between fits of fury at the inept Southern generals and fits of despair at how much he was suffering from the effects of the war. Lucy Ann pouted because she didn't have any new clothes and plotted her escapades with Zeb. Cat had gotten quite adept at catching the gleam in her eye when she was planning and had managed to thwart her schemes quite a few times. It actually became like a game for her to see to what limits she could push her sister-in-law, but she also realized a life was at stake. Cat couldn't bear the thought of anything happening to Zeb.

It was growing harder now because Penelope depended on her so. She wanted Cat near her constantly, which wasn't too much of a burden because Penelope would tell her stories about Ty when he was a boy. The stories helped to keep him close. They helped to keep the loneliness at bay, except for the long, hot nights when her body ached for him. Cat was afraid of not remembering what he looked like. There was a painting of him as a young man, done before he had gone to Europe on his tour, but the face in the portrait was still soft and innocent. It wasn't the face of the man she loved, just the boy he had been before she knew him. The only thing about the painting that made it truly recognizable as Ty was the sensuous lower lip; even as a baby he had had that lip. Penelope had admitted to giving in to the baby Ty many a time when he stuck out his lower lip in a pout. Cat would gaze on the painting at night before she went to bed, hoping it would inspire dreams of her missing husband, but instead she fought the sheets in frustration, forever looking for him and never finding him.

She wrote to Jenny of her fears, knowing that she

had lived through them. Jenny's replies counseled patience; it was all she could offer, along with her prayers that they all would return safely home. Cat longed to see the babies, who were now two years old and full of mischief, according to letters from her father and Jenny. How had so much time passed while her life was on hold? She wanted to go home, she wanted to feel her father's arms around her, she wanted to walk down to Grace's cabin in the twilight of evening and listen to Zane talk about nonsense. Most of all, she wanted her husband back, safe and whole.

"He's still alive, Cat."

"The papers say we lost more than twenty thousand men at Gettysburg."

"What does your heart tell you?" The bones in Penelope's hand felt as fragile as the papery skin that covered them, but the grip was firm as she reached across the small round table and clasped Cat's hand in her own.

"He's alive." A tear trickled unbidden from beneath dark lashes that sheltered green-gold eyes. "But is he safe?"

"Looks like a bad place for a fight, sir." Ty, who now wore the rank of major, stood with several other officers on a wooded ridge overlooking what was known as The Wilderness, south of the Rapidan River. The densely wooded countryside stretched out for miles before them. Scouts had reported the underbrush thick and the area crossed with ravines and creeks. Creeping vines and sticky briars added to the desolation of the sparsely populated area.

"At least we won't have to worry about artillery," another officer commented.

"Looks like our kind of fight." Were they trying to convince each other or themselves?

"You have your orders, men," the general said. "We'll see you on the other side."

"As near as I can tell, this is the one remaining place in Virginia that we haven't fought over already." Jake snorted as Ty rejoined his growing command.

Ty checked his weapons again. *When did Jake get to be so bitter?* His horse tossed its head, feeling anticipation for the coming battle through its rider. *God be with us.* Ty shook his head, knowing that the same prayer was being said on the other side. *Cat . . .*

"Going to be hard to maneuver the horses through that mess."

Ty blinked, trying to catch what had just been said. *Don't think about her; thinking about her will get you killed.* He wondered when it had gotten so easy to remove her from his mind. There had even been times when he had almost convinced himself she didn't really exist, but the dreams reminded him. He always found her waiting for him in the soft world of slumber and then he would wake beneath his lonely blanket on the hard ground and ache with wanting her.

The bugle echoed through the ridges and ravines. Jake let out a war whoop, and his horse jumped forward. Willie was right behind him. *Damn fool's going to get us all killed.* They plowed into the battlefield, each now a well-trained killing machine, each living the day one second at a time, knowing that it was kill or be killed.

The woods were alive with the enemy, but for the men of the South, it was a natural way to fight. The trees soon became thick with the smoke of fired weapons and the attempt by the artillery on both sides to make a difference in the outcome. Each man fought as if alone, not knowing if those who fought beside him were friend or foe. The smoke added to the deep gloom of the forest until it was impossible to tell night from day. The horses were of no use to the men under these conditions, so they turned them loose and sent them galloping back toward the south, knowing they were well-trained and would wait for their masters.

The shot, when it hit him, surprised him. Ty spared an instant to look down at the blood that stained the shoulder of his coat before he slashed his sword across the chest of the man who was coming toward him with his rifle butt raised. It was hard to breathe. How long had he been fighting? He looked up toward the treetops, hoping to see the sky, but there was nothing to see except dense smoky fog and a strange glow coming from the east. *The woods are on fire!* Ty heard footsteps behind him and turned, raising his sword to take the impact of the blow. He saw the rifle butt coming but was too late to stop it. He sank into the soft floor of the dense woods and watched the booted feet of his attacker move on to the next unsuspecting victim. *Cat* . . . He lost her face in the darkness.

* * *

Cat sat up in a rush, drawing in great gulps of air. Her heart was pounding in her chest. She looked over at Penelope, lying still as death in her bed. A small intake of breath reassured her. Cat gathered her robe from the foot of the cot she was now sleeping on in Penelope's room and softly padded to the window on bare feet.

She had seen Ty in her dream as clearly as if he were standing in front of her. She leaned her forehead against the clear cool glass and recalled the image to her mind. She saw him again, resplendent in his uniform, a revolver in one hand, a sword in the other and behind him a fire with flames shooting high into the darkness of the sky. Was he safe? "God keep him safe. Keep all of them safe."

"Cat?"

The voice from the bed was weak, barely audible, but Cat had become attuned to it and was by Penelope's side in an instant.

"I'm here."

"Where's Ty?" How many times had she asked that question this spring, along with others that couldn't be answered? Where was her husband? Where was her son? What's wrong? What's happened? And why won't the good Lord just let me die instead of torturing me with this long, lingering death? The nights were the worst for she became disoriented and couldn't comprehend the answers Cat gave her. She no longer recognized Lucy Ann, she called Parker by his father's name and she insisted that Ty was hiding from her.

"Ty will be here soon, Penelope." *Please let him*

be here soon. "You go back to sleep and when you wake up he'll be here." She wouldn't remember what Cat had told her when she woke up and they would go through it again, both of them needing to believe in her words.

Cat smoothed the translucent skin of Penelope's forehead and gathered one of the frail hands in her own. Perhaps it was better for her, not knowing. She didn't have to deal with the worries and the reports from the front and the fact that there had been no letters except for a brief one at Christmastime scribbled on the back of one of Caleb's drawings. Penelope settled back into her world of half sleep with a sigh. The cot that had been Cat's bed for more weeks than she could count did not call to her in the same way, so Cat settled into the rocking chair and pulled the afghan she had knitted under her chin.

May 6, 1864. Yes, it was past midnight so it was May 6. They had come from Wyoming almost three years ago. Had any of them thought it would go on this long? How much longer could she wait living this half life? What if Ty never came back? He had to come back. She had finally written and told him about his mother's illness after keeping it a secret from him for more than a year. He had to come back before she died. He needed to come back soon.

A creak of the floorboards alerted her to movement in the hallway. Cat was across the room and out the door in an instant, startling Lucy Ann, who was creeping down the stairs.

"My goodness, Cat, you scared the life out of me."

She was on her way out, Cat surmised by the look

of frustration that crossed her face. "Would you mind sitting with Penelope for a while?" Cat took her victories where she could find them. "I'm feeling a bit under the weather, and I would hate to expose her to anything." Cat could just imagine the wheels turning in Lucy Ann's head as she searched for an excuse to be awake yet not able to sit with Penelope.

"Oh, well, I was feeling a bit weak myself." Lucy Ann's hand went to her stomach, feigning an imaginary ache. "Must have been something we ate for dinner."

"I'll ask Portia about it in the morning," Cat volunteered, not wanting Lucy Ann to take out her frustration on the cook. "Can you make it back to your room all right?"

Lucy Ann looked at her closed portal down the hall and then at the elegantly curving staircase that would lead to her satisfaction. Cat could almost see the wheels turning in her head as her sister-in-law searched for an answer, for any excuse that would get her out of the house and on to her perverted rendezvous. Cat was almost tempted to search the pockets of the robe she wore for the knife that she used to keep Zeb under her power.

"Lucy Ann?"

She turned a syrupy smile on Cat. "I'll be fine." Cat watched until she was safely behind her door and couldn't resist a self-satisfied grin as she went back into Penelope's room. But when the door was closed behind her and the house returned to its silent state, the worries came tumbling back, one upon the other.

Is he safe?

Chapter Ten

"We're not getting any younger, Grace." They were sitting on her porch in the swing, gently rocking as they enjoyed the cool peace of late evening in early May. Grace raised her head from Cole's shoulder and gathered her shawl about her. "It's been three years . . ."

Had it been so long since Cole had showed up on that snowy winter's day? Three years since Jamie died; three years since Cat, Ty, Jake and Caleb went off to war. Three years this summer that the babies had come into their lives. More than three years that his niece, Amanda, had been missing. Where had the time gone? Had it been lost in the small day-to-day activities that made up life on the ranch or had it just stood still, wrapping all of them in the small valley in a cocoon of safety. It had been two years since Cole returned from New Orleans, frustrated by the dead ends he had found in his search for Amanda and unable to follow the small lead to Nassau until the war was over. Three years of sitting in the swing after the chores were done, discussing the small events of the day, three years of unfulfilled longing for each other because he was unable to ask Grace to marry him until he had done the best he could by Amanda.

"So what are you waiting for?" Cole looked down at her with amazement as Grace looked away, suddenly ashamed of her boldness. "I'm no inexperienced virgin, Cole. I've done some things I'm not proud of."

His finger turned her chin toward his face. "You did what you had to do to survive."

Grace smiled and the scars disappeared into the lines of her cheek. "Not always. Some of it was just for the pleasure or the companionship." How had they avoided talking like this for so long?

"It's been the same for me. You don't live the type of life we lead and not get lonely."

Grace walked to the end of the porch and looked up toward the ridge. Justice thumped his tail as she went by, now as devoted to her as he was to his master. "Jamie and I were together for a while." Cole came up behind her. "I felt so foolish at first since he was so much younger than I, but he had this way about him. That boy could sweet-talk his way around anyone," she said, laughing. "It was because of our scars." Grace's hand trailed down the left side of her face, seeing Jamie's scars in her mind as she did so.

"None of Caleb's drawings show his scars," Cole remarked, not sure of where the conversation was leading.

"It was a passing thing between us, nothing more. I loved Jamie, but not in that way. Not in the way that a woman loves a man with her entire being. Not in the way that Jenny loves Chase, or Cat loves Ty. I never thought that kind of love was possible for me. I always thought it passed me by as a punishment for my sins."

"Grace . . ." Cole gripped her shoulders and turned her to face him.

"Until I met you." Deep brown eyes stared up into his cool gray ones. "What are your intentions toward me, Mr. Larrimore?"

That had been the burning question in his mind since the day he had met her. Old habits died hard, especially when a man got to be his age, but then again some things were worth the risk, no matter what the lessons of the past had taught him. Cole found himself at the top of a precipice, teetering on the edge with the rest of his life laid out before him. The choice was his as to how he would spend the rest of it, but would she have the patience and understanding that others before her hadn't been willing to share? It would be a long, lonely road if she didn't. He realized that even in the uncertainty of his life there had been one consistency. And she was standing right here before him. "I love you, Grace."

"But?"

"But I don't know what's going to happen with Amanda. And as long as we're bringing up ghosts of the past, you should know that I was married a long time ago. It was a big mistake, and she's been dead for years."

"So you're a widower?" She wasn't surprised; he was much too attractive to have remained a bachelor all these years. He had to have had a past.

"I guess that's what you call it. I preferred the term free at last when it happened." Cole smiled down at her, noticing that she had suddenly turned coy.

"But you do love me?"

"Yes, but how about you? I haven't heard a declaration from your lips yet."

Grace placed her hand in his. "I love you, Cole." She smiled up at him. "And at some other time I want to hear all about this dead wife of yours. But right now, I think we have more important things to talk about." She led him into the cabin. Justice got up to follow, as usual, but was met with a door firmly closed in his face. He watched it for a moment with bright eyes and a tilted head, then turned and lay down across the stoop.

Across the small valley the Duncan family had retired early for the night. Jenny had decided a long time ago that keeping up with two precocious boys who were close to three years old was much harder than nursing two babies. Especially when one of the boys was Chance. Just that morning he had singlehandedly turned over the wash tub, drenching not only himself but Fox and Justice as well. Justice had wisely retreated to a safe place beneath the porch while Fox crinkled his wide blue eyes and clapped his hands gleefully at his sudden bath. From then on the day had gone straight downhill. Chance had thrown his picture book down the privy and then cried when Jenny refused to get it out. He threw his lunch at Dan, which brought gales of laughter from the hands along with more applause from Fox and led to another lecture from Jenny on how the men shouldn't encourage Chance's bad behavior. She was finally able to get both boys down for a nap in Grace's cabin so she could spend some time training Storm Cloud, who at two years of age was looking more and more like his sire, Storm. Chance woke up while Grace was getting the laundry off the line and snuck out of the cabin. Jenny found him in the corral surrounded by yearlings that were in the process of being weaned from their mothers. She couldn't fault him for that, she thought to herself as she scooped him up from between the long legs of the yearlings. He came by his fascination with horses naturally. It was in his blood, just as his restless wandering was. How many times had her mother chastised her as a child for being adventurous and getting herself into sticky situations? Jason had already put the search out for ponies for both of the boys in his neverending quest to spoil them rotten.

Jenny also realized that she couldn't stay mad at her son for long either. No matter how much he frustrated her, he was a part of her. One look at the dark head peacefully asleep in the double bed that he shared with his cousin was all it took to melt her heart. If only he would stay this way. She fell into bed that night exhausted from her day. She fell asleep before her head hit the pillow, missing the good-night kiss that Chase gently brushed on her cheek as he rubbed her back, amazed once again at the patience she showed with their boys.

Jenny found her dreams to be just as frustrating as her day. As she drifted on the ocean of the big bed she found herself in a misty dream land searching for something she couldn't find. Her mind could not settle on what was missing as she ran from place to place, finding only locked doors and empty rooms. She found herself pounding on a portal at the end of a long hall and suddenly it opened and she tumbled out onto a mound of soft green grass.

The light in her dream was so bright, she shielded her eyes and slowly turned as she scanned the horizon. She saw the small valley where she lived lying peaceful in the night. In her cabin she saw the forms of the boys asleep in the room Chase had added on and then she saw the long body of her husband sprawled on his back with an arm thrown over his head, his wide chest slowly rising and falling in slumber. Her place beside him was empty. The image funneled away from her mind, growing smaller in the distance. She felt as if she could reach out and touch it, even in its miniature form, but eventually it faded away until it was no larger than the head of a pin.

A noise behind her caught her attention and she turned, finding the source of the bright light. A fire was raging and beneath it a battle was going on. She saw Ty, Jake and Caleb, all covered in blood, all fighting desperately for their lives. Then she realized Cat was there also, wielding a sword, slashing at the enemies that continued to come. Above the battle, the flames still raged and danced until they took form. The form became a face and Jenny realized that she was looking into the face of Wade Bishop. He was the one who controlled the fire and he controlled the battle. There was no way her friends could win. They were lost because of him.

Jenny blinked against the darkness of the night. Beside her she could hear the steady breathing of Chase. His mouth was against her ear and his arm placed protectively over her stomach. She slid from beneath it as quietly as she could and crept to the door that linked the new room with the old.

The boys were both sleeping peacefully. Fox on his stomach, as usual, with a worn rag doll stuffed under his arm and his hair flopped into his eyes. Chance lay on his back with both arms spread above him, snoring slightly from a stuffy nose, no doubt the result of his dousing with the laundry water. Jenny rearranged their quilt and deposited soft kisses amid swirls of hair.

"Momma?" Chance drifted up from his dreams.

"Shh, go back to sleep."

Back in the main room of the cabin, a letter from Cat lay on the table. It was full of her worries for Ty. She had reached out to Jenny because Jenny had lived through similar fears when Chase had gone on his pursuit of Jamie's killer. What would she have done if he had been gone as long as Ty? Would she have survived the waiting if it had been years instead of months? Could she have gotten through the birth and the day-to-day living without Chase by her side? She couldn't stand to think about it, but she had to because Cat needed her help. But how could she send her words of reassurance when her dream had just told her Ty, Caleb, and Jake were in mortal danger? She was sure of it now, just as she was also sure they had managed to remain unharmed for this long. But what did Wade Bishop have to do with it? Why was he mixed up in her dreams of her friends?

The Bible lay next to Cat's letter. How did it get from the carved angel box on the nightstand to the table? Chase must have left it there; he had been poring over the Old Testament lately and telling her stories of conquests from the days before Christ. Jenny turned up the lamp and sat at the table.

She said a silent prayer and flipped the worn pages open. Her eyes were immediately drawn to the top of the page, the second column, Philippians 4:6. "Be careful for nothing; but in every thing by prayer and supplication with thanksgiving let your requests be made known unto God."

Ask God to take care of Ty. How many times had she prayed that prayer when Chase had been gone? *Keep him safe, God, and please bring him back.* It had become a constant for her, almost like breathing.

God had answered her prayer. But why, then, had He not kept her parents alive or Jamie? Why had He let her suffer the trials she had gone through before she had come to this place of happiness? She would never know the answers to those questions but she was so grateful for the blessings that she had.

Would God answer Cat's prayer and keep Ty alive, along with Caleb and Jake? Only God knew that. It was up to those who prayed to have faith.

"Are you all right?" Chase's voice was soft and full of concern as he sat up in the bed, looking for her.

"Yes." No need to worry him with her dream. Not

just yet. He was all light and shadow against the white of the sheets and the dark wood of the headboard. "I was just writing to Cat."

"She sounded scared in her last letter."

"She's worried about Ty. He's been gone for a long time."

"He's just doing what he has to do, Jenny. They all are." His voice sounded distant in the darkness around the bed. He was remembering his time away. Jenny rose from the table; she knew the demons couldn't be far away. She had vowed to fight them. His eyes glowed silver in the darkness, creating a familiar ache deep inside her. She shed her gown as she came to him, her body already shivering in anticipation. Jenny slid under the sheet into Chase's waiting arms. They enclosed her as she molded herself to his body, and his lips found hers. This feeling of being carried off into the big night sky swept away the images that haunted the corners of both of their minds. Jenny silently said a prayer for the safety of her friends before reason left her and passion took over. She also said a prayer of thanksgiving that her husband was with her. That he had come back to her. That he would never leave her again.

Chapter Eleven

The mixture of different smells, none of them pleasant, made his stomach turn, or was it the wave of pain that rolled through his shoulder? Slowly the dense fog lifted from his weary brain and Ty found himself lying on a splintery plank with the late afternoon sun shining in his eyes. He turned his head away from the light and saw a scarred table covered with stained and bloody medical instruments. A rather thin and bent man of indeterminate age was wiping his hands on an apron that looked as if it had been found on the floor of a slaughterhouse.

"Where am I?" Ty had to force the words through a throat that felt like charred wood. His tongue was swollen and his lips dry, and he wondered if the man would be able to understand him.

"Field hospital." The man picked up an instrument. "It would have been better if you'd stayed out of it for a while longer, Major. I haven't had a chance to dig that bullet out of your shoulder yet."

Ty looked at his shoulder where his sleeve had

been ripped away and then sat up on the plank. "Where are my men?" he croaked. His throat felt as if it was on fire and it hurt to breathe. Ty searched with watery eyes for a familiar face and a drink of water.

"Getting ready to ride to Spotsylvania for another battle from what I hear. Two of them carried you in here." The man placed a hand on Ty's arm. "Now why don't you lie back down and let me dig that bullet out."

"I don't suppose they said anything about my horse?"

"No, they didn't. Would you please lie down now?"

Ty looked in disgust at the bloody instruments and the man's soiled hands. "Are you a doctor?"

"I'm the closest thing you're going to find to one."

His head and shoulder throbbed in unison. The bullet needed to come out, but the chance of infection scared him more that the wound. "Have you got any whiskey?"

The man produced a jug from under the table. Ty took a swig of the vile potion that burned his already parched throat and then poured some on his shoulder, clenching his teeth as he did so.

"Hey, you're wasting it!" the man protested.

Ty grabbed the hand that held the instrument and doused it along with the sharp metal probe. He then lay back on the plank with the jug firmly grasped in his hand. "Get on with it."

The man handed him a piece of wood, which Ty placed in his mouth. Then he braced his hand against

Ty's arm and jabbed the metal probe in the wound. Ty bit on the wood and grasped the edge of the plank as the pain shot through his arm and shoulder into his chest. He felt each movement of the probe as it searched through the wound. His eyes had begun to water when he heard the clink of steel against lead. Finally the shot was out and the man threw it in a bowl on the table at the same time that Ty spit out the splintered piece of wood. Blood poured forth from the wound and Ty liberally doused it again with the whiskey.

"Wrap it up," Ty gasped. "And try to use something clean."

The man looked at Ty as if he were insane, but complied. Ty's head protested when he found his feet but his resolve conquered the pain, and he soon was on his way toward the general army.

He caught up with Caleb and Jake along with the rest of his men as they were forming up to ride out. "Where's my horse?" His voice sounded better but it still hurt to talk.

"How about thank you for finding me before I got cooked in that fire pit that used to be a battlefield?" Jake leaned casually across his saddle as Willie took off to get Ty's horse from an officer who had confiscated the faithful gelding after losing his own in the battle.

"Shouldn't you be in the hospital?" Caleb asked with concern showing in his warm dark eyes.

"Only if I want to die. And I'm not quite ready to do that yet." His throat still hurt and he coughed. Caleb handed him a canteen and he gratefully took it, leaning his head back to take great gulps of the cool water. Caleb handed him a kerchief when he was done with his drink.

"Your face is covered with soot," Caleb explained.

"I don't suppose you two picked up my weapons while you were hauling me out."

"Nope." Jake leaned casually across his saddle horn. "But Willie did. He put everything on your horse and then let some fool captain take it from him."

"Did we lose anybody?"

"We lost Murphy."

Willie rode up triumphantly with Ty's horse behind him and a big grin on his face. "That captain sure was mad when I told him the major was looking for his horse."

"I guess it's a good thing I outrank him," Ty said as he swung up. His head swam and his shoulder ached. The horses tossed their heads as they felt the agitation and anticipation of the men, who were all tired of waiting for the order to ride. They all knew they had to beat the Federals to Spotsylvania. The battle just fought had been a vicious one with many of the wounded dying in the fire. But there was no time to take stock of what had happened and prepare for another day. They were all men on a chess board and it was time for a bold move. The Federal army was mustering up to head south, and the race was on.

The sound of the bugle echoed through the wilderness. "Caleb, Jake . . ." They both turned and looked at their commanding officer and their friend. "Thanks for saving my life."

* * *

How much longer could they continue to cheat death? They had been fighting every day since the first of May. For twelve straight days they had battled bitterly for the crossroads. Ty and his men had followed Stuart to the Yellow Tavern in the Richmond suburbs where Stuart was mortally wounded.

And now, finally, there was a brief lull in the campaign. Ty flexed his left shoulder and was grateful that the wound had closed with no sign of infection. Jake had griped the first time he had seen him pour whiskey on the gaping hole but soon realized the danger and had even miraculously produced a bottle from the vicinity of the tavern. Caleb had started fussing over him about the same time. Ty had thought he was doing a good job of hiding the headaches and the coughing from the smoke, but Caleb still watched him as if he was waiting for him to pitch over and die. Ty watched from his bedroll as Caleb approached with a big grin on his face. He pitched an apple to Ty, who caught it in his right hand and immediately took a bite.

"Where'd you find this?" The apple was tart and juicy, and Ty knew it was the best thing he had eaten in a long time.

"There's an orchard down below the mess. I made Willie climb up since all the fruit close to the ground was long gone."

"Thank you." Ty settled back with the apple and tried to will his tired, overworked muscles to relax.

"I found something else, too."

"It's not a pie to put this in, is it?"

Caleb laughed. "No, although one of Grace's would taste good right now."

"Yes, it would." Ty found himself not caring what Caleb had found, although he could sense his friend's worry. The only thing he cared about at the present was ending the war. Jake had accused him several times in the past few days of trying to win it all by himself as he fought viciously against the Yankees. Ty just knew that when the war was over, he could go home. "Do you ever think about home, Caleb?"

Caleb's confusion showed on his face. "Are you talking about your plantation?"

"No, I'm talking about Wyoming. Home. Where the prairie runs for miles and miles and the mountains reach up to the clouds. Doesn't it seem like the sky was bluer there? You can't even see the sky here for all the smoke."

"Yeah, you're right." Caleb settled into his own bedroll as Ty went on.

"I'd give anything to be sitting around Grace's table right now, listening to Zane run on about some nonsense."

"I want to see what the little boys look like."

"It's hard to believe that they're almost three years old and we haven't ever laid eyes on them."

"What else do you miss?"

"I miss all of it." Ty almost felt foolish, talking about things that were so far away.

"How about Cat? Do you miss her?"

"Of course I do." Why did he suddenly feel so defensive?

"Then why don't you write her?"

"I have written her." Ty could not believe that Caleb had the nerve to ask him that.

"One letter in the past two years?" Caleb snorted. He rose from his bedroll and threw an envelope on Ty's chest. "Here's another letter for you to ignore, Major." Caleb stalked off, muttering something about fools and pride.

Caleb didn't understand. Ty leaned close to the fire as he opened the letter. Caleb didn't know that he couldn't tell Cat the war was wrong. He couldn't tell anyone that even though it was wrong, he still had to fight because he had committed himself, along with his friends, to do so. How could he explain all that in a letter to his wife? He could only tell her face-to-face. He needed to beg her for her forgiveness and promise that he wouldn't let his foolish pride make decisions for them anymore.

He couldn't explain that to Caleb any more than he could explain it to Cat. He just wanted the war to be over so he could make it up to her. He shouldn't have gotten so foolish with Caleb, talking about home. It was just that he was so tired.

He quickly read the letter by the light of the small fire and then folded it and placed it inside his shirt. Ty blinked a few times and poked at the fire. The smoke had taken a turn and was making his eyes water. He lay back on his bedroll, exhausted. Caleb found him sound asleep when he returned and joined him in his own pursuit of rest.

Chapter Twelve

Cat pulled the sheet over Penelope's face. It would be dawn soon; no need to wake anyone now. Over the mountains in the distance she saw the flash of lightning that promised a morning shower for the Kincaid plantation. She rubbed her arms to combat the chill. She had just watched a woman she had grown to love breathe her last breath.

Cat had never known her own mother. Her aunt in New York and Grace were the closest she would ever come to having one. The time she had spent with Penelope had opened her eyes to what it was like to be a mother. Penelope had lived her life for her children's happiness. And during the last months of her life she had relived her own mistakes in raising her two sons. Her biggest regret had been not stepping between Ty and his father as she watched them grow farther and farther apart during the years of Ty's growing up.

Cat had learned a lot in the months she had sat by Penelope's side through the long nights of her suffering. She hoped she would remember it all and learn from her mother-in-law's mistakes. If only she would have a chance to use the lessons just learned, if only she would have a chance to be a mother.

Was this her fate then? Would she be forever childless and forever waiting for her husband to come home? Would she be a widow before she turned twenty-five? Cat looked through the window at the coming dawn and saw a long, lonely road stretching before her. There was nothing left to hold her at the plantation except the hope that she was closer to Ty here and he knew she was waiting. Where was he? Why didn't he write? *Is he safe?*

Cat had decided that the entire process was too morbid for words. When Jamie had died, they had buried him the next day before the ground froze hard again. This entire process of laying the dead out for viewing was pointless as far as she was concerned, but Lucy Ann seemed to be enjoying all the attention it created. She had actually fallen across Penelope's body and sobbed loudly at one time in the afternoon when the house had been full of visitors, who were more interested in the table laden with food that Portia had prepared than the fact that the Kincaids were in mourning. Parker had taken her away with the help of Silas, dutifully acting out the role of son and surviving heir since his brother was off fighting for the glory of God and country, leaving Parker to bear the burdens at home alone.

Parker and Lucy Ann had retired early to rest for the funeral the next day. Cat sat with the body, alone, nothing but the mourning from the slave quarters to keep her company. She heard the pitiful cries fade and knew the slaves were crying more for themselves than the departure of their mistress. Who knew what the future would hold for them now without the grace and wisdom of Penelope to temper Parker's judgment.

The body was dressed in black and draped with a fine lace veil to keep away the gnats that had arrived with the latest summer storm. Cat wore a mourning gown of black satin, hastily made over by the plantation seamstress from one of Penelope's own that she had worn when her husband had died. The high neck and long sleeves were comfortable now in the cool of the night but Cat knew that the next day would bring more heat and humidity. She longed for the cool wind coming down from the mountains of Wyoming as she sat on the straight-back chair next to the body. The tall clock kept time in the hallway and the gentle snoring of Silas, asleep in his chair, was strangely comforting.

How many nights had it been since she had slept from dusk to dawn? Penelope had slept in fits and starts, calling out for her every time she had awakened. Cat felt herself drifting as the gentle ticking lulled her into a state of half sleep. She could see herself sitting in the chair as if she were drifting above. A sound from outside jerked her back to consciousness, and she stood as she heard Silas open the door.

How long had it been since she had seen Ty? At one time she had thought she could count down to the exact second the time that had passed since he had walked from the room they shared. His golden-brown hair seemed lighter now and flowed in waves down to his shoulders. He was thinner than she remembered, but hard, like the sword he wore at his side, polished and lethal.

As he walked into the parlor, Cat trembled, wrinkling the fine linen handkerchief she held into a tight ball. The light from the candles caught his eyes, and she saw the lines around them. Where had the lines come from? He was dressed in a gray coat with gold braid running up the sleeves. She knew he had been promoted, but did not know enough to recognize the rank on his shoulder.

The room started spinning around her. Was she dreaming? Strong arms caught her as she began her descent to the floor. She felt herself crushed against a hard chest, Ty's chest, but she did not recognize the scent of him. How long had it been? Was he really here?

"Ty?"

"Yes, it's me." Had he always sounded like this? Why couldn't she remember? Cat raised her head and with a trembling hand touched his cheek. There was a small scar over his brow. When had he gotten it?

"You're alive."

"Yes." He looked beyond her to where Penelope's body lay. "When?" His voice was hoarse. Cat was able to stand again and he released her, walking past her to the table where his mother rested.

"Early yesterday morning."

"I came as soon as I got your letter." His back was turned to her as he stood over the body. He picked up Penelope's hand and gently stroked it.

"But I wrote it months ago, last spring."

"We're at war, Cat."

She felt the sobs welling up inside her. "I know. Don't you think I know . . . that . . ." Cat wrapped an arm around her stomach and placed a hand over her mouth to stem the tide of emotion that threatened to overtake her. Was this how Jenny felt when Chase had come back? Ty's body was standing before her, but where was Ty? How could he be so cold and callous? She had to do something, and since her legs were trembling again, she sat down in the hard chair next to the table.

Ty replaced the hand beneath the lace veil. Cat shuddered as she fought to control the storm that threatened to carry her away.

"Cat?" She looked up at him through tears that wouldn't be stopped. He dropped to his knees in front of her. Strong arms crept around her waist and his head found her breast. She touched his hair; it was still soft and silky as she remembered it. "I love you, Cat."

They were burying his mother and yet Cat felt nothing but joy. Ty had fallen into bed the night before, weary and exhausted. Cat had found him sound asleep after taking care of Jake, Caleb and Willie, who had discreetly waited outside for a bit to let Cat and Ty have some time together. She had spent what remained of the night watching him. She could sleep later, when he was gone again. She knew without a doubt that he would leave. He took his responsibilities so very seriously. Caleb had confided to her that the only reason they had come was because their commanding officer had ordered it. It troubled her to know that her husband had to be ordered to come home, but then again, he was here and she would enjoy his company while she had it.

She wondered at the dreams that caused fleeting expressions to chase themselves across his handsome face. She knew they had all seen horrors; it was ever present in their eyes. Images of Chase kept creeping into her mind and she continually reminded herself that he was fine, and he and Jenny were happy.

The rising sun cast a rosy glow about the room, turning his body golden in the soft light. Cat lightly touched the puckered scar on his left shoulder and wondered at the story behind it. She couldn't stop her trembling as her hand trailed down to where his heart lay beating in his chest. A better shot would have gone through that precious part of him, and she said a prayer of thanksgiving for the very busy guardian angel who was watching over her husband.

Long, lean fingers crept up her back and steel-blue eyes found uptilted ones that had turned gold in the morning light. Ty's other hand touched her cheek and pulled her down to waiting lips. His kiss was soft and searching, barely whispering against lips that trembled in response.

Ty rose beside her, and his hands grasped her upper arms. Cat placed her hands on his shoulders and met him halfway. She felt the strength in his arms and Ty felt the melting of her body. Ty's next kiss was questioning, and then it became demanding. He seized her lips with his own, claiming her as his wife, leaving no doubt in her mind as to how much he wanted her.

Cat poured her soul into her answer, desperately seeking his body, heart and soul with her own. The two of them fell back against the mattress, wrestling with the sheets and her gown, a sob catching in her throat as she reached for him, a growl in his as she guided him into her softness.

Their bodies remembered each other. Their eyes stayed open and found answers in each other. They hung on to each other as if to a life line as the dance as old as time began.

She was thrilled beyond measure to know that she had not forgotten what this felt like. He knew without a doubt that she was his salvation. Finally, when the passion overtook them, their eyes closed in unison as if arranged by previous agreement, and they clung to each other, both of them promising that they would never let go.

The house slowly came awake around them. Portia was in the kitchen, preparing a homecoming feast from the depleted larder. Silas tended his mistress in the parlor, performing his last duties for her. Parker paced in his office, impatient for news of the front from his brother. Lucy Ann plotted in her room, knowing that she still had to get around Cat, who wouldn't have Penelope to distract her anymore. In the barn, Zeb carefully groomed the team of matching blacks to take their mistress on her last ride. Jake, Caleb and Willie slept comfortably for the first time in a long while on soft beds beneath clean sheets. And in the room that had been Ty's since childhood, husband and wife found each other again, and again, until they were spent and knew it was time to greet the day.

Even with the solemn crowd and mournful faces, Cat's heart was singing. She knew that Penelope had gone on to a better place. She had sat with her night after night while the woman begged for death. It was a time for rejoicing because Penelope's suffering was over. It was a time for rejoicing because her beloved husband was by her side.

Ty was resplendent in his uniform. The coat had been brushed, the buttons polished, and the navy pants with the bright gold stripe pressed. He shook hands with the mourners and humbly dismissed any rumors of his bravery on the battlefield while Willie protested his modesty and launched into tales of valor that included Caleb and Jake. Cat shuddered to think about what the three of them had been through in battle. It was enough for her that they had survived this long.

She knew they were leaving the next day. Ty had told her that they were to rendezvous with the rest of his troop; meet up with the smuggler, Wade Bishop; and transport ammunition from their secret stash in the mountains of what was now the separate state of West Virginia. They would deliver it to a ship that was in hiding somewhere along the Cape Fear River. Bishop was to deliver the ammunition to points south where the Union blockades made getting in and out almost impossible, except for the ghost ships that smugglers like Bishop used.

Cat had the rest of the day and all of the night to be with Ty. She watched him from across the study, which was crowded with landowners and townspeople who had come for the funeral. The afternoon sunlight danced off the golden streaks that ran through his freshly washed and trimmed hair. His teeth flashed white against sun-bronzed skin and the scar over his brow added an element of danger as he talked to the men, who all wanted news of the war.

There was nothing he could tell them. The South had lost a lot of good men and the North had lost a lot of good men. The North had more men to throw into the fight than the South. The prisoner exchange had been halted because the men of the South were returning to the battlefield. Now there were horror stories coming from the prison camps on both sides. Would that slow death be better than one on the battlefield? Neither would serve any purpose, Cat decided as she listened to the debate.

She needed time with Ty. She needed to talk to him about little things, but she also needed to tell him about the big things. He needed to know what Lucy Ann was up to. He needed to know that the plantation was on the edge of bankruptcy and Parker refused to acknowledge it. But most of all, he needed to know how much she loved him, that her life wouldn't be worth living if something happened to him.

Maybe then he would be more careful, instead of charging full bore into battle. She had heard the stories Willie was telling everyone about his major and

Jake and Caleb. She had never doubted their bravery, but she also knew that their honor would overrule their common sense on the battlefield. She had plans for them all and they included growing old together. Very old. Very together.

The close quarters and the heat of the day were contributing to a headache that was now pounding against her temples. She made her way through the company of men who had all gathered around her husband. His arm encircled her as she came to his side with polite apologies to the throng. A moment later found them in the peaceful solitude of the garden and the privacy of the corner arbor.

"Thanks for rescuing me." Ty kissed her hand, which was clasped in his own as they sat on the bench. Heavy boughs of wisteria dripped over the arbor, granting them shade and seclusion from anyone who happened to be about. The blooms of purple and blue gave off a heady fragrance that was refreshing after the close contact of many overdressed bodies. "And thank you for what you did for my mother." His arm slid around her shoulders and her head found the familiar resting spot beneath his chin. "Portia told me you were the one who took care of her, until the end."

"It was the least I could do, Ty. After all, she gave me the most precious gift."

"What was that?"

"You."

She felt his smile against her upswept hair and his arm around her tightened.

"I'm sorry I haven't written more."

"I understand why you haven't."

"You do?"

"It's hard enough, what you're doing, without having to worry about me and whether or not I'm happy."

"But I should at least let you know that I'm alive."

"I knew you were alive."

"How?"

Cat rose up and placed her hand over the left side of his coat, where his heart beat firmly in his chest. "I felt it here. Your mother told me that my heart would know when yours stopped beating, just as hers did when your father died. I knew you were alive. I just worried about how you were, how you were doing."

His hand caressed the softness of her cheek. "I'm doing fine, Cat."

"Are you?" Her eyes had turned as green as the leaves that sheltered them. "The thing that scares me the most is what this war is doing to you, Ty. Remember what Chase was like when he came back from killing Logan? I'm afraid the same thing will happen to you, and I won't be strong enough to save you." A tear slipped from beneath dark lashes and trickled into his palm.

"As long as I know I have you to come home to, I promise I will be fine." He pulled her into his lap and cradled her against him like a child.

"That's something that you won't have to worry about." Her arms crept around his neck, and her head found his shoulder. "I miss home, Ty. Do you think this war will be over soon?"

"Yes. It can't go on much longer. The battles we've fought this summer have been futile, and we're running low on men and supplies. I don't know how much longer the South is going to be able to hold on."

"Then why are you still fighting?"

"Because I gave my word that I would fight, until the end."

Cat knew it was useless to enter into that debate.

"You talked to Parker?"

"Yes."

"What did he tell you?"

"A lot of ranting and raving about England and France not supporting us and there's no credit to be had anywhere. I guess things are looking pretty bad for everyone."

"I have to give Portia credit, she can make a little go a long way."

"It will be over soon. You'll be eating Grace's cooking before you know it."

"That will be fine with me." She had put it off long enough. "Have you talked to Zeb at all?"

"No, I haven't had time. Why? What's wrong?"

Cat sat up and faced him on the bench. "You're going to find this pretty hard to believe and I want you to think about it before you do anything." Cat explained the incident she had witnessed between Zeb and Lucy Ann and the conclusions she had come to regarding the slave whose beating Ty had attempted to stop years earlier. He listened with a look of disbelief on his face, but as she told her story he obviously came to the same conclusion.

"She deserves to be stripped and whipped herself!" he exclaimed with a curse when Cat was done.

"I think I've put an end to it somewhat. I've kept a pretty close eye on her since I realized what's been going on. I just don't know what to do about Zeb. I think he'd be mortified if anyone knew about it."

"You're right about that. Do you think Lucy Ann knows that you know?"

"I don't know. She's not going to come up and ask, that's for sure. I caught her quite a few times trying to sneak out of the house in the middle of the night, and she always came up with some excuse, but I don't know how many times she got out without me knowing about it. I wonder if Parker knows what's going on."

"That's a good question. I don't think he'd stand for it, but for him the embarrassment of having it known would be worse. It sure does explain a lot."

"I always wondered why they never had any children. It must be because she can't." Unbidden tears for her own childless state gathered behind her eyes. Cat willed them away. She refused to give up on having a child with Ty. "What should we do?"

"I don't know right now. I don't know what we can do at this point. I will have a talk with Zeb."

"Ty, don't tell him what I saw. It would kill him."

"I won't. I just wonder how long this has been going on."

"It probably started sometime after you went to Wyoming."

"Years. Poor Zeb. I wondered why he never married any of the women on the plantation. Now I know why."

"Wouldn't being married have protected him from Lucy Ann's advances?"

"You don't understand Zeb's sense of honor. He wouldn't marry any of them because he would feel that he wasn't good enough for them. He's caught in a trap."

"And he couldn't say anything because it would mean his own death sentence."

"It doesn't seem fair, does it?" Ty was agonizing over his friend's plight and had not realized what he'd said.

"No, it doesn't. And this is what you're off fighting to preserve." The words spilled out of her before she could stop them.

She could have slapped him and done less damage. Cat wanted the words back as soon as she said them. Ty saw the truth of her statement and realized he was in the same situation that Zeb was in. Trapped by his own sense of honor.

"I'm sorry . . ." Her voice trembled. She hadn't meant to hurt him. She would rather die than hurt him.

"I don't want to waste time fighting with you, Cat. I have enough of that to look forward to. Right or wrong, I'm committed to this cause and I have to see it through." He felt so weary. He wondered briefly if it showed.

"I know." Cat bit her lip. When would she learn to think before she spoke? Would he leave with the bitter words ringing in his mind? How could she bear it if he left without forgiving her?

"I'm going to talk to Zeb and then we'll figure out what we're going to do about the situation."

"Ty?" She was afraid he would leave.

He bent to kiss her. "We've got a lot of time to make up for, Cat. Like I said, I don't want to waste it." She watched as he walked away, so handsome in his uniform. She hated it.

Chapter Thirteen

Ty found Zeb in the coolness of the barn, polishing the carriage that had carried the family to the cemetery. He paused just inside the dim interior and watched Zeb as he worked.

Hands that could crush his jaw worked at the intricate carvings in the brass fixtures that trimmed the carriage. Because of his great height, Zeb knelt beside the carriage, which brought his arms to a perfect level for the cleaning and polishing. The tattered shirt he was wearing was too small, and Ty marveled that the seams held the great breadth of chest and shoulders that strained the stitching. How could such a strong man be forced into subjection by Lucy Ann? Ty knew the answer and hated it, because he was part of it.

He had excused slavery all these years because it was the way things had always been. That didn't make it right, and he knew it. Generation after generation had been handing the problem down to the next to deal with, which led to nothing being done. Acceptance of the issue had become a way of life and no one had had the courage to look for an alternative. But now it was being forced upon them.

Ty had long ago realized that it was time for things to change; unfortunately the realization had come too late to be of any use to him. He was trapped by his sense of honor, just as Zeb was trapped by the color of his skin. He was fighting to keep his friend a slave and his friend, subjected to slavery, was not in a position to fight for his own freedom. It was up to strangers from the north to do that for him. Ty had to shake his head at the irony of it all.

"How are you doing, Zeb?" Ty casually laid his arm across a wheel.

"I be fine, Mister Ty." The dark head was bowed as Zeb concentrated on the task at hand.

"Are you sure?"

"Yes, sir." The brass gleamed in the dimness of the barn as Zeb continued working on an imaginary spot.

Ty laid a hand on the bigger man's shoulder. "If things weren't fine, would you tell me?"

"Mister Ty, you gots enough to worry about without adding me to your troubles."

"Zeb, I consider you to be my friend and friends talk to each other about their problems."

Zeb stopped his polishing and looked up at his master. He quietly unfolded himself to his great height and looked down at Ty.

"That's a nice thing for you to say, Mister Ty, but you ain't allowed to be my friend. Mister George done tole me that a long time ago. And I don't have no problems that you need to be worrying yourself over."

"You're wrong about that, Zeb. I can be your friend; I don't need anybody's permission to be so. And I do worry about you, and so does Cat."

"Did Miz Catherine tell you to come down here and talk to me?"

"She's noticed some things, Zeb," Ty said, wading in. "Some things that I know you'd rather not talk about." Zeb sighed and with the sigh he became smaller as he turned into himself. "If you will let us, we can help you."

"I don't need no help, Mister Ty. And you tell Miz Catherine that I be just fine and I can take care of myself."

Ty looked up into a familiar face that had closed him off a long time ago. "I'm sorry, Zeb, for everything." He walked away.

"Mister Ty—" Zeb wiped his hands on the cleaning rag that he was still holding—"it ain't your fault."

Zeb's words rang in his ears as he came into the big house. He had been granted forgiveness from a man who could lose his life at the whim of his owners. Did he deserve it? Portia, as always, was in the kitchen, supervising the cleanup from the funeral banquet. Silas was helping with the polishing of the silver and rose from the table as Ty entered the room.

"Mr. Parker is looking for you, sir."

"Thank you, Silas." Ty looked at the stooped, elderly man who had been a part of his life for as long as he could remember. If circumstances allowed, would he and Portia choose to be there? Had they not been treated well through the years? How would he feel if it had been his lot to live in servitude to another man?

"He's in his office."

Ty searched for words to convey his feelings, but they failed him. He nodded in response to Silas's direction and went to the office. Parker was sitting at what was once their father's desk, looking at some papers. Memories of entering his father's office and standing before that desk, waiting in trepidation for his father to tell him that once again he had been found wanting crossed Ty's mind. His father had been dead for years but Ty still resented the man's inventory of his actions.

Parker looked up from his perusal of the papers. The evening sun cast its brilliance through the west-facing window and caught Parker's face in its light. Ty settled into the worn leather of the burgundy chair opposite the desk and realized that his brother had aged greatly in the past few years. Parker had just recently reached the age of thirty-two and yet he looked older. Or maybe he just looked worn. Ty wondered how his own face looked to others. He had barely noticed it lately except for a passing glance in some cool stream where he had knelt to get a drink. Had he looked in the mirror just this morning while dressing for his mother's funeral? Little things, once so taken for granted, escaped him. He vowed to enjoy them once again, when this was all over, if it was ever over.

"Silas said you were looking for me."

"Where'd you disappear to?"

"I was talking to Zeb." Ty wondered once again if

Parker knew about Lucy Ann. "He's unhappy, Parker."

Parker dismissed Zeb with a shrug of his shoulders. "He's a slave."

"He might not be much longer."

"What are you talking about?"

"Lincoln freed the slaves more than a year ago."

Parker snorted. "Lincoln had no authority over the Confederate States of America."

"The Confederate States of America aren't going to be around much longer, Parker."

Parker leaned back in his chair and gave his younger brother a skeptical look. "How can you sit there in that uniform and talk such treason?"

"It's because I'm wearing this uniform that I can." Ty leaned toward the desk. "Eventually we will lose this war. We don't have the resources or the finances to win it."

"When England supports us . . ." Parker protested.

"England and France are not going to support us. They're just sitting across the ocean, biding their time, hoping that we will kill each other off and they can come in and take the spoils of war."

"If you feel that way, then why are you still fighting?"

Ty leaned back in his chair and shook his head. "Because I committed myself to this cause, Parker, and right or wrong, win or lose, I'll see it through to the end."

Parker slumped his head into his hands and leaned against the top of the desk. "Then what's to become of us?"

"What do you mean?"

"We're broke, Ty. I had hoped that mother had some property or bank notes, or something stashed away, but there's nothing. All she had was some jewelry, and Lucy Ann has already picked her way through most of it."

"Then save it for after the war. Sell it for food and taxes."

"What about you?"

"Do you mean do I want my part of the inheritance?"

"I need to know, Ty."

"When this is over, I'm going back to Wyoming. It's my home now. You can have whatever's left here. I don't want the land and I don't want any money."

The brothers looked at each other for a moment and each realized that besides the name and some history, they had nothing in common. The tall clock in the hallway ticked the seconds away as they searched for a reason to continue. Finally, Parker slid a flat box covered in black velvet across the desk. "I managed to find this before Lucy Ann did. I think Mother would want Cat to have it."

Ty opened the box to find a strand of pearls with an emerald pendant gleaming against the satin lining. A matching pair of earrings completed the set. "I don't ever recall seeing her wear these."

"Father loved to spoil her. She had drawers full of things she never wore."

"She was practical, Parker. Perhaps she knew that you would have a better use for them."

Parker nodded in agreement as Ty closed the box

and tried to hand it back to him. Parker threw up his hand, stopping him. "I want Cat to have those, Ty. She took care of Mother; she was a better daughter to her at the end than I was a son." Parker looked earnestly at his brother. "Please."

"She'll cherish them." Ty slid the box into the pocket of his jacket. "I'll be leaving again at first light."

"So I heard."

Ty turned on his heel to leave.

"Ty?"

He turned to look at his brother, who remained sitting at his desk in the dimming light. For a moment, Ty saw the image of his father sitting there, but the moment passed as Parker spoke.

"Stay safe."

Cat brushed her hair as she waited for Ty to come back from his talk with Zeb. She had watched him from the window as he crossed the yard and entered the kitchen below. The house remained quiet. There was no uproar over Lucy Ann's sins, so she knew there was still a secret to keep and she would be the one responsible for keeping it.

If only the war would end and they could all go home and take Zeb with them. She imagined the big man caring for the mares and the magnificent stallion Storm, Jenny's legacy from her own father. The Lynch ranch would soon be famous for its horses and the business would grow. They could use a man with Zeb's talents.

Having thought of a solution, Cat decided that her

father would agree. Now if only Ty would go along with it. How would he feel about having a slave that he had owned working for her father? Would he continue to treat Zeb as a slave or would he treat him as an equal?

As she stroked her hair with the brush, she thought about the time she had spent around Ty and the slaves. She had never seen him treat them as anything other than people who were doing their jobs. He approached Portia and Silas with affection and respect. He never asked any of them to do anything that he would not do himself. Having Zeb in Wyoming would not be a problem for Ty. She was sure of it.

With that settled in her mind, she looked forward to the night ahead. She could not take back the harsh words she had said about the war, but she could show Ty how much she loved him. If all she was to have of him were passing moments, then she would make the best of them.

She heard his footsteps on the stairs and placed the brush on the washstand. While his hand was on the door she checked her appearance once more in the mirror. When he entered the room, she hurried to his side, where she offered help with his coat. Ty lowered himself into the brocaded seat of the wing-back chair that sat in front of the empty fireplace while Cat hung his coat in the wardrobe. She placed it where it would be handy, for she knew he would have need of it in the morning. His weapons lay where he left them upon his arrival the night before. She was grateful for them, but hated what they represented.

Cat knelt before the chair and silently picked up

one of his legs to remove one of the freshly polished boots that graced it. Her father had taken her request to heart and had sent new boots for all of them two years ago. They had stayed in their boxes unused until today. There was even a new pair for Willie, something he had never hoped to see, and he had admired them all day long.

"I think you should go home, Cat." Ty's hand touched a golden-brown curl that had fallen over her shoulder. Cat placed the boots side by side on the hearth and turned to look up at him. "It will be safer for you there."

"Do you think the war is going to move into these parts?"

"I don't know."

"I don't want to leave you, Ty. I'd be so far away from you in Wyoming."

"I know." He didn't want her to leave any more than she wanted to go. But he felt he should be doing something for her, to protect her. Cat had proved time and time again that she was able to take care of herself. But so far the only thing she needed protection from was the heartbreak he had given her. Ty glanced at the wardrobe where the jewel case was hidden in his pocket. He wanted her to have it, but felt ashamed that it had come from his brother, not him. The only thing he had ever given her as his wife was the gold band that she wore on her finger. He had not spent a Christmas or a birthday with her since the day they were married. He couldn't even give her a child, something she so desperately wanted. He was as much a failure as a husband as he had been as a son.

"Wherever you go, I go." Cat laid her head on his lap. "It was a part of our wedding vows, Ty. I would follow you into battle if you would let me."

A slight smile graced his lips as he caressed the shiny crown of her hair. She would, if she thought she could get away with it. "You also promised that when I said it was time for you to go back home, you would."

Cat raised her head. "It's not time yet." She placed a hand on either thigh and knelt between them.

"It's not?" He leaned toward her, and his hands gripped her upper arms.

"No, it's not." She met his lips with her own as his arms moved behind her and beneath her, pulling her into his lap.

She was right, it wasn't time. Sending her to Wyoming would only make it easier for him to die, and he didn't want to die. He wanted to be with Cat. He wanted to go back to Wyoming and make a home with her, have children with her, grow old with her.

"I love you," she breathed against his lips.

"Why?" His mouth slashed across her cheek and assaulted the hollow of her neck. "Why do you love me?"

"Because you're Ty. Because you're the one meant for me." It sounded so simple when she said it.

He stopped his caresses and looked at her. "How do you know that?"

"What are you saying?" Cat didn't know if she should be shocked or scared of his questions. "What have I done?"

"It's not what you've done; it's what I've done, or

haven't done. I haven't been a good husband to you, Cat, and yet you still love me."

"Do you still love me?" What if he didn't?

"Yes, I love you. I love you with every breath I take." He looked away from her, toward the weapons, toward the door. "I just don't know how you can."

"It's for better or for worse." Her hand on his cheek brought his eyes back to hers. "We're just getting the worse out of the way. When I said I loved you, it was forever and I was hoping it was the same for you."

"It is." His arms closed around her and they trembled as he held her as tightly as he could without crushing her. "I'm just afraid that forever is not going to be enough."

"If all we have left is tonight, Ty, then it will be enough." Her mouth moved against his chest, seeking the skin beneath the crisp mat of hair. "It will have to be."

"I'm so sorry."

Cat leaned away from him and looked up with eyes moist and glowing in the dim light of early evening. "Like you said, we've got a lot of time to make up for, and I don't want to waste any of it." Ty's eyes turned a deeper shade of blue as he leaned forward and kissed her, using his lips to convey the words that escaped him. Cat rose up to meet him as she always did. This was Ty, and he was where he belonged for the moment. She knew it was all she would have until the war was over.

"Where did you get this scar?" Her voice was soft as a slim finger traced the narrow white slash on his brow and her lips followed.

"Chancellorsville." His hand trailed down the length of her spine and the other pulled the sheet around them as she shivered against him. "I don't remember how."

"And this?" Her lips gently touched the puckered scar that was still fresh on his shoulder and then her cheek settled against it.

"In the Wilderness." He wrapped his arms around her and held her close. "I would have died there if Jake and Caleb hadn't pulled me out. There was a fire."

"You don't have to talk about it."

"There's nothing to say except we survived. Others weren't so lucky."

"It can't last much longer."

"No, it can't." Whether they were talking about the war or luck, neither wanted to know. They were content to hold on to each other as the night fell around them and sleep, too long delayed, took them both away.

Chapter Fourteen

The realization that morning was upon them came as a shock. They had not meant to sleep so late; they hadn't meant to sleep at all. The usual sounds of plantation life drifted up to their room with the dawning of the day, bringing regrets for the time together they had lost. Cat watched from the middle of the bed as Ty dressed once again in his uniform. He patted a bulge in his jacket and then looked at it in surprise. Cat curiously tilted her head as he walked toward her with a black velvet box in his hand.

"Parker wanted you to have these." A twinge of regret tickled his mind. There were so many fine things he wanted to give her. Cat was used to the best things in life but had also proved that she could get along just as well without them. He would make it up to her. "They belonged to Mother."

"I'm surprised Parker was able to keep them away from Lucy Ann. I swear, she was in there taking inventory of Penelope's jewelry every day."

"I just wish I could be around to see her face when

you show up wearing them." Ty settled on the bed next to Cat and handed her the box. Her mouth formed a perfect "O" as the morning sun caught the brilliance of the square-cut emerald and the glow of the pearls against the black velvet.

"Oh, Ty, are you sure Parker wants me to have these?"

"I'm sure. He gave them to me last night."

Cat bounced off the bed and hurried to her dressing table with an earring in her hand. She pulled her hair up off her neck and examined her reflection with the earring held up to her ear. She caught the steel-blue of Ty's gaze in the mirror and turned.

"I won't wear them until you can be here to see me in them."

"I want you to enjoy them."

"Oh, I will." She playfully moved into his arms. "Because the next time I see you, these will be the only things I will be wearing."

"If you plan on greeting me like you did the last time I came home, it might be a bit uncomfortable." Her unruly curls tickled his mouth.

"What are you talking about?"

"Remember when you slid down the banister and knocked Parker on his behind?"

Cat dissolved into a fit of giggles. "How about if the next night we spend together, this is all I'll be wearing?"

"I think that will give me something to look forward to." His hands slid up her back as she leaned into him. Ty sighed. It was already late and he knew Jake, Caleb and Willie would be waiting.

Cat sensed his frustration, and for one fleeting moment thought about tempting him as she would have a few years earlier. Instead, she stepped away.

"I have something for you too. Actually, I made one for each of you." She opened the wardrobe and searched amid the boxes on the shelf.

"You made something?" The corners of his mouth twitched as he willed the laughter that welled up into submission.

Cat stopped her plunder of the wardrobe and turned with hands on hips. "Yes, I did. I haven't just been sitting around here for the past few years looking pretty."

"Thank goodness. I would hate to think that Lucy Ann would be out of a job." Cat threw a shoe in his direction and resumed searching the wardrobe. She finally emerged with a striped hat box and carried it over to the bed. She removed the top and pulled out a finely knitted muffler of soft blue wool.

"I know it's a little too warm to wear it now but since I probably won't see you again before winter . . ."

Ty took it from her and wound it around his neck. "You made this?"

"Yes. Your mother taught me how to knit. I started with mufflers and then went to socks. I've even made a few blankets. She showed me how to spin the wool, too, although you have slaves to do that."

"Catherine Lynch Kincaid. You amaze me." He dropped a kiss on her forehead and examined the fine rows of the muffler again. Cat glowed under his perusal and took pride in her accomplishments.

"I made one for Jake and Caleb, too."

"They will love them."

The mention of Jake and Caleb made them realize that more minutes had somehow slipped away. It was time once again for Ty to leave. Cat suddenly felt weepy and weak and turned her head away, determined not to give in to the sudden tide of emotion. Ty went to gather his weapons. Cat watched with the mufflers for her friends gripped in her hands as he buckled the belt that held his gun and sword. He was going back to battle and the only armor he wore was a silly blue muffler around his neck. She should have made him a suit of iron instead of a scarf of soft blue wool. Ty held out his hand to her. "Walk down with me."

She was still dressed in her robe and her hair was a mess but she didn't care. She took his hand and walked with him down the stairs.

Caleb, Jake and Willie were waiting with the horses. Jake and Caleb accepted Cat's gifts with sheepish grins and immediately wrapped the mufflers around their necks, even though the day was already steaming. Cat looked at the three of them, Ty in blue, Caleb in red and Jake wearing a pale gray, and couldn't help thinking that they represented the red, white and blue of the nation's flag. No, make that the Union's flag. It suddenly dawned on her that she wasn't living in the United States of America; she was in the Confederate States of America and had been for a long time. How had they come to this point in their lives? She wrapped an arm around the porch column as Ty swung up on his horse. Parker and Silas joined her as the warriors waved their good-byes and took off down the long drive. The men went back inside but Cat stayed, watching the dust cloud that followed her men until it faded from sight. She stroked a plate-sized blossom from the purple clematis that trailed up the column of the porch and wondered how many seasons it would see before Ty came home again. *Please God, keep him safe.*

Chapter Fifteen

Within a week's time, life at the plantation returned to its normal pace as if nothing had changed, but for Cat everything had changed. Without Penelope there to ground her, she drifted from room to room, never settling in one place long enough to get comfortable. In all her explorations of the house, she noticed the abundance of clothing and fabric that was stored in the rooms and attic and marveled at the waste of it all. She had seen the rags and tatters that the slaves wore during the week, saving the one piece of new clothing they got each year for Sundays and special occasions.

Cat found Parker in his office one morning and approached him with an idea that had been burning in the back of her head.

"Parker, I've noticed that this house is stuffed from top to bottom with clothes that nobody wears and there are bolts of fabric just rotting in the attic."

"Most of the clothes are things that Ty and I outgrew a long time ago." Parker leaned back in his chair and peered down his nose at Cat. "I had no idea about the fabric, except to say I know that Mother was always saving things for what she called a rainy day."

"I think your rainy day has arrived."

"What are you talking about?"

"You have all these things just going to waste sitting here in this house and you have all these people outside who are in desperate need."

"Are you talking about the slaves?"

"Yes."

Parker snorted. "I suppose you think I should start coddling them?"

"No, but times are bad for all the planters. Think of how much worse they are for the slaves." Parker looked startled as Cat continued. "What would happen to the plantation if the South loses and all the slaves are freed?"

"That's not going to happen."

"But what if it does? Where will they go? Who will work the fields? How will you pay the hands you will have to hire to work the fields?"

Parker ran his hand through his thinning hair. Cat had just touched on the very thing that kept him awake at nights in his lonely room. "What do you suggest?"

"Take care of your people. Lay the groundwork for them to stay. They are as worried about what's going to happen to them as you are worried about this place. Wouldn't it make things easier if they decided to stay on and work for you when this is all over, that is if they have that choice to make?" Parker chewed on the end of his pen. "It won't cost you anything, Parker."

"So all you're suggesting is that we give them the clothes and things that nobody is using?"

"Yes."

Parker sighed. "Go ahead. Do what you want to do. Lucy Ann and I are going to Raleigh for a few days, so you'll have the house to yourself and won't have to worry about disturbing anyone." Cat knew he was talking about Lucy Ann. She wouldn't put it past her sister-in-law to suddenly decide that she needed all the stored fabric for her own plans.

"Thank you, Parker." Cat stood to leave. "And by the way, I never thanked you for the jewelry either. I will cherish the necklace and earrings because I cherished the woman they belonged to."

Parker stole a look toward the hall as he came around the desk and took Cat's hand. "Thank you for what you did for Mother. Besides, I knew they'd look better on you than on, er, someone else." Cat smiled sweetly. "Just do me a favor and put them someplace where you know they'll be safe."

"I have," Cat assured him. The morning Ty had given her the jewelry she had taken care to hide the case in the false bottom of the small trunk that contained the cash her father had given her in case of an emergency. "And I assure you that it will be our secret."

Parker squeezed her hand. "You're a good match for Ty. I'm glad he found you."

"Thank you, Parker." It was the most conversation Cat had ever had with her brother-in-law. She almost felt sorry for him as she left the room. He was trapped in a way of life that was slowly dying before him. He would have to change with the times or become a failure. He was trapped in a loveless marriage to a shallow, selfish woman, but at least he wasn't deceiving himself about his relationship with Lucy Ann. Cat wondered again if he knew the truth about Lucy Ann's perversions. She hoped he didn't. Cat found that she could respect him as long as he wasn't turning a blind eye to his wife's liaisons.

Cat found Portia in the kitchen and shared her ideas with her. The woman chuckled her approval as she cast an exploring eye over Cat's pale face. "Chile, you look a bit peaked. Are you feeling alright?"

"I'm fine; it's just that it's so hot in here." Cat grabbed the back of a chair because the heat was making her dizzy. Portia fanned her with a towel while one of the younger slaves fetched her a glass of water. "Can you find someone to help me sort through all the clothes?"

"Sho 'nuff. I'll get Ruth. She's 'bout due her time and can't do no work. And don't neither of you go carryin' no stuff. I'll get Zeb to fetch some boxes and tote that stuff down these stairs."

The thought of Zeb in the house was enough to send Cat into a panic, but then she remembered that Parker and Lucy Ann were going to Raleigh and would be gone for most of the week. She could certainly use his help in getting things out of the attic but knew she was capable of carrying clothes down the stairs. Why would Portia ask her not to do so simple a task?

Ruth was summoned and a spare bedroom was set aside to sort the clothes into piles according to size. Cat became teary when she opened a drawer that contained an exquisitely embroidered and smocked christening dress and accessories carefully wrapped in pure white paper. It had been set aside for Kincaid grandchildren that would probably never exist, but there was always hope. Cat carried the garment to her room and placed it in the small trunk for safekeeping.

Cat and Ruth soon found other items that were more practical. Pants and shirts that had been play clothes for the Kincaid boys when they were growing up were arranged into stacks according to size. Ruth knew the names of each child who could wear the garments. Cat and Ruth worked throughout the day, sorting and stacking. Cat found that she could hardly keep her eyes open at dinner that night and went to bed as soon as she reached her room, exhausted.

She awoke the next morning to an upset stomach and wondered what she had eaten that could have caused it. She heard the sounds of people already going about their morning routine and hurriedly washed her face and tied her hair up. Through the back-facing window Cat saw Ruth arranging the clothes on a table that Zeb had set up in the yard, where they were going to make the distribution to the slaves. Cat rinsed out her mouth and slipped into her pants and shirt. She didn't have time for breakfast, and the thought of it turned her stomach. A mad dash down the stairs left her dizzy and she wondered for a moment if perhaps she should eat, but the smells coming from the kitchen quickly changed her mind and she hurried out to the back.

The day was spent passing out the clothes to the children, and then letting the women go through the piles that had belonged to George Kincaid for the men. The women were also given bolts of fabric to make dresses for themselves and their daughters. Some of Penelope's simpler dresses were passed out also. The joy on the faces of the women and children were wondrous to behold as they held each cherished article close to their chests. The women caressed the brightly colored calicos and stripes of the bolts of fabric and fingered the soft wools as if they were solid gold. Cat wished she could carry her plan a step further and provide them with shoes and coats for winter. But she knew Parker's finances would not allow that, and she was determined to save her hidden funds for an emergency. The one thing she did have was time and she vowed that she would start using her knitting skills to make life a bit more pleasant for the slaves. She could take enough money to buy some yarn and decided that she would go to town to do just that.

Cat ate dinner that night in the kitchen with Portia, Silas and Zeb. Since she was alone in the house, she saw no need to make them go to the trouble of serving her in the dining room. The easy conversation about the day's accomplishments reminded her of home and the friendly banter that had always been a part of any meal in Grace's cabin. Even Zeb was relaxed and smiling, and the three of them seemed to be amused when she quickly cleaned her plate and asked for seconds.

"I don't know what's wrong with me," Cat commented as Portia ladled more portions on her plate. "This morning the thought of food made me sick and now I'm putting it away like one of the field hands."

Cat missed the look that Portia gave Silas as her own head was bent toward her plate. Zeb grinned broadly as Portia refilled his plate also.

Cat decided to take advantage of the easy company she was enjoying. Zeb needed to know that he could trust her and that she was on his side. "Zeb, I was thinking about going into town tomorrow and doing some shopping. Do you think you could drive me?" They all knew she was quite capable of driving herself, but Portia nodded at her son that he should take on this task.

"Yes, ma'am." Silent communication passed between Portia and Zeb. "I'll have the buggy ready to go first thing."

"I just hope I don't feel the same way tomorrow that I felt this morning." Cat looked over at the yellow cake that was sitting on a counter. "Is that for dessert?"

Portia chuckled as she went for the cake. "Yes, ma'am. And I believe we's got some late strawberries left too." She cut Cat a big slice and placed it in front of her, knowing full well that she would lose it come morning. But she would enjoy eating it, that was for sure.

Cat hit her pillow again that night, exhausted. She realized that she had not worried about Ty at all that day. Keeping busy was a good thing and she had accomplished something of which she was proud. She decided to write him about it. She'd tell him about her gentle truce with Parker, about taking care of the slaves and about the wonderful dinner. She would tell him how much she missed him, how much she loved him. Cat fell into a deep sleep as she imagined the words filling the page.

Cat's knees hit the floor in front of the chamber pot with the bright light of the morning sun streaming through the window. As she retched and gagged, a dark hand wiped the back of her neck with a wet cloth. "That's all right, chile, just let it come on out. You'll be fine sho 'nuff in a minute or two."

"Portia?" Cat had not heard her come in. She laid her head on trembling hands and waited for the tide to subside.

"Yes, ma'am. Zeb done got the buggy waitin' and we was beginnin' to worry."

"I guess I ate too much last night."

Portia chuckled. "Well, you's eatin' for two now. Best get used to it."

"What?" Cat sat up and instantly regretted it. When she quickly grabbed the pot, the smell of strawberries mixed with the bile, and she vowed never to eat the fruit again.

"It won't last long." Portia used the cloth to wipe the corners of Cat's mouth and then fanned her with it.

"What did you say earlier?"

"I said you was eatin' for two. Don't you know the signs, chile?"

Cat's eyes grew wide as she looked up into the kind face of the woman who had raised Ty. "You mean . . ."

"You done made a baby, you and my Ty. I asked the good Lord to give you one and he done answered my prayers. Surely Mister Ty will come home now and stay."

"I'm pregnant?" Cat couldn't believe it, but Portia nodded in agreement. "I'm pregnant." She quickly began counting days in her head as her mind whirled with the possibility.

"You has to be. Can't be nothin' else." Cat flung her arms around Portia's neck with a squeal.

"Are you sure?"

"Yes, I am, but why don't you go see that town doctor today and make sure."

"Oh, I will, I will." Cat felt like spinning in joy but the dizzy spell that overtook her as she jumped to her feet changed her mind.

"You get dressed and come on down to the kitchen. I got something that will make that stomach of yours feel better," Portia assured her. "Zeb ain't in no hurry to go to town. He can wait all day if he needs to." Portia moved to the door. "We finally goin' to have a baby in this house. Praise be."

A baby. Cat stood in the middle of the room, unable to move. After all this time, a baby. She had begun to think it would never happen, and when she had finally given up on ever having a baby, she was pregnant. She wrapped her arms around herself and imagined the look on Ty's face. On her father's face. On her friends' faces. "Thank you, God. Thank you." A delicious grin lit her heart-shaped face. "I hate to disappoint you, Portia, but this baby is going to be born back home. In Wyoming." If only she could tell Ty in person, then maybe she could convince him to leave this war before he was killed. Panic instantly overtook her. What if the baby was God's way of telling her he was going to be killed? Maybe this baby was her consolation for losing her husband. She turned to the mirror. "Get a grip on yourself, Cat. You're going to have a baby." Her hands slid down to her stomach and stroked the flatness of it beneath her gown. "A baby." Her reflection smiled back, joyously. Cat flung her arms out and spun and laughed until she fell on the bed, drunk and dizzy. "Oh, Ty, we're going to have a baby . . ." She threw a hand over her mouth and raced once again to the chamber pot.

The doctor had confirmed it. Cat leaned against the corner of the buggy, tired from her visit, tired from her shopping. She looked at the bags that were gathered around her feet. She felt foolish for buying baby things, knowing that they were one more thing she would have to pack up and take home, but she hadn't been able to resist. She had literally floated out of the doctor's office and into the store. When shopping for yarn, she had kept going to the soft pastels instead of the brighter colors that the slaves liked to wear and had finally given in to the impulse and purchased the skeins, imagining tiny booties, bonnets and sweaters along with cozy blankets.

Zeb had dutifully followed her all day, smiling at her antics, loading the purchases in the buggy. She had already taken care of a list for Portia, though she was unable to find all of the necessities because of the blockade. The storekeepers seemed grateful for her presence. It wasn't often that they had customers who carried real gold instead of Confederate paper or asking for credit.

On the way home she chattered on about Wyoming until Zeb began to ask her questions about that part of the country and the horses they were breeding. Cat told him about Storm and the mares; then she talked about Jamie and his magic with horses. Zeb seemed to take it hard when she told him of Jamie's death and the waste of it all but smiled when she told him about Fox. He chuckled over stories about Zane and the incident involving Jake and the mud puddle. She had never heard him talk more than just to reply, and it amazed her how animated he became as he asked her questions. She decided once again that Zeb would go to Wyoming with them when the time came, if it ever came.

Dusk had settled over the plantation when they arrived. Silas rushed to meet the buggy as Zeb pulled around to the front door.

"Miz Catherine, I hate to tell you this but you done missed Mister Ty."

"Ty was here?"

"Yesum, he swung through here 'bout lunchtime. Said he was on his way back up the mountain and just wanted to take a minute to see you."

Cat slumped back into the buggy as Silas held out his hand to help her down. "I can't believe it. Today of all days. How long ago did he leave?"

"It was early afternoon, ma'am. He knew there weren't no chance of seeing you, so he just ate a bite and left to meet up with his men. He said he'd stop back on the way down the mountain."

Cat's mind whirled as she counted the hours in her head. He had only a day's head start on her. She had a general idea of where he was going and knew that he would probably have pack animals with him. She could find him. She knew she could. She knew how to track and she knew she could survive a few nights in the open on her own. There had not been any sightings of Union troops in this area and they wouldn't bother her anyway. She was handy with a rifle and had been in wilder country than this. First thing in the morning, she was leaving. She was going to find Ty. She was going to tell him about the baby, and she was going to convince him that it was time to go home.

"I hope Portia saved some supper for us, Silas. I don't know about Zeb, but I'm starving." Zeb grinned over the packages as she entered the house with her skirt swishing around her.

Chapter Sixteen

"I can't believe that you found us." Ty ran his hands through his hair just to keep himself from wringing the neck of his beautiful wife, who stood proudly before him. He had been angry since the moment Jake had informed him that the person who had been determinedly following their trail was his impetuous wife.

"It's not hard to track twenty mules through mountain country," Cat retorted impudently. Ty fought the urge to take the muffler that still dangled from his neck and choke her with it.

"I'm not talking about your tracking abilities; I'm talking about how stupid it is for you to be here. We're in the middle of a war, Cat, or haven't you noticed?"

"Yes, I have noticed. I hate it. It's keeping you away from me and keeping us away from our home in Wyoming."

"You knew what you were getting into when you came here." Ty couldn't believe they were having this argument, at this moment, standing out in the middle of nowhere.

"That was before. Now it's different."

"What's different now? We've been fighting this war for three years. The only thing that's changed is the list of dead and it's growing every day."

Cat saw that his anger was rising, so she laid her hand on his arm to gentle him. "The difference is now we're going to have a baby." She carefully watched his face for his reaction to the news.

"A baby?" Words failed him for a moment as his steel-blue eyes looked at her in wonder. "Are you sure? After all this time I didn't think it was going to happen."

"I'm past my time and I've been sick every morning. The doctor says it's a baby, but more important, Portia says it's a baby." The words tumbled out as Ty gathered her into his arms. "Can we go home now, Ty? Please? You said yourself that the South can't win this war. The three of you have managed to survive this long and I'm afraid our luck is going to run out. I want to go home."

"You know I can't." She felt his mouth moving against the top of her head. "I have to see it through."

"Even if it means the death of you and Caleb and Jake?"

"They made their own choices."

"What about my choices? When do I get to have some? I want a home with you and a family." She pushed away from the solidness of his chest. "I want to grow old with you, not visit your grave in some cemetery. I want your child to know you as a father, not some headstone with a name carved on it. 'Here lies a war hero. He was glorious in battle, may he rest in peace.' A headstone that we will never see because you'll be buried here and we'll be back home. And that's if we even find your body. You could get blown to bits and I wouldn't even know about it until the war is over and you don't show up."

"Cat . . ." He had seen her like this many times before, gathering her words like ammunition as she paced before him.

"No." Her righteous indignation fueled her. "I've been patient long enough. You are going to be a father." She enunciated each word with a delicate finger pressed into the solid width of his chest, bypassing the soft blue yarn of the muffler and striking the bleached whiteness of his shirt. "You need to think about the future instead of worrying about the past. There is nothing for you here, Ty. Kincaid Plantation is going straight to hell. Your mother is dead and your family is bankrupt. You are fighting a war for a brother who doesn't have enough courage to fight it himself. Your future is in Wyoming with me and your child."

Her finger in his chest hardly dented him but the words hit his gut like a swift punch. She was right. He had known for a long time that he had no business being here. He hoped by not saying it that no one else would know it. Hearing Cat say the words out loud was something he had not been ready for. The horrible visions of the battlefields he had seen flashed through his mind. What was he doing here? He slid to the ground with his back against a sturdy tree trunk and his head dropped against his chest. His hands covered his eyes as if to shut out the horrors of war that he had seen. It was a miracle that they were all still alive. What purpose would it serve if they died?

Why had he come? Had it been to defend the principle of each citizen to live his life without the interference of the government, or was it to prove to his long-dead father that he was a man worthy of carrying on the family name? When his father had died, Parker had inherited the plantation because he was the elder son, even though Ty knew in his heart that he could run it better and make it more profitable. What was he trying to prove and to whom was he trying to prove it?

Cat knelt in front of him and gently placed her hands on his knees. "I love you, Ty."

"I know." His hands scrubbed through his hair as if they could erase all the problems circling in his brain. The steel-blue eyes were moist with unshed tears as he reached for her. "I'm so sorry, Cat. Sorry I've put you through this. Sorry that we came here. We never should have come."

She held him as he buried his face in her chest, for one moment letting her carry the responsibility that weighed so heavily on him at times. But he knew that they were vulnerable, so the moment passed quickly as he sought to regain the steady composure that had carried him through so far.

"Can we go home now?" She was afraid to ask but she had to know.

"No." Ty shook his head. "We have to finish this

mission. It's not just me, Cat; there are a lot of people depending on us."

"I know. You have to do your duty. But I had to ask." Her smile was sweet as she leaned back on her heels, giving him time to get his emotions under control.

"I have learned through the years not to expect anything different."

"And I have learned that if you want something, it's best to ask for it."

Ty felt a great weight lifting from his shoulders as he considered her sweet, heart-shaped face for a moment. The war couldn't last forever. He had survived this long; he would make it through to the end. Cat wouldn't stand for it any other way. The corners of his mouth turned up in a playful grin. "You mean like you wanted me?"

"Oooh, Tyler Kincaid, sometimes I just want to beat you." She swung halfheartedly at his arm as boundless joy bubbled up inside her. He was going to be fine; they were going to be happy. They were finally going to be parents. Now if this war would just end.

"Careful. Got to watch out for the baby." His arms encircled her as she swung and she landed against his chest with his face buried in her hair. "I promise, Cat, as soon as I can get us out of this mess, we will go home. All of us."

"I want the baby to be born in Wyoming."

"I'll do my best." At the moment, that seemed impossible, but he had to try because he loved her.

Oh, how he loved her.

Chapter Seventeen

"Couldn't stand it, could you?" Jake grinned maliciously at Cat as they rode down into the Greenbrier River. The horses were hot and took advantage of the chance to splash water up under their bellies with uplifted hooves striking the water.

"Couldn't stand what?" Cat rubbed Scarlet's neck as the chestnut mare buried her muzzle in the shallow water.

"Us off having all the fun."

"You call this fun?"

Jake laughed and slapped the rump of her mare. "Compared to what we've seen, it's a picnic."

"You didn't get anything you didn't ask for, Jake, when you came out here."

"You got that right."

The horses sought for footing amid the rocks on the bottom of the river. Jake rode on and Caleb fell in beside her as they made their way up the opposite bank.

"He sure has changed a lot since this war started," Cat observed.

"Who, Jake?" Caleb looked ahead, where Jake had pulled up alongside Bishop. Willie, as usual, had fallen in behind him. "We've all changed, when you think about it; it just shows on some more than others."

"Well, with Jake it's kind of scary."

"You ought to see him when the shells start flying." The woods were deep and cool and the traveling was easy as they followed the curve of the river. "I think it's the circumstances. Jake was raised with violence and he had to learn how to deal with it by facing it head-on. Sure, he didn't say much when we were back home but that's because he was learning how to live a peaceful life. He was never sure if the peace was going to last because he had never known peace."

"Does he ever talk about his family?"

"Not a word beyond that one time when he first came to the ranch. And I think he was trying to scare us more than anything. I wouldn't have believed him if I hadn't seen the scars on his back from the beatings."

"I've never seen them."

"He doesn't want you to. He has his pride but he also had to live with us, so he just owned up to them and got the uncomfortable part out of the way." Caleb was bemused as he caught Cat studying him. "What are you looking at?"

"You." Cat smiled. "You never cease to amaze me."

"Why?"

"Your insights into people. You seem to have everyone figured out."

Caleb blushed under his tan. "I just spend a lot of time observing people. I like to study them."

"I guess that's why your drawings are so good. You capture the inside as well as the outside."

"Well, I don't know about that."

"Caleb, please, you know your drawings are good." He grinned at her. "I am not going to ride beside you and tell you how wonderful you are. You can just forget it."

"Gee, Cat, I think you have me confused with Zane." They both laughed and Caleb continued. "About Jake. When the fighting starts, there's no one else I'd rather have around than him and Ty. But one thing scares me. It's almost as if he doesn't care. Sometimes it seems as if he wants to die."

"Because his father made him feel like he was worthless?"

"Yes, and if he dies in battle, then he's died for something. And something else that he'll never admit—he's fighting for the South because his father was against slavery. Jake said he used to preach these fiery sermons against it and said the slave owners would pay the price. I guess he was right about that anyway."

"Yes, he was." Cat placed a hand over her still-flat stomach. "I guess I will never understand how any man can abuse his own child."

"Me neither. We might not have had much, but I knew my father loved me. I never got a chance to know my mother. She died when I was born."

Women died every day giving birth. It was something Cat hadn't considered but Caleb had lost his mother that way. The birth was a long way off and with luck she would be home by then. If she was going to die, then she would do it in Wyoming in her own bed.

"Cat?" Caleb's soft query brought her back to the present. "I know you and Ty have been trying to have a baby. Don't worry. It will happen."

Cat reached over and squeezed his hand. "It already has."

"Really?" Caleb's smile was contagious. "I thought you might be when you showed up."

"You know me too well, Caleb."

"I'm really happy for you. Gosh, between you and Jenny there's going to be babies everywhere."

"How about you, Caleb? Have you ever thought about being a father?"

"Yes, but so far I haven't met the right woman. And as you can see, there haven't been that many come across my path lately either." He waved his arm around to encompass the wild countryside of what was now West Virginia. "Come to think of it, I really haven't had much exposure to the kind of woman a guy would want to marry."

"Well, maybe you should quit spending all of your free time visiting the whorehouse with Zane and look somewhere else."

Caleb laughed out loud. "That's a good idea. Of course, you know I'll have to make a few visits when I get back just for old times' sake."

"Most of the whores will be old-timers by the time

you boys get back." The two of them dissolved into laughter as they rode, drawing a few stern looks from the rest of the troop.

"We'd better keep it down, Cat." Caleb suddenly became aware of his surroundings. "We don't want to draw any attention to ourselves."

"But we haven't got the ammunition yet."

"If they find us now, they can follow us to the cave or else ambush us on the way back."

"I guess I forgot that we were in the middle of a war."

"Yeah, I did, too, for a minute. It was nice."

Cat smiled warmly at his dear, sweet face. "Yes, it was."

They made camp that night beneath a rocky outcropping. Ty went off to check the surrounding area and post guards, leaving Cat to enjoy the camaraderie of the Ridge Riders around the small cook fire. She knew Ty had lost some of his men in battle, but those that remained respected him. He had shown himself to be brave and willing to sacrifice himself for all of them. They couldn't ask for any more in a commanding officer.

The smuggler, Bishop, made her uncomfortable. It seemed as if he was always watching her, his dark, narrow eyes running over her as if she were a fine mare at auction. His dazzling white smile beneath his narrow mustache never seemed to show in his eyes. He seemed out of place among the hardened soldiers. His manner was much more refined, as if he were a gentleman, but beneath the polished exterior was something else. She knew that Jake was suspicious of him, but Jake was like that with everyone. Cat decided to keep her distance from the man.

She had noticed that Caleb and Jake had wandered off during the telling of an outlandish story by one of the mountain men. A while later Jake came back and quietly motioned for her to follow him. Cat slipped off and he led her up a small trail to a ledge above their camp. She could make out Caleb in the dim light of a stub of a candle that had been placed in the middle of a hollowed-out rock. Two bedrolls had been placed together and strewn with Queen Anne's lace and black-eyed Susans.

"We thought you might like to celebrate," Caleb explained.

"Don't worry," Jake volunteered. "We'll keep the varmints away."

Cat threw her arms around both of them. "Have I told you lately how much I love you two?"

Jake immediately saw a wild creature stirring beyond the bedrolls and went to chase it off with stamping feet. "We love you, too, Cat." Caleb's dark eyes were smiling in the dim light of the candle. "And Ty, although Jake would never admit it to anyone." He squeezed her shoulders reassuringly. "We'll go see if we can find Ty."

"We'll probably have to hog-tie him to get him up here," Jake growled, satisfied now that the threat to Cat's boudoir in the wild was gone.

"What he means is Ty will feel like he has to stay with his men instead of being alone with you," Caleb explained as he smacked Jake in the back of the head.

"Oh yeah, that's what I meant, Cat," Jake apologized sheepishly. "Why don't I just leave now?"

"Before you say something stupid?" Caleb chastised him.

Cat's soft laughter followed the two of them back down the trail. She turned to survey their handiwork. It wasn't much, just a blanket and a candle, but the ground beneath was cushioned with sweet grass and the sky above was dotted with bright stars. She could see the three-quarter moon tickling the top branches of the evergreens that grew between the cracks and crevices of the ledge she was on. Fireflies danced amid the trees, giving the illusion of magic to the night. The air was warm, with a breeze that kept the air from being muggy and sticky, a fact for which she was grateful as she pulled off her boots. Below she could hear the soft conversation of the men as they settled in for the night and beyond the occasional shifting of the horses and mules in the picket line. The crickets and tree frogs decided that the men were not going to be a threat to them and began their nightly chorus as the forest settled around them for the night. Cat shed her clothes and slid between the blankets with a sigh.

She heard him coming up the trail a few minutes later. The scattering of pebbles and a sudden rush of a bird disturbed from its slumber announced his presence on the ledge. Cat sat up, holding the blanket across her breasts and folded down his side invitingly.

The moonlight illuminated her from behind, casting a glow about her hair and shoulders but leaving her face shrouded in the shadows. Ty knelt at the end of the bedroll, dipping his head to see her face.

His eyes caught the light of the moon, causing their intense blue to glow like a flame. Cat felt suddenly shy, as if his eyes were those of a stranger, and she nervously pulled the blanket up under her chin.

"Are you cold?" he asked.

"No." Her curls bounced around her shoulders as she shook her head. He removed his gun belt and sword and placed them beside the blanket. His boots were next, followed by his shirt. The muffler remained in place, however, and he flashed a grin at her as his eyes raked over her with passion. Cat could not believe how nervous she felt, so much so that she was shivering.

"I thought you said you weren't cold." Ty's arms slid around her.

"I'm not." Her teeth chattered. "I guess it's just that everyone down there knows what we're doing."

"They don't mind." He rubbed the tip of his nose against her hairline. His short growth of beard scratched against her temple. "You also promised me that the next time we were together, all you would be wearing would be pearls."

"I didn't think they were proper attire for the trail." His mouth traced her ear and then trailed down her neck. "Ty?" Her stomach dipped. "Are you happy about the baby?"

He moved his head away so he could look into her eyes. "Yes. Why would you think anything else?"

"I don't know. I just . . ." His mouth closed over hers, ending the discussion before it had a chance to get started. Cat melted against him, her body molding itself to the familiar contours of his, skin meeting skin as he tenderly carried her once again to the heights that were theirs alone. The trees whispered above them as the gentle breeze caressed the branches and danced along the strong outline of Ty's back while he sheltered her from the night.

Chapter Eighteen

"I don't know which is worse, herding cows or herding mules." Jake popped a well-laden mule on the rump to goose him across a meadow that was covered with wild asters and waves of blooming clover. A swarm of pale blue butterflies attacked the air around them in protest at the unruly disturbance.

"Well, it's a lot easier than trying to get wagons over these mountain trails." Ty was having his own problems as the mules balked at the heavy loads of gunpowder and the ups and downs of the backwoods trails that led out of the mountains from the caves.

"I think our job will be easy compared to what Mr. Bishop has to do," Caleb commented. "I'd much rather wrestle mules than sneak around out in the ocean trying to get by Federal ships."

"We all have our jobs to do." Bishop smiled. "And we try to do our best. My crew is one of the best out there and my ship has the reputation of being one of the fastest." Jake snorted at the comment, not sure if he was insulted. He still wasn't sure about this Bishop fellow, no matter how much faith the Confederacy had in him. How could he get around ships and blockades when no one else could? Luckily Ty had exercised caution and had not taken him to the Organ Cave where they made the powder, but to a smaller one where it was stored. Supplies were getting short enough without having a Yankee spy discover one of their best-kept secrets. It was bad enough they'd trusted him with this much.

Their orders were to carry the powder and Wade Bishop out of the mountains and into Raleigh, where the gunpowder would be loaded onto wagons and taken on toward the coast. There, Bishop supposedly had a ship waiting that would smuggle the powder into New Orleans. He was one smooth operator if he could do all that, Jake had to admit, but he still didn't trust him.

It was strange how you could sense things before they even happened. A slight tingle on the back of the neck, an itch in the palm of the hand or a sudden quiet that filled the air as the creatures who called the fields and forest home sought shelter against the coming storm. They had left the meadow where they could all ride abreast and were riding single file down a game trail that lay between a heavily forested ridge and a quickly moving stream that had carved a gully into the forest floor. On the left was the dense brush of low-hanging hemlocks and dense mountain laurel. On the right the rocky stream bed ran some ten feet below the trail. The mules had spooked every forest creature for miles around, leaving a silence in the background that made the creak of leather and the sounds of hooves striking dirt sound ominous.

There was no warning. One instant they were making their way through the dense forest and the next the air was filled with flying body parts as men, horses and mules were suddenly blown to bits.

"Idiots!" Bishop exclaimed as his horse reared.

"Take cover!" Ty yelled as he drew his gun. "Let go of those mules!"

Riders struggled to control their horses as terror seized the animals on the trail.

"Willie, let go of that mule." Jake drove his horse between the dazed boy and the mule he was still holding on to.

"Jake, cut back and see if you can get behind whoever's doing this." Ty had been leading the group while Jake had been bringing up the rear. The explosive had split the group of men, killing several as it hit the powder kegs carried by the mules. "The rest of you take cover in the brush."

"Ty!" Cat screamed as she surveyed the forest behind her. "Where's Caleb?" Ty turned his horse, searching the carnage behind him. He saw Jake charging back up the trail with Willie and another Ridge Rider on his heels. Several of the mules had gotten caught up in the mad dash and were carried along. The kegs clanked and the mules brayed, creating a wild cacophony that accompanied their charge. Beyond the confusion Ty could see Union cavalry riding toward them with weapons drawn. Bishop was beside him, still fighting to get his horse under control while the remaining men took to the dense underbrush.

"Cat, take cover." His voice was steady and firm,

taking on the responsibility his rank afforded him.

"*Ty,*" she sobbed as she fought to control her mare.

"*Caleb?*" Ty managed to grab Scarlet's reins as the mare danced around. "Cat, take cover now."

Jake plowed into the Union riders with both guns blazing. Ty watched in horror as horses and men flew into the air as another explosion rocked the forest around them.

"*Jake!*" Tears ran down Cat's face as she screamed at the vision of her friend being blown into bits.

"He's gone Cat." Ty's face was rigid as he dismounted and jerked Cat from her saddle. Scarlet, finally free of her rider, took off up the trail, following Wade Bishop, who had left them to their fate. "*Take cover.*" He shoved her into the brush. Cat swiped dirt and tears across her face as she crawled up the ridge beneath the deep canopy of a mountain laurel. *Oh God, please save us. Oh, Jake . . .* She backed up against the roots and listened to the sounds of men and horses crashing around, and beyond that, the soft moans of the dying. She slammed her fists against her ears to block out the sounds and squeezed her eyes shut as she saw again the image of Jake disappearing before her eyes. One moment he was there with his pale blond hair flying and guns blazing and the next he was gone, and the boy Willie with him. There was no way anyone could survive that. And where was Caleb? He had been riding behind her, but so had Bishop. Where was he? She was shivering despite the summer heat. She couldn't stop shivering.

"Oh God, Jake." Ty shook his head as his mind saw once again the rapid destruction of his men. His men. His stomach heaved as he tripped over a body. The hair was gray, not warm and brown like Caleb's. Was it Beroth or Tuttle? He didn't want to know.

"Ty?"

"Caleb!" He lay partially sheltered against the ridge with a body thrown over him. Ty pulled the body off. It was Tuttle, which meant the other was Beroth. Ty moved the body away. "Oh, God."

"Is it bad?" Caleb rose on his elbows to look. His eyes widened, and he swallowed hard against the bile that suddenly rose in his throat.

Ty looked at the bloody mess of boot and skin that comprised what had once been Caleb's left ankle. "Let's get you out of here." He quickly ripped Tuttle's belt off and made a tourniquet for Caleb's leg.

"Where are Cat and Jake?" Ty pulled Caleb up and placed his arm over his shoulder. Caleb turned pale and his eyes swam as his hand grasped Ty's sleeve.

"Let's get you to cover."

"Leave me. Get Cat and get out of here."

"Let's go." Ty half dragged, half carried Caleb back to where he had hidden Cat. Ahead he heard the sound of hoofbeats—Bishop running away, the coward. Above and behind them was the sound of the Union soldiers coming down to claim their victory.

"Cat?" Ty stopped close to where he had last seen her.

"I'm here." Her face appeared and she managed a timid smile until she saw Caleb's mangled leg.

"Take him."

"What?"

"Take him. I have to cover the signs or they'll find him."

"*No!*" Cat and Caleb responded in unison as Cat wiggled out of the brush.

"You will never survive a Yankee prison. Not with an injury like this." Ty's steel-blue eyes bored into Cat. "Drag him into the brush and keep quiet. No matter what you hear, keep quiet."

Cat's green-gold eyes grew wide as she realized what her husband was planning.

"Now, Cat." His voice was firm and his manner commanding. He expected to be obeyed. He was the commanding officer and responsible for their lives. She nodded and grabbed Caleb by the armpits, dragging him back from the trail. Ty stuck his head under the brush and watched as she pulled him back. "When this is over, when Caleb recovers, I want you to go home."

"I'll get him there." It was hard to respond as she dragged Caleb over tree roots and rocks.

"No, I mean home to Wyoming." She stopped, trying to see his eyes through the dense brush. "It's time, Cat."

"No, I won't leave you." Her chin trembled.

"I love you," he whispered and disappeared from her sight.

"Ty . . ." She saw his hand slide over the ground, smoothing out the signs of their passage as she backed Caleb into the undergrowth. The dense foliage of the mountain laurel surrounded them, creating a cave. She slid down the trunk of a hemlock and pulled

Caleb into her lap, his back against her breast and his head falling onto her shoulder.

"I'm sorry, Cat." She barely heard him.

"Shhh, it's not your fault." Below she heard the sure steps of her husband as he led the soldiers away from their hiding place. "It's not your fault," she whispered into the dark shaggy hair that was matted with sweat and blood. Caleb's hands sought hers as she held his trembling body against her, neither one of them daring to breathe as they heard the sounds of shots fired, running feet, men yelling and then the slash of swords and the impact of fist against skin as they fell into hand-to-hand combat. "Oh God, please don't let him die." Cat mouthed the words over and over while Caleb squeezed her hands. She realized he was saying it with her as the two of them huddled together, waiting for the sounds to go away.

An eternity passed for the two who were hiding in the deep woods against the ridge. Cat finally realized that the horrible sound she was hearing was the beating of her heart. Slowly she felt the forest come alive around her as the birds and smaller creatures returned to their normal routine of survival. Caleb was as still as death against her chest which caused her a moment of panic until she heard the sudden intake of his breath when she shifted beneath him.

"Do you think it's okay now?" She hated the trembling in her voice.

Caleb quietly cleared his throat. "I don't know." He tried to sit up. "We need to look around first."

Cat eased out from beneath him and gently lowered him against the tree trunk. Her hair caught in the wandering branches of the mountain laurel, which pulled it out of the rawhide thong she had tied it with earlier. Caleb helped her with the tangle and she couldn't help noticing how his hand was trembling and how pale he looked in the dim filtered light beneath the hemlock.

"Don't worry, Cat. I can't feel a thing," he assured her when he saw the look of concern that crossed her features. She nodded and turned over to crawl on her stomach down the slope toward the trail.

She cautiously stuck her head out from beneath the undergrowth after holding her breath to make sure she didn't hear a human sound. If Ty was near, he would have come for them. If Ty were still alive . . . She didn't want to look for fear of what she would see but she also knew that Caleb's life, along with her own and that of her unborn child, depended on what she did next.

The trail was empty except for the bodies of the men, horses and mules that lay in a tangle of limbs and gore where the first shots had hit. Cat moved out and stood silently, her ears tuned for the slightest sound that did not belong.

"Caleb?" She tried saying his name quietly but her voice sounded as loud to her ears as the explosions that had rocked them earlier.

"Coming." She saw the underbrush sway with his movement. How could he even move with his injury?

"Wait. Let me help." She ran into him coming down as she turned to go back up. He was sweating with the pain and exertion. *Oh God, whatever am I to do?*

Cat helped him the best she could and finally he made it to the trail. The next problem was helping him up. Caleb was nearly as tall as Ty but not as heavy, so they managed to get him standing with an arm around her shoulder and hers around his waist.

"Should I loosen the tourniquet?" He was trying to hold his lower leg at an angle to keep it from touching the ground but it was taking all of his strength to do so.

Caleb looked down at his leg with a grimace. "No, I think that's all that's holding it on right now." Cat's green-gold eyes grew wide as she looked down at his calf. "Help me sit." A fallen tree paralleled the trail across from them, and she supported him as he leaned and hopped the few steps. Caleb's face reflected the pain he felt but his voice was steady as he handed her his gun. "We need more weapons, Cat. And a horse."

Cat nodded and swallowed hard as she looked up the trail in the direction she had last seen Ty. The question of what had happened to him remained unspoken, but they needed to know that also. She held the gun firmly as she made her way back up the trail where the mangled remains lay. There was no sense in checking there. There wasn't anything left to check. She moved on. She found the boy Willie lying facedown. His body was remarkably whole. She knelt and placed her hand against his neck, checking, hoping for a pulse, but there was none there. She rolled him over and fell back in shock, scrambling to get away from the faceless mask that greeted her. She turned and gagged. Then her stomach heaved and she lost what little she had managed to eat for breakfast in the middle of the trail.

"Cat?"

"I'm okay," she managed to get out as she wiped her mouth with the back of her hand. She glanced back at Willie's body. She just couldn't leave him like that, could she? Cat walked on trembling legs back to the edge of the trail and looked down in the gully. A horse lay half in and half out of the stream, its head twisted at a strange angle. She recognized it as Jake's. She looked around again, afraid of what she would find. There were bits and pieces of someone or several someones, but nothing that would identify anyone. *Oh, Jake*... Cat swallowed back her tears and went on up the trail, cautiously following the curve of it. A sudden breeze caressed her face, bringing the slight hint of an approaching thunderstorm and sending the high branches of the trees into a wild dance. Sunlight bounced through the swaying branches and threw back a reflection against something shiny that lay in the trail.

Ty's sword.

Cat grasped the handle and lifted it, turning it slowly back and forth as if the blood dried on its length would answer all the questions that tumbled about in her mind. The brush around the trail was broken down. Obviously a fight had taken place. She swung the tip of the sword over the broken and bent undergrowth. She found his revolver and the chambers were empty. Ty had made his stand here—she was sure of it. How many had he killed? Was he wounded? They would have left his body if he were dead, wouldn't they? She tried to wipe the tears that were running down her cheeks and realized her hands were full of weapons. She stuck Ty's gun in her belt along with Caleb's and proceeded up the trail with his sword in hand.

There was nothing else. She found signs that horses and men had been there, but where they had gone would remain a mystery. Whoever had survived had been taken away, and there was nothing she could do about it.

Ty was gone.

Chapter Nineteen

The sound of thunder off in the distance brought Cat back to the reality of the moment. She stood in the middle of the trail with Ty's sword in her hand and felt herself incapable of making a decision. Her mind screamed in agony at the realization that Ty was gone without a trace.

Caleb. Caleb was waiting. *Turn around and go back to Caleb.* She didn't move. Fear consumed her. What should she do? Caleb could very easily die from his wound. What could she do against these odds without horse or supplies? *Think, Cat, think.* When they had rescued Jenny from Randolph Mason several years ago, Chase had made a sled to drag behind his horse when she became too ill to ride. Cat looked at the sword in her hand. Could she do that? Could she drag Caleb all the way back to North Carolina? Where else could she go without fear of him being taken? He would surely die if captured by the Yankees. The wind kicked up again as the thunder rumbled. Cat surveyed the darkening sky above the tips of the trees and turned back down the trail.

He was waiting where she had left him. He had been crying. She could still see the tracks of the tears on his cheeks.

"Anything?" he asked. Cat shook her head. "Cat, what happened to Jake?"

"He's gone, Caleb. There's nothing left."

"Willie, too?"

Cat's stomach heaved again as Willie's faceless body swam before her eyes. Would she see his death mask for the rest of her life? "Willie, too."

The wind whirled through, stirring up dead leaves and swirling them down the trail.

"They won't hurt him, Cat. He's an officer."

Cat looked at the ground and nodded as she fought to suppress the tears that threatened to erupt from her body. She felt her body shudder, and then Caleb pulled her into his arms.

"What are we going to do?" Cat sobbed into his chest. Caleb had no answers as he held her and patted her back while she cried. He did not know how much longer he could go on. The numbness in his leg was spreading up his thigh. He knew he would bleed to death if he took off the tourniquet, but keeping it on wasn't helping much either. *Please God, help us . . .*

A crashing below brought both their heads up.

"It's Scarlet!" Cat's horse was standing in the creek with her reins dragging and the whites of her eyes showing.

"Bless her heart, she came back." Caleb laughed weakly as Cat slid down the bank to catch the shiny chestnut mare. She ran her hands expertly over the mare's legs and flanks.

"She's okay!"

"Thank you, God," Caleb said, sighing. Cat quickly mounted and turned the horse downstream to search for an easy way up the bank. She was back on the trail in a short time.

"I think I saw a cave farther down. At least it will be some shelter until this storm blows over." Caleb saw her through a tunnel as blackness threatened the corners of his mind. "Can you mount?" He shook his head to clear the fog that was coming over him. "Caleb, stay with me for a few more minutes. Please!" Cat grabbed his shoulders. "*Caleb!*"

"Wha . . . yes . . . I'm here . . ."

Cat didn't like the looks of him. He had been so brave and yet he had to be in pain. She pulled him up and wrapped his hands around the top of the saddle.

"You've got to pull yourself up." Caleb laid his face against the cool leather of her saddle. Scarlet shifted her weight, nervous at the smell of blood and powder that covered him. "*Pull!*" Cat shoved with all her might. He managed to make the stirrup with his right leg but he couldn't swing his left one over.

"You've got to do it, Cat." He was drenched with sweat and was barely hanging on. Falling off would be the end of him. Cat gingerly grabbed his knee and swung it over Scarlet's back. Caleb groaned and pitched over the mare's neck, unconscious, but mounted.

The cave was big enough for the three of them. It

was sheltered by a dead tree, which provided plenty of wood for a fire. The hardest part was pulling Caleb off Scarlet. She wasn't strong enough or tall enough to hold him and had to use her body to break his fall. She made him as comfortable as possible and was grateful he was still unconscious. Cat had put off looking at the wound to his leg as long as possible.

She knew he carried a small sketchbook inside his shirt and she regretted using the blank pages as tinder for a fire. From her saddlebags she pulled a knife and the change of clothes she had packed. The shirt would make a cushion against the wound and the heavier fabric of the pants a bandage. She ripped at the seams of each, destroying the garments. She stuck a cooking pan outside to collect water as the rain came in a sudden sheet that blocked the view of the stream tumbling wildly beyond. Cat's wild imaginings conjured a sudden flash flood but she dismissed it. She would not let her fear conquer her. She had enough to deal with at the moment.

She began by cutting away Caleb's pants at the knee. The fabric below was in tatters and lost amid the ruined leather of his boot. Caleb's boot had to go; there was no way to save it. She sliced through the side facing the other leg and peeled it back and away from his calf. Her stomach lurched when she realized his foot was coming away with the boot.

"Oh God, no . . ." Caleb's ankle was hanging by nothing more than a piece of skin and some muscle. Shards of bone stuck out through the tissue. There was nothing left. Nothing to save. It would have to come off. Cat rocked back on her heels and covered her face with her hands. "Dear God in heaven, give me strength . . ."

Caleb lay as still as death on the blanket.

Could she do it? Her eyes found Ty's sword. She had carried it with her while she led Scarlet. It had even come in handy to clear some of the brush out of the way. Could she cut off Caleb's foot with Ty's sword?

Cat picked up the sword and tested its weight. She swung it down in a practice motion. The light of her fire flickered against the walls of the cave. The ceiling was high enough that she could raise it over her head. What if she missed? Caleb lay before her on his back. She cleaned the blood and dirt from the sword as best she could and then placed the blade in the fire. She looked at Caleb lying on the floor of the cave and then bent his good leg up under and away in case she missed. He didn't make a sound.

"Oh, Caleb, please forgive me." The blade was glowing in the fire. Tentatively she reached for it and placed the edge of it above the wound, judging the distance and the force she would need. "God, make this work because I don't think I can do it twice." She lifted the sword to the ceiling and swung down with all her might.

Ty gratefully lifted his face to the rain that would wash away any signs that Cat and Caleb might leave behind. It also washed away the blood that was trickling from a gash above his eyebrow. His hands were tied behind him and he was kneeling beneath a tree with four other survivors of his troop, waiting to be interrogated by the commanding officer of the unit that had captured them.

"Riders approaching."

Ty turned to watch as the sentry made the announcement. *Please don't let it be Cat.*

Three Union soldiers rode in with Wade Bishop in tow. He was bound and gagged and looked ready to explode as he was hauled off his horse and shoved into the commanding officer's tent. Ty let out a sigh of relief. Thank God they had never taken him to the real cave. Ty knew that the men under him would never give away its location and the only thing that would force him to give it up would be a threat to Cat, and he prayed to God she was safely away. He hoped Caleb would be all right. He hadn't liked the look of his leg. He didn't want to think about Jake, or Willie or the rest of the men who lay dead along the trail without hope of a proper burial. He would see their faces for the rest of his life and curse himself for letting down his guard, for letting Cat distract him from his job, for getting them killed.

He heard angry voices coming from the tent. The drone of the rain drowned out the words but he recognized Bishop's deep drawl alternating with the clipped tones of the commander.

"Which one of you is Major Kincaid?"

"I am." Ty rose to his feet.

"Come with me."

Ty followed the soldier to the tent. The man lifted the flap for him and Ty ducked under it.

"Untie his hands." The Yankee colonel ordered. Ty's eyes narrowed when he realized he knew the man; he just couldn't remember how. "Major Tyler Kincaid of North Carolina, I am Colonel Joseph Myers of Massachusetts. Am I correct in assuming you have surrendered your troop into my custody?"

"Yes sir, I have." Colonel Myers rose from behind the folding table that served as a desk.

"Do I know you from somewhere, Major Kincaid?"

"I don't know." Ty rubbed his wrists as the Yankee came closer. "You do seem familiar."

"Did you capture his wife?" Ty looked at Bishop incredulously and decided then and there that Bishop had to die.

"Mr. Bishop, the actions of my troop are none of your concern." Obviously Myers was not impressed with him either.

"It's my concern when your troop fails in its purpose."

"Which was?" Ty knew the answer in his heart, but he still wanted to hear the words.

"To find the source of the powder, Kincaid. This stupid Yankee was supposed to follow us to the cave and capture the facility. Instead he got lost and wound up blowing every bit of powder we had to kingdom come."

"The cave you went to was not the source, Mr. Bishop. Apparently Major Kincaid did not trust you any more than I do. These men would rather die than give up the location. My orders were to keep the powder out of rebel hands. I believe we accomplished that task rather effectively."

Ty didn't know which one he wanted to kill first.

Bishop had betrayed them. Myers dismissed the death of his men. Myers was closer.

Two soldiers grabbed him from behind before he had a chance to wrap his hands around the colonel's neck. He was shoved into a chair while Myers looked on with a bemused expression.

"You brought your wife with you on a mission?"

Ty fought against the hands that held him.

"She followed us." Bishop was a font of information.

"Having trouble controlling your wife, Major Kincaid?" Myers was obviously amused. "What is your wife's name?"

"Catherine. He calls her Cat." Why couldn't Bishop just shut up for once? Ty imagined what it would feel like to choke the life out of Wade Bishop.

"Catherine Lynch of Wyoming?"

Ty's eyes widened as the realization struck him. The Colonel Myers standing before him was the same Captain Myers who had taken Cat to the Christmas dance in Wyoming before the war started. The same Captain Myers that he and his friends had brawled with right before Jamie died. It seemed like a lifetime had passed since those carefree days. Several lifetimes had passed. Jamie's, Jake's, Willie's, his mother's, along with the thousands of men who had died in this war. Ty couldn't help it; he laughed.

"What is so funny?" Bishop fumed. "His wife is out there. If you find her, you can make him tell you where the cave is."

"So you did marry her." Myers nodded to the men

holding Ty and they released him. "Brave man." Myers turned to Bishop. "We don't make war against soldiers' wives, Mr. Bishop. Put him with the other prisoners."

"You can't do that. I work for the Federal government," Bishop protested.

"Mr. Bishop, you work for whomever serves your best interests. You are a traitor to your own people. You are now my prisoner. That is all." The men escorted an incredulous Bishop out of the tent.

"Should I go find your wife, Major Kincaid?"

Ty thought about it. She would put up a fight, but she was no match for the Union Army. They would eventually let her go and probably give her safe escort. Caleb would receive medical attention but after that there would be prison. They would be separated since Caleb was an enlisted man and not an officer. He wouldn't survive; there would be no one to look out for him.

"No." He smiled at the thought that Cat and Caleb would survive. "Besides, she's long gone by now."

"Good." Myers settled back into his chair. "I don't feel the need to lose any more of my men today."

"And what about my men?"

"Your men are now prisoners of the Union Army. There will be no more prisoner exchanges."

"My men who died."

"Oh, of course." Myers steepled his fingers as he considered Ty. "Will you give me your word of honor that you will not attempt to escape if I free you and your men to dig graves for the dead?"

"Yes."

Myers extended his hand to Ty. "The war for you is over, Major Kincaid. I will allow you this one last duty. To see to your men."

Chapter Twenty

Typical of a summer afternoon storm, the rain was over as quickly as it came. Caleb was still miraculously unconscious. Cat dreaded his waking. Whatever would she tell him? She had done all she could do. The wound had been cauterized and bandaged. What was left of his foot she had buried and then covered with rocks so the animals wouldn't dig it up and drag it away. She had managed to eat some food from the provisions Portia had packed in her saddlebags. The prospect of how she was going to get Caleb home was more than she could deal with. She sat within the entrance to the cave and watched the stream roll merrily along.

The snap of a branch alerted her to someone on the trail above. Cat silently went to Scarlet and placed her hand over the velvet nose to keep the mare from spooking and giving away their location. She listened to the slow, steady plod of a horse walking above and held her breath until the sound faded into the distance. Maybe she should try to rouse Caleb at dusk so they could make their escape under the cover of darkness.

Cat knelt and smoothed the shaggy dark brown locks away from his handsome face. He looked at peace for the moment, his face free of the cares and worries that weighed it down when he was awake. Had she ever really looked at Caleb before? He had been around for so long that she had taken him for granted, like the weathered buildings of the ranch. She remembered when her father had brought him to Wyoming after one of his many business trips. Jason had found him on the streets of St. Louis trying to support himself by drawing pictures for pennies. He had been a skinny, gawky kid with huge dark brown eyes and thick, unkempt hair. Fresh air, hard work and good food had helped him grow into his frame. Baths and regular haircuts had taken care of his shaggy locks. But the eyes hadn't changed. They still saw everything.

Cat dreaded the pain that would be there when he realized his foot was gone. He would have a home forever with them, but would his pride accept his changed circumstances? She picked up his hand and admired the long, slender fingers. So much beauty sprang forth from this hand. She smiled wistfully at his little finger, which seemed to have a permanent smudge from the blending and shadowing he did on his drawings. What if he had lost his hands instead, or his wonderful brown eyes? Or worst of all, what if he died before she got him home?

Cat realized that the what-ifs could go on forever. What if she hadn't followed them into the mountains? Had her presence made Ty careless of his duties?

Would he have realized they were riding into an ambush? Would he have hidden with Caleb? She knew the answer to that one. He would have fought to the end with Caleb right beside him. Was there anything that any one of them could have done to make the outcome of today any different? She could go insane thinking about all of it.

At least she knew Ty was alive. Penelope had told her on a fine spring day in the garden that she would feel it with her heart if something happened to Ty. Her heart was still beating strong and sure and beneath it a baby was listening. Ty was alive. And as soon as she took care of Caleb, she would find him.

Someone had been here. Ty and his men grimly surveyed the carnage that had once been the Ridge Riders. The bodies had been robbed. Boots were missing, pockets were turned inside out.

"I found Willie," someone called out. "Or what's left of him."

"Any sign of Jake?" Ty dreaded the answer but he had to know.

"I see his horse."

"Permission to look for my lost man?" Ty asked the Union officer who was in charge of guarding the prisoners.

"Go ahead." The man took off his hat and ran his hand through his hair. A few of his friends had been killed also.

Ty slid down the muddy bank. Jake's horse had torn up the area in his descent into the gully. The hard shower just passed had raised the water level until the horse was trapped and floating between two huge boulders. The saddle and bridle were gone, taken by scavengers for the price of the leather. There was nothing left but the bloated, twisted body of what had once been a fine animal. Nothing left to say that Jacob Anderson had died there, nothing left to say he had lived a life except the private memories of those who knew him and loved him, in spite of himself.

"Find anything, major?"

"Nothing." Ty took a deep cleansing breath. The water from the stream tossed merrily along, the birds sang their songs and he was facing a bleak life, alone and without any control over his future. It was probably the same way Jake felt all those years ago before he left home and struck out on his own. "Things could have been different. They should have been different for you, growing up, but you turned out good. You were a good man, Jake."

"He must have been blown to bits," someone offered from above. They were strange words of comfort.

"I guess it's the way you wanted to go . . . my friend." That was it, Jake's epitaph. Ty looked downstream toward the south and the way home. *Cat* . . .

"Let's go, major." The Union officer had been patient long enough. Ty made sure his muffler was secure around his neck and then struggled back up the muddy hill. He had bodies to bury.

How long had she been asleep? Cat blinked against the darkness that had come with the warm summer night. The moon was still rising so it had to be early evening. The reflection of it was mirrored in the stream that still gurgled merrily along, carrying with it the remnants of the death and destruction that had marred its surface earlier that afternoon.

"Cat?"

Caleb was awake. Did he know what she had done? "I'm here." She made her way over to his pallet in the darkness. "How do you feel?"

Caleb made a weak attempt at sitting. "I'm alive, I think. My leg hurts like hell." He moved his back against the wall of the cave. The movement surprised him, causing him to look in shock at the darkness where his legs lay.

"Caleb—" She gently touched his arm. "It's gone."

"What?"

The light was too dim too see his face. Cat found her saddlebags and the stub of a candle. The warm glow of it bathed their faces in a surreal light as Cat held it up, then trailed it down his leg. Caleb's hand followed, the touch confirming what his brain did not want to accept. He flinched when he touched the heavily bandaged stump where fortunately the blood had dried after she had cauterized the wound with her knife.

"Oh God." His hand covered his face.

"I'm sorry, Caleb, it was gone. There was nothing for me to do but take it off." The words tumbled out in a rush and a sob as she dropped the candle, leaving them once again in darkness.

"I can't believe you did it."

"I'm sorry. I'm so sorry." She couldn't stop shaking as the tears overcame her.

Caleb pulled her to his chest. "No, no, I can't believe that you were able to do it, Cat. I don't blame you; it's not your fault. You did what you had to do. Shhh, it's all right." Her arms circled his waist and they clung to each other in the darkness, each trying to comfort the other.

"Oh, Caleb, what are we going to do?"

"Go home."

She nodded against his chest and wiped her nose with her sleeve. "Do you think you can ride?"

"I guess I'll have to. I'm not much for walking right now."

"Oh, Caleb." Cat felt around in the darkness for the candle.

"See if you can find something for me to use as a crutch." His face looked pained in the small circle of light. "And hurry . . ."

"You need to take it slow."

"Some things won't wait, Cat."

"Oh." Cat felt her face flush as she backed out of the cave. The fallen tree supplied several likely candidates for a crutch and with a few adjustments, made courtesy of Ty's sword, she soon had something that would work. She found him trying to rise so she quickly went to his aid.

"I'm okay," Caleb insisted, bravely. Cat prayed that he wouldn't fall as he made his way with great difficulty to the outside. The sounds coming forth soon assured her that he had achieved his purpose. She waited a few moments more, then checked on him.

Caleb was resting his forehead against the rocky

entrance to the cave, leaning heavily on his crutch. "Caleb?"

He turned his head and looked at her sideways. "We might as well start now. I don't know if I have the strength to get up again."

"Do you want something to eat first?"

"No. I don't think I can keep anything down right now."

Cat gave him a worried look before she brought Scarlet out of the cave. "Do you think you can mount?"

"I'm going to have to, aren't I?" Caleb wearily grabbed the saddle horn as Cat moved Scarlet next to him. With the help of her shoulder and the crutch, he was able to haul himself up, but Cat could tell he had used what little reserves he had gathered while unconscious. "You'd better ride behind me. I don't know how long I'll be able to stay upright." Using the dead tree as a step, she swung up behind him and, gathering the reins, turned Scarlet toward the south, and home.

Caleb fought to stay upright. Occasionally his head would fall back against Cat's shoulder and then he would jerk himself up again with his back held ramrod straight. Cat kept her arms wrapped around his waist, but she knew that if he started to topple over, there would be nothing she could do to stop them both from going down. She was afraid that Caleb hitting the ground in his condition was something neither one of them would survive. Cat once again began considering building a travois of some type as Caleb jerked against her. Night would soon be upon them and she was afraid that they would both fall asleep and wind up in worse shape than they were at the present.

"Cat, look," Caleb said weakly.

She followed his gaze into a small clearing along the trail. Ty's horse stood at attention with ears pricked toward them.

"He's been trained to wait. He just went on a little farther that he was supposed to," Caleb explained.

"All the explosions must have spooked him."

"Maybe. He should be used to it by now." They pulled up and Scarlet nickered a greeting. "Go on. He's used to me. Just ride up to him and grab his rein." The horse waited as Caleb had said he would and Cat soon had him by the rein.

"What do we do now?"

"Tie me to the saddle."

"What?"

"You can't keep holding me up and if I fall, I'm a goner for sure. And if I take you with me, you might lose your baby." Caleb's head hung forward with his hair in his eyes. Each word was an effort. "My foot is gone and my leg is sure to follow if you don't get me home soon. It's a four-day ride from here if nothing goes against us. Tie me to the saddle and keep going."

Cat couldn't stand the thought of it, but she knew he was right. She had to get him home and then have the doctor come look at his leg. She knew the riding couldn't be good for it and wasn't sure if what she had done had helped him or hurt him. The only thing to do was get him home as soon as possible. She did as he asked and mounted Ty's horse. Caleb slid into unconsciousness soon after they started up again. He lay against Scarlet's neck but stayed put on her back.

The moon was full and cast enough light on the trail for the horse to find his way. Ty's animal seemed sure of his steps and Cat realized that he had made this trip many times. It was miraculous that the horse had survived this long and she caressed the animal's neck in gratitude for the fine service it had given her husband. Heart was not something you could breed into an animal, but it was something for which they all hoped.

Where was Ty? What had happened to him? Was he at this very minute at the mercy of Union forces? Cat knew that the men in the field treated each other honorably, but she had heard stories of the prison camps and hated the thought of Ty being subjected to the horror that they offered. Was he hurt? Had he been wounded in his attempt to save them from being taken prisoner? What kind of care would he receive? Would he survive what was to come? The questions tumbled in her head like water over a fall. They broke the surface and were driven down only to come bubbling up again, tormenting her with the fact that she had no answers and would not have any for a long time to come. Not knowing was the worst part of it. The not knowing and the waiting. How long would she have to wait for the answers to her questions? *Was he safe?*

Caleb groaned from his saddle. The moon was waning and Cat suddenly realized how tired, scared and hungry she felt. She knew Caleb couldn't make it all the way home tied to the back of a horse. It couldn't be good for his leg, or what was left of it. And she had the baby to think of. Spending days and nights on the trail couldn't be good for it either. They had to stop and rest for now. She was too tired to think about what to do after that.

She soon found a suitable place to make camp and Caleb roused as soon as she stopped.

"Where are we?" His voice was slurred and weak.

"Somewhere down the trail." Cat rushed to his side and untied the rope that was holding him on. Caleb weaved and blinked as he tried to get his bearings in the darkness. "Hold on." Cat reached up to support him and found his shirt to be soaking wet. He was running a fever, the first sign of infection. He managed to swing his leg over and land on his good one between the support of Cat and Scarlet. "Can you hang on for a minute?"

Caleb nodded, his hands clutching the saddle and his face buried in the side. Cat hastily spread a blanket over a bed of long grass. She wrapped Caleb's arm over her shoulder and with her arm about his waist managed to guide him the three hopping steps to the blanket. Getting Caleb down proved to be a problem but she finally dropped to her knees and he flopped over on his back.

She made him as comfortable as possible under the conditions and went about the business of making camp. She turned the horses out to graze and gathered wood for a fire.

"Caleb, you need to eat something."

"I can't." His dark eyes were glassy in the flickering light of the fire. Cat wiped his face with a kerchief that she had soaked in a nearby stream. His head tossed as she wiped his forehead.

"You've got to keep your strength up to fight the fever," she pleaded.

His reply was lost as he slid beneath the weight of his illness. Cat lifted his head and poured some water from her canteen between his lips but whether any of it went down or not she could not tell.

With the light of the fire as her aid she turned to check the bandages on his leg. As soon as she touched the stump with her hand he flinched and she knew the pain must be bad indeed to reach him in his semiconscious state. "Oh, Caleb, what should I do?"

There was no answer except that of his agitated murmurs and the chorus of crickets and tree frogs beyond. Cat stared dumbly at the fire, feeling her weariness and despair settling over her. *God, help us . . . please . . .* She found her blanket and made a pallet as close to Caleb as she could, seeking comfort in the fact that she could be close to him, even though his mind was a million miles away. She finally slept knowing the dawn would soon be upon them and the problems to which she had no solutions would be waiting.

In the cabin in the small valley in Wyoming, Jenny dashed the tears from her eyes as she burrowed into Chase's wide chest. He immediately wakened and wrapped his arms around her.

"What's wrong? What happened?"

"Oh, Chase." Her voice trembled as she fought the

sobs that threatened to consume her. "I saw them in my dream and they were all dead."

"Who?"

"Ty, Cat, Caleb and Jake. I saw them lying in a meadow and they were dead." She dissolved into tears, and her words were lost against the dampness of his skin.

Chase stroked her hair and held her as she gave in to the fear that had awakened her. His mind raced as he considered her words. Surely they couldn't all have been lost. The chances were great that the three men would not survive, but Cat, too? She was supposedly safe and waiting out the war at Ty's family home.

"It's just a dream, Jenny. Everything will be fine."

"It's not, Chase. I know in my heart that it's not."

Even though his mind screamed that logically there was no way she could know what had happened hundreds of miles away, his heart knew that her dreams had proven to be a portent of future incidents. It had occurred too many times to just be coincidence. What did this mean? He refused to accept the fact that the four of them could all be dead.

"I dreamed of this disaster before. I saw all of them being consumed by flames." Jenny sat up in the bed and wiped her eyes with the heel of her hand. "Wade Bishop was there, too, and he was laughing at them. It was as if he was the one who did it." She pounded the mattress with frustration. "I just wish I knew what it all meant."

Chase propped himself against the headboard as he listened to Jenny's rant. "I don't know what to tell you." His hand caressed the end of a golden lock of hair that had tumbled over her shoulder. "I wish I knew what your dreams meant; I wish I knew where they came from. I know that a lot of times they seem to come as a warning. I don't know how Wade Bishop got mixed up in dreams of Cat and Ty except that maybe it's because they are all constantly on your mind. The only thing I'm sure of is that he is nowhere around here and if he was, Cole would be on him before he had a chance to turn around." Jenny lay against his chest and his hands stroked her back as he sought the words to bring her comfort. "There's a good chance that something could have happened to Ty, Caleb and Jake but not Cat with them. There is no way Ty would let her anywhere near a battlefield."

"But you know how stubborn she is."

"Yes, anybody who knows her knows that she likes to have her way but where her safety is concerned, Ty wouldn't care about her feelings."

"I just wish there was some way we could know for sure."

"We have just got to believe that she's fine, that they are all fine." His hand tangled in her hair as she relaxed against the solid strength of his chest. "Aren't you the one who said we have just got to have faith and believe that God will take care of them?"

"Yes."

"Then we just got to keep the faith, Jenny."

"I love you, Chase." Her arms wrapped around his waist as he continued his gentle stroking. Another day awaited them in just a few hours. For Chase there would be many long hours of preparing for the annual drive to St. Jo. For Jenny there would be taking care of two very active boys, along with numerous household chores, plus work with Storm's offspring who were already giving the Lynch ranch a reputation of breeding excellent horses. The day would wait; for now it was enough just to be Chase and Jenny, together.

"I love you." He wanted to crush her in his arms, he wanted to hold her and never let her go. The depth of his love for her frightened him sometimes. The three little words did not seem enough to express what he felt. She was the center of his world, the sun in his sky. His life revolved around her, his children, the growing cabin in the small valley in Wyoming. He marveled once again over the circumstances that had brought them together, that had placed them there, where they had made a life and found happiness, even amid the tragedies that had befallen them.

"Keep the faith, Jenny." They would wait and see what happened. If their friends had met their end, then they would deal with the sorrow. It was all they could do.

Chapter Twenty-one

"Talk to me, Caleb." They were coming down to ford the New River. Cat was afraid he would slide over and drown. She needed him to be conscious for the crossing.

"Wha . . ." His head jerked upright. His hands were wrapped tightly in Scarlet's mane. Cat knew the area around the amputation was swollen and infected but there was nothing she could do about it. She was afraid to unwrap it to see what she would find. She was afraid he would bleed to death or she would do something to make the infection worse. Her best course of action was to get him home and to a doctor as soon as possible. They had ridden all night after getting a late start the morning before. It had taken Cat a long time to rouse Caleb sufficiently to get him back into the saddle. She was afraid he wouldn't have the strength to do it again.

There wasn't a part of her that didn't ache. She realized that she was a long way from Wyoming and the girl who used to tag along on the drive, just for the fun of it. She was tired and afraid, but mostly she was tired of being afraid. She wanted Ty, she wanted her father, and she wanted everything that had happened to them to just go away. She wanted to go home.

"Caleb!" The horses picked their way down the bank to the ford. Caleb blinked and searched for whoever it was that wouldn't let him sink back into the oblivion that consumed him. "Talk to me. Talk to me about home."

"Home?"

"Wyoming. Home. What do you miss about home?"

Cat watched as his dark brown eyes focused on her and then on their surroundings.

"Is this the . . . New?"

"Yes." Her heart leaped for joy when she realized that he was still functioning.

"Then we're close to home."

"I hope so."

The river was down since the summer had been dry. The horses moved on into the hip-deep water. Cat lifted her feet to keep them dry and noticed Caleb letting the water swirl around his. It probably felt good and helped to cool him down. Portia would know what to do. Portia would take care of him and the doctor would come and probably fuss at her for not taking care of herself.

Caleb's head bobbed. "What's your favorite thing to eat?" Cat literally shouted although he was right beside her.

"Eat?" His lips were cracked and dry from the fever and his voice weak.

"That Grace would fix, what's your favorite thing?"

"Apple pie."

Cat felt bad for making him talk when it was obviously so painful for him. But she was proud of him for trying. He had not complained once although she knew he was in great pain.

"Yeah, me, too." She tried to sound encouraging. He just needed to stay awake until they were safely across the river.

"Her biscuits."

"Uh-huh. How about her blueberry cobbler?"

"Jenny's sugar cookies were good."

"You mean the ones that got baked instead of thrown around?"

Caleb managed a smile as they made their way up the opposite bank. "And her ginger cookies . . ." He leaned over Scarlet's neck as her powerful hindquarters propelled them up onto solid ground. His hair hung limp and damp in his eyes and his breath was labored as if he had done the climbing himself.

"Remember that ham we had the last Christmas at home?"

"Yeah, it had—" he was trying so hard to keep up the conversation—"pineapple? That was the funniest looking fruit I've ever seen."

"Grace had a hard time figuring out how to peel it and slice it."

"Your father . . ." He was fading fast. "Your father always found the most wonderful things." His dark brown eyes lost the faraway look for a moment as they settled on Cat. "He always knew how to make things special . . . for all of us." Caleb shivered as the water rolled in sheets off the horses. If only he could hold on a little while longer. "That was the last Christmas we were all together. . . ." Cat felt him drift off with the words as the images from the past filled her mind. The last Christmas they had all spent together. The next one the four of them had been gone and Jamie and Sarah were dead. How many more Christmases before what was left of the gang was together again? Would Caleb survive to see this one? Would Ty be alive and spending it in some Yankee prison camp?

Cat decided that she very much wanted them all to be together for Christmas. It was five and a half months away. All she had to do was get Caleb to a doctor, find out where Ty was and bust him out of whatever camp he was in. She might need some help, she decided. Chase would help her. He said he owed Ty his life. Ty had been the one who found him sick and dying in the pasture that day. Surely he would help Ty escape. So she needed to go home. Find out where Ty was, take Caleb home, get help, come back and break Ty out of prison. Surely she could get that done by Christmas. And the fact that she was expecting a baby shouldn't interfere with her plans at all.

The horses crested the rise and began the descent that would bring them out of Virginia and into North Carolina. "We're going to be home tonight, Caleb. Just hold on a little while longer."

* * *

The inhabitants of the Kincaid Plantation had turned in for the night but sleep would be difficult for them with the muggy air that had settled over the piedmont. The heat had raised Caleb's temperature and sent him into a semi-conscious state. A lone lantern on the post outside the house was the only welcome to be had as Cat led Scarlet up the long drive to the house. The barking of the dogs brought Zeb around from the barn wearing nothing but a pair of pants.

Cat wondered wearily what to do next. Caleb's skin felt close to boiling as she reached over to place a hand on his forehead. Portia would know what to do. The doctor would come and take care of him.

"Miz Catherine?"

"Zeb!" Cat repressed the urge to throw herself into the big man's arms and cry her eyes out. Things still had to be done. "Mister Caleb is hurt bad. We need to get him in the house and then someone needs to go for the doctor."

A light appeared in the doorway and Silas took in the scene as he held a lamp above his tightly curled white hair. Caleb was cut free and slid from the saddle into Zeb's waiting arms. The big slave carried him through the front door with Cat on his heels.

"Mister Ty?" Silas asked fearfully.

"Captured." The fear she had held at bay through most of the long trip down the mountain came flooding back. She didn't know. *Is he safe?*

"Someone needs to go for the doctor." Cat followed them up the stairs. Portia appeared in the hallway, fastening her robe at the same time that Parker appeared on the landing above.

"Good Lord, Cat, where have you been?" The thin strands of his hair literally stood on end as he took in Caleb's appearance. "Where's Ty?"

"We were ambushed and he was captured. He led the enemy away from us because Caleb was hurt." Cat started to shake and wrapped her arms around herself to stop it. "Jake was killed. That's all I know."

Parker opened his mouth to speak and then closed it when he saw the extent of Caleb's wound. Silas led Zeb down the hall to the room that Caleb had shared with Jake while staying at the house. The bed was turned down and Portia began stripping his uniform before Zeb even had him settled.

"I'd best go for the doctor," Parker volunteered when he saw that Portia had the situation well in hand.

"I'll go saddle your horse." Zeb turned to go.

"Then get right back up here when you're done. We're going to need you to help turn him and hold him down," Portia ordered. "Silas, go put some water on to boil and bring up my box of medicines. This boy is in a heap of trouble and we gots to make sure he survives all these troubles that the Good Lord has heaped on him." The men left to do her bidding, and Cat crept to the end of the bed to stand as Portia disposed of the uniform that had once looked so handsome on Caleb's lean frame.

Once again Cat realized that she had never really looked at Caleb. His skin glistened with sweat from his fever but looked soft and smooth beneath the moisture. His chest and arms were dark from the sun. He was painfully thin, as most soldiers were from short rations but the long line of his muscle stood out, showing good health and a strong constitution.

Portia took a pair of scissors and cut away the dark blue pants with the gold stripe running up the side. The long line of his thigh was revealed, and then the sharp contrast of the bandages and what lay beneath brought a lump to her throat. Caleb was beautiful, like a work of art, Cat realized and she had never appreciated his beauty until it was destroyed. As far as she was concerned, he had just been another part of the ranch, like the cows and horses and buildings. He was fun to talk to and she admired his talent but she had never really known Caleb, deep down inside.

Nor had she known Jake, not really, and now she never would. She could excuse it all by saying he was an employee of her father's but they had all lived together as a family for years and she had been too wrapped up in her own shallow little world to notice the people who were an important part of her life.

Cat came around the bed and picked up the graceful hand that could make a pencil and paper come to life. *I promise I will always be your friend, Caleb.* She heard Silas as he came into the room with a pitcher of water and Portia's box of herbs. Portia wrung out a cloth in the fresh water and handed it to her. Cat gently wiped the sweat from his forehead. She tenderly smoothed back the damp heavy dark hair from Caleb's pale face. He lay as still as death beneath their ministrations. Portia worked quickly and efficiently, bathing his body before she attempted even to look at the leg beneath the heavy bandages. Cat got the feeling that she was avoiding it.

Zeb appeared and reported that Master Parker had gone off to fetch the doctor on one of the fastest horses. They shouldn't expect him before dawn. He had also awakened one of the men to take care of Scarlet and Mister Ty's horse. Portia took advantage of his presence and asked him to hold Caleb up so she could wash his back. She was soon satisfied that she had done all she could to clean him and stood back with hands on her hips to examine the bandages.

"Tell me what happened to this poor boy."

Cat had settled into a chair and blinked as if waking from a dream. Portia had covered Caleb with a sheet, leaving his leg out. There was a pillow propped under his knee. Cat wondered if Caleb had felt all the hands on his body, despite his fever.

"We were ambushed on the trail," she began. "The powder kegs blew up and Caleb was close to them."

"They blew his foot off?" Silas asked with eyes wide.

"No." Cat shook her head and pushed back the unruly curl that fell into her eyes. "It was still attached but just by some skin and muscle. I cut it off."

Three dark faces looked at her in shock.

"I had to; there was nothing else to do. I used Ty's sword . . ." Cat wiped her sleeve across her eyes and willed the tide of tears into submission. "I didn't know what else to do . . ."

Portia laid a hand on her arm. "You did the best you knew how. You took care of him and you brought him home. Can't nobody ask for more than that." Cat nodded, her chin trembling. "You go on and get some rest. We'll fix you a bath and you can get to bed."

"No. I can't rest until the doctor comes. I have to be here when the doctor comes."

Portia looked over Cat's tangled curls at Silas. "All right, chile. We'll just fix you a bath then so you can get cleaned up. The doctor won't be here for a while and ain't nobody going nowhere. We'll take care of Mister Caleb. Ain't nothing more you can do for him right now. You gots to take care of yourself and that baby for when Mister Ty comes back."

Cat looked at Caleb's dear, sweet face as he lay still as death on the four-poster bed. Portia's words ran through the weary paths of her mind. "Take care of yourself and take care of your baby for Ty . . ." She left the room to seek the comfort of a bath and clean clothes, knowing she could refresh her body but her mind would not rest . . . Ty was out there somewhere . . .

Chapter Twenty-two

The sound of hurrying footsteps on the stairs jerked Cat upright from the chair where she had been dozing since her bath. Her head felt foggy and her back was killing her, but the sight of Caleb's face, covered with sweat and tossing against his pillow brought her into quick awareness of her surroundings. Portia wrung out another cloth to place against his feverish forehead as Parker and the doctor entered the room.

The doctor was all business as he rushed to Caleb's side and immediately examined the injured leg that was propped on towels above the sheet. "You did this?" he asked Cat as he gently probed the area.

Cat bit her lip and nodded, dreading what the doctor would say next.

"For someone who was supposed to come home and take care of herself, you've been very busy."

"Will he live?" she asked with trembling lips.

"Most likely, but he'll wish he were dead first." The doctor removed his coat and rolled up his sleeves. "You probably saved his life, but there's still work to be done. The stump is infected and we need to remove that before it turns gangrenous and kills him. I'll need to remove about six inches of the bone and fashion him a flap so he can be fitted with a wooden leg." Cat's face turned pale as he talked. "The good news is that we will probably be able to save his knee, so he should be able to get around without too much trouble. The bad news is I have no morphine."

"You mean you're going to cut him, bone and all, and he'll feel it?" Cat felt the nausea rising in her stomach along with a sudden cramp in her lower back.

The doctor raised one of Caleb's eyelids for a quick examination. "Let's just hope he stays unconscious for a while longer."

It was decided that the surgery should be done in the kitchen on a sturdy table, and Portia and the doctor went down to prepare for the operation. Zeb picked up Caleb to carry him downstairs and Parker and Cat followed. They ran into Lucy Ann in the hall. She stood there with tousled hair and blinking eyes as she fastened the high neck of her robe.

"Parker, whatever is happening?" Lucy Ann drawled, obviously annoyed by the activity that had interrupted her beauty sleep.

"Ty's been captured and Caleb is hurt. Cat brought him home."

"Ty's captured?" Lucy Ann blinked at the two of them in disbelief while Zeb went on down with his precious cargo. "What is Zeb doing with Caleb?"

"The doctor is here and says he must take off part of his leg. He's going to do it now."

"The doctor is going to remove Caleb's leg, in our house?" Lucy Ann was incredulous as she stood in the hall with her perfectly manicured hands braced on her well-curved hips.

"I'm afraid so, dear. He might die if we don't." Parker's tone was condescending, as if he were talking to a child.

Lucy Ann wrinkled her nose in disgust and went back into her room. The slam of her door echoed through the hall.

Cat and Parker did not spare her another thought as they rushed down the stairs to the kitchen. Zeb had laid Caleb on the sturdy wooden table.

"Where am I?" Cat could see Caleb's head turning as he tried to get his bearings. She rushed to his side and smoothed the dark, sweaty locks of his hair away from his forehead.

"You're home." She tried to keep her expression calm even though her insides were crying because he had awakened from his unconscious state. "We're in the kitchen."

Caleb surveyed the faces surrounding him. The doctor was a stranger to him, and he blinked as his feverish mind tried to place him. He attempted to rise but several pairs of hands gently pushed him back onto the table. "What's happening? What are you doing?"

The looks on the others' faces made Cat realize it was up to her to do the telling. "Caleb, the doctor is here and he needs to operate on your leg. It's infected and he has to take some more of it off so you'll be able to use a wooden leg." Caleb's dark eyes were wide in his pale face as Cat spoke. Behind her she could hear the sounds of the doctor's instruments being lined up on the counter. Caleb's eyes flicked from face to concerned face as Parker, Zeb and Silas hovered around the table. "The problem is there's no morphine because of the blockade. We were hoping you would sleep through it . . ." Words failed her as terror seized her. How would he survive it? He was sick and weak and the pain would be incredible. She looked at the dark brown eyes that were suddenly huge in his face. Heavy, dark circles stood out against his pale skin. Caleb licked dry chapped lips as he glanced down the table toward his leg and saw the doctor standing there with a saw in his hand.

"Cat?"

"Shhh, Caleb, it will be all right. You just have to hold on."

The doctor nodded to the men, who all took a firm hold of Caleb. Zeb placed both hands on his upper arms, Silas held his good leg and Parker took the bad. With a small scalpel the doctor began to cut away the infected tissue. Caleb gasped. Cat ran her hands through his hair and swallowed the bile that rose in her throat as a mixture of blood and pus streamed onto the table. Portia immediately began to sop up the mess with a towel as the doctor worked.

"Caleb, I'm creating a flap to cover the end of your bone," he informed his patient as he worked. Cat wondered if Caleb really needed the details of what was going on. Caleb fixed his eyes on the ceiling as he took in short gasps of air, only to blow them out again. The doctor's hands were sure and steady but

Cat wondered why he didn't work faster. Surely he could see how much he was hurting Caleb.

Portia produced a pan and the doctor flung sections of infected tissue and muscle into it as he cut them away from Caleb's calf. The sound of pieces of Caleb hitting the pan made Cat's stomach twist into knots, and she felt a wrenching pain in her back and sides. She felt as if she were soaked with sweat. She could even feel it as it trickled down her legs. *Please hurry; I don't know how much longer I can stand this. . . .* If only Caleb would pass out.

The doctor nodded to Portia and she handed him the saw. The men took a firmer hold as he lined it up on the bone that was protruding from Caleb's raw flesh. Cat was amazed at how white the bone was. She had never seen anything so purely white, as if it has just been cast down from heaven. The blade was placed against the bone and the doctor drew it back to begin his stroke.

Caleb's back arched against the table, raising his shoulders. Zeb pushed him back down and placed his weight across his chest.

"Keep that leg still!" the doctor barked.

Cat grabbed his face between her hands and looked down at him from the top of the table. "Caleb!"

The sound that came from between his tightly pressed lips nearly tore her heart out.

"Caleb. Look at me."

He couldn't. His eyes were tightly shut and tears slid from beneath the incredibly long, dark lashes.

"Caleb!" she called again.

Zeb blocked her view of the proceedings. Caleb's shoulders flexed and his head between her hands jerked. She could see his fists clench as he fought the pain and Zeb moved to cover more of his arm to keep him from moving. She held his head as tightly as she could without hurting him. She felt a tear slide down her nose and watched it as it slowly splashed onto Caleb's cheek, where it mingled with those sliding from beneath his dark lashes. "Oh, Caleb, I'm so sorry. I'm so sorry . . ." A cramp moved up her side. She needed to let go; she was holding him too tight. Her back protested as she leaned over the table, holding on to Caleb for all she was worth because she was so afraid of losing him. Afraid that if she let go, he would be lost, just as Ty was.

From the end of the table the doctor nodded.

"Praise be," Portia added. The men relaxed their hold.

"It's over, chile. You can let go of him now." Portia looked at her with wide, dark eyes full of sympathy. "He's gonna be all right."

Cat heard the words as if they were coming through a tunnel. The room swayed around her. Beneath her she could see Caleb's face as it relaxed, the dark eyes now open and blinking as relief flooded his body.

"Cat?" She saw his mouth move but the sound was lost as she heard the blood rushing through her body, roaring into her ears. She felt as if she were being sucked backward into a tunnel, hurling toward darkness. She looked for the light but it grew small until it was nothing but a pinprick that was miles away from her. She wanted to reach for it but she couldn't move. Cat fell to the floor in a faint, landing in a puddle of blood.

Chapter Twenty-three

Two weeks was long enough for anyone to lie abed but for some reason she couldn't get up. Cat pulled a pillow up to her stomach and curled around it, hoping that it would help to fill the hollowness she felt inside. The baby was gone. Ty was gone. Why should she get up? What purpose was there in her getting out of bed and going through the motions of living?

She knew Caleb was recovering in his own room down the hall. She knew Zeb slept on a cot in Caleb's room to help him when he needed it. She had heard the sounds in the hall of Caleb learning how to walk with the aid of crutches as the strength of his body was slowly restored.

She knew that others on the plantation were going about their business as they always had. She heard Parker go down in the mornings and come up in the evenings. She heard Lucy Ann on the stairs and knew that she paused outside of Caleb's room on several occasions. Cat knew Zeb was inside and bound to be a temptation to Lucy Ann but surely she wouldn't do anything while he was in the house. Surely she had more sense than that. And even if her sister-in-law did attempt something, Cat knew that she didn't have the strength to prevent it. She simply didn't care what anyone else did, as long as she was left to her bed in peace.

Portia came to her room twice a day, bringing food on a tray that Cat simply rearranged to make it look as if she were eating. She would take a bite or two but there was no taste to it. It was just something that kept her alive, just as breathing kept her alive. She wasn't even sure if she wanted to be alive. Portia made her sit in a chair or walk around the room that had been Ty's and she complied because it was easier to do what the woman said than to put up a fight. There was no reason to do anything else, and she didn't have the energy to think about it.

A gentle knock on the door sent her head under the covers in the hope that whoever it was would just go away and leave her alone. She knew better though when she heard the slow opening of the portal.

"Miz Catherine?" It was Silas. "I has a letter for you."

"Leave it on the table." Her words were muffled in the pillow and she hoped that he understood them.

"I think it's from Mister Ty."

Cat jerked the blankets down. Her hair was filthy and hung limply in her face. She pushed the tattered curls back out of the way as she sat up. "What did you say?"

Silas nervously shuffled the envelope before he handed to her. "It looks like Mister Ty's hand."

Cat's green-gold eyes widened in disbelief as she examined the envelope. It couldn't be from Ty. It had only been three weeks since he had been captured. She recognized the fine neat slant of his hand, however, and tore the letter open with trembling hands.

Dearest Cat,

I hope you are home and I hope both of you are safe. I am so sorry for allowing this to happen and for putting you through this. How typical of him to take the blame when it was all her fault. If she hadn't foolishly chased after him, he wouldn't have been distracted and surely would have avoided the ambush. *Please tell Caleb how sorry I am and that I hope he has recovered from his wound.* Oh Ty, you don't need to take on another burden; you need to take care of yourself. *As you may have guessed, I was captured that day along with a few of my surviving men. Jake and Willie, I'm sorry to say, were not among them.* How his heart must ache for Jake, who had been by his side for so long. And Willie, too. Cat knew the boy had wormed his way into all their hearts and they had looked after him as if he had been of their own blood. The sight of the gaping wound that had once been his face still haunted her and she prayed that Ty had been spared that ghastly sight. *I have been told that I will be sent to Governor's Island in New York to sit out the remainder of the war. We do not know how much longer this conflict will last, so I want you to go home to Wyoming. I want our baby to be born there surrounded by family who will love our child.* He didn't know. How could he know that the baby they had long planned for was gone, another victim of her foolishness? *The colonel who captured me has graciously allowed me this opportunity to write you and tell you that I am without injury and will be kept safe on Governor's Island until this war is over. I believe you know him. Remember Captain Myers from the Christmas dance?* Cat's mouth dropped open as she realized whom he was talking about. Ty's captor was the same man who had fought him several years ago when she was trying desperately to make him jealous. Apparently it had been a stroke of luck for both of them since the man had allowed Ty to write to her and had obviously mailed the letter. *I will find you and our child safe in Wyoming when this is over. Until then, be careful and remember that I love you. I will always love you . . . Ty.*

Governor's Island in New York. She knew the place. It was located in the mouth of the harbor. She had sailed by it many times on social outings during her numerous trips to visit her aunt there. She knew where Ty was. She was going to New York, but first she was going home. She had to take care of Caleb and she needed help to get Ty off of Governor's Island. Her father would know what to do and Chase would help her. After all, he owed Ty his life. Her mind was made up. She was going home.

"Silas, tell Portia I need a bath." Cat kicked the covers off and her feet hit the floor. "How's Caleb doing?"

"He's fine, Miz Catherine, and he'll be tickled to see you up and about." Silas grinned from ear to ear as he shut the door behind him.

Cat looked around the room as if to get her bearings. She felt as if she had just awakened from a deep sleep and needed a moment to regain a sense of normalcy. She caught her reflection in the mirror and moved closer to get a better look.

Her hair hung dark and limp around her face and shoulders. Her face was pale and thin. She had lost the usual healthy glow of her skin that frequenting the outdoors had given her. She needed a good long soak in the tub; she'd had only sponge baths since she had lost the baby. Her scalp itched; a thorough washing would restore its natural bounce and shine. She suddenly felt incredibly hungry and realized that her stomach was absolutely hollow.

Her hand lingered over her stomach and she wondered if the hollow feeling was due to hunger or to the loss she had experienced. For a brief moment in time it had seemed as if she was close to having all her heart desired, but once again things that she had no control over had invaded her life and taken everything away. Ty was destined to sit out this never-ending war in a prison camp on a small island in the waters of New York City. The baby they had longed for was gone, a victim of her own foolish whims and recklessness. If she had stayed home where she belonged, the babe would still be safe inside her. But then again, if she had stayed home, what would have happened to Caleb? Was it because she had chased after Ty in her impulsive desire to tell him of their impending parenthood that they'd been ambushed, or had her being there helped to save Caleb's life? Once again her mind chased in endless circles, worrying about circumstances over which she had no control.

She found herself too exhausted to deal with it.

The bath refreshed her but also brought back memories of Ty as her mind saw him soaking in the tub as he had on each visit home. How would he deal with the indignities of being a prisoner? With quiet resolve, she had no doubt, but he would still suffer. He was a man who was used to being in control of his life. Turning that control over to someone else would chafe his spirit.

Was he being fed? Was he sheltered from the elements? What would happen to him when the weather turned cold as it surely would eventually? His heavy coat had been tied to the back of his saddle during the high heat of summer days.

Cat sank beneath the water to rinse her hair and a slight smile lifted the corners of her mouth when she remembered that Ty had been wearing his blue muffler when he had been taken. She had seen no sign of it in the trampled grass of his last battle so she felt sure that he was still wearing it. Somehow it comforted her to know that he still had it. It felt as if a part of her was with him.

She closed her eyes and remembered him as she had last seen him before their world had been blown apart. She pictured him as he had been in the meadow with the mules jumping in protest and the swarm of butterflies taking flight at their invasion. He had been smiling, his eyes crinkling with delight as Scarlet shied and danced into his gelding. She recalled the intense blue of his eyes in his tanned face and the way the blue of the wool muffler had made their color seem even brighter. She saw again the flash of white teeth between his sensuous lips as he grinned broadly at the nonsense of it all, just enjoying the day, even in the middle of war. That was how she would think of him until he was free again. She didn't want to remember the pain that had filled his eyes when Jake had died and he had seen the gravity of Caleb's wound. She knew he felt responsible for all of it.

The water was cooling around her. Her stomach growled at the neglect of the past few weeks. Caleb was down the hall in his room and she needed to talk to him and tell him of her plans. No doubt he would call her foolish for wanting to free Ty from his prison, but he would agree that it was time to go home. "We're going home." She rose from the tub and reached for her towel. Enough time had been wasted crying over things that could not be helped. It was time to go home.

The smile on Caleb's face when she knocked and entered his room was brighter than the afternoon sun that streamed through his window.

"Wait right there," he said from the chair by his bed. He tossed his book on the mattress and stood with the aid of a pair of crutches. Five swinging steps had him in front of her. His hair had been neatly trimmed, his beard was gone and his color was good, although he had lost his usual sun-bronze hue. "I've been waiting to show you how well I can get around now. I still haven't figured out how to go down the stairs, but Zeb and I have been working on it." His deep brown eyes glowed with pride over his accomplishment.

"Oh, Caleb, I'm so proud of you." Cat impulsively leaned forward and planted a kiss on his cheek. He grabbed her arm to steady himself as the crutches slid a bit. He regained his balance and moved his hand down to take hers into his own.

"I'm so sorry about the baby. I know how badly you and Ty wanted it."

"It's not your fault, Caleb, and I don't want you thinking it is."

"You saved my life, Cat, and I will never forget it." His dark eyes sought hers. "I'm just afraid the price you paid was too high."

"Caleb, we could all spend the rest of our lives torturing ourselves over things that we've done wrong. If I had stayed put, I might not have lost the baby."

"But then again, if you hadn't have been there, Ty and I both probably would have died fighting."

"See, that's why we can't dwell on it. We all make our choices and we have to live with the results. Would I have traded this baby's life for yours and Ty's? That's a choice that was in God's hands. It's up to us how we choose to live with it."

"At least you know that you and Ty will have a chance to have more children."

"And I plan on working on that as soon as possible."

Caleb laughed. "There's no doubt in my mind that as soon as this war is over you will."

"I don't plan on waiting that long." Cat pulled Ty's letter from the pocket of her dress. "I know where he is, Caleb. He's on Governor's Island in the harbor of

New York City. And I'm going to get him out."

Caleb looked at her skeptically as he read the letter she handed him. "Dang, the captain from the dance. What are the chances of that happening?"

"I know. It's a small world, isn't it?"

Caleb folded the letter and returned it to her. "So what are we going to do now?"

"Go home."

"Home." Caleb turned and made his halting way over to the window that looked over the front of the house. "It sounds good, Cat. But I don't know what I'll do when I get there."

Cat followed him to the window. "Caleb, you'll do just what you used to do."

"I won't be able to work like I did before."

"You'll still be able to ride and once we get you fitted with a new leg, people won't even notice what happened to you."

"Your father has been good to me, Cat, but I've always been able to earn my keep. I don't want to take advantage of his goodwill."

"Caleb Conners!" Cat's eyes threw sparks as she stamped her foot. "Don't even think that way. You are a part of our family, just like everyone else back home. We are not going to throw you out just because you are missing part of your leg. You will simply have to figure out what you can and cannot do, and we'll take it from there." She turned away from him and stomped across the floor. "If my father was here, he would probably have you horsewhipped for talking such nonsense." Cat picked up his book and snapped it shut. She then began straightening his bed coverings with short, jerky motions, all the while muttering under her breath about the stupidity of men in general.

Caleb grinned at her tirade and then swung around the bed with his peculiar gait. Cat stopped her rant and watched him with hands on hips. "What?" she asked as he grinned down at her.

"Just wanted to know when we're leaving, ma'am."

"As soon as you feel you're ready."

"The only thing that's holding me up is those stairs."

"Well then, let's go work on that."

Chapter Twenty-four

Cat had fallen into bed exhausted after spending the rest of the afternoon helping Caleb learn how to navigate the many steps of the curving staircase. Zeb had been there to help in case Caleb started to fall, but after a few scary moments he soon had it figured out.

Cat still wanted to take the big man with her back to Wyoming. He would definitely be needed to help Caleb on the train and then the stage. She also knew Parker wouldn't like it. She decided to talk to him about her plan first thing in the morning and then she would approach Zeb.

She had eagerly sought her bed after eating dinner with Parker, Lucy Ann and Caleb in the formal dining room. Lucy Ann had talked incessantly the entire time and seemed to be excited about something. Cat wondered briefly if it was due to the fact that Zeb had moved back into his sleeping quarters in the barn after Caleb assured him that he was able to get along by himself. It would have been impossible for Lucy Ann to go after him when he was sleeping on a cot in

Caleb's room with the door safely locked.

It was a good kind of tired that enfolded her as she slipped under the covers. She knew she was weak from lying around for so long but felt pleased that she had accomplished something today. She mentally made a list of things to do the next day. She would talk to Parker about Zeb, she would talk to Zeb, and she would look into travel arrangements. She had to arrange for her trunks to be shipped home. The small trunk with the false bottom would travel with her. Cat fell asleep with her head full of little chores that needed to be taken care of before they began their long trek to Wyoming.

The pounding on her door penetrated the dream that had captured her. Her mind couldn't make sense of the sound or put it in its proper place. It wasn't until Caleb laid a hand on her arm that she awoke fully.

"Caleb, what's wrong?" He stood over her, wearing nothing but his pants.

"Something awful is happening, Cat." Caleb made his way to the window and pulled back the curtain. "I heard Thompson in the house and Portia started crying. Everyone's out back now."

Cat pulled on her robe and joined Caleb at the window. In the yard beside the barn, torches were flickering and they could see the slaves gathered there. Suddenly Zeb stumbled out of the barn, with Thompson pushing him along. Behind them was Lucy Ann, who seemed distraught as she clung to Parker's side.

"That conniving bitch!"

"What's going on?" Caleb asked as Cat went to her wardrobe.

"Zeb's in trouble and we've got to stop it." Cat jerked on her pants. Caleb blushed and turned back to the window when she lifted the gown over her head. "Lucy Ann has been after him for years."

"What do you mean after him?" Caleb asked the window.

"After him, you know . . ." Satin slippers and fine leather dress shoes hit the floor as Cat dug into the back of her wardrobe, looking for her boots.

"You mean, she's been . . ." Caleb searched for words that wouldn't sound offensive.

"Yes, she has, she forces him. I saw it."

"How could she, why . . . Oh, my God." Caleb turned back, hoping that Cat was safely covered. "What are we going to do?"

"We're going to stop this. Now." Cat tossed her curls back over her shoulder. "Where's your gun?"

"My revolver is in my room. Ty's is in the office downstairs. Parker had them all cleaned."

"Get yours. I'm going out there." Cat stopped to look at Caleb, who still seemed to be in shock. "Can you make it?"

"Go on, I'm right behind you."

Cat clattered down the stairs and rushed into Parker's office. She took a rifle from the gun rack and quickly loaded it. She stuck Ty's revolver in her pants after checking to make sure it was loaded also. On her way out of the room, she noticed Ty's sword lying on the mantel and she picked it up also. She heard the sounds of Caleb beginning his descent but she didn't have time to wait. She hurried down the hall and out the back, with a sword in one hand and a rifle in the other.

She heard the sound of the lash as it whistled through the air and landed on flesh. Zeb's flesh. It should be Lucy Ann. Cat flew into the circle of light. Zeb was stretched between two posts, his toes barely touching the ground, his arms tied above his head. The muscles in his back were taut and he dripped with sweat and blood from the slice that the lash had made in his back. Portia had dropped to her knees and was sobbing while Silas and Ruth, who was holding her newborn baby in her arms, tried to comfort her. The rest of the adult slaves stood in stony silence with resentful faces as they tried to shelter the children's eyes from the torture they were witnessing. Cat dropped the sword and leveled the rifle at Thompson in one smooth motion.

"*Stop*. Now." She cocked the rifle, and the sound of the shell entering the chamber echoed in the silence that filled the yard. Thompson gave her a fleeting glance as he pulled the lash back for the next stroke. In the next instant he danced away as a bullet bit the dirt before his feet.

"Cat, put the gun down." Parker said. "You don't know what's going on here."

"Yes, I do." Cat cocked the rifle again. "Now cut him down."

"Cat, you need to leave this to us," Parker said as if he was talking to a child. "It's none of your concern."

"As long as I'm Ty's wife, this is my concern. Do

you think he would stand by and let Zeb be beaten like this?"

"You don't understand." Parker was quickly losing his patience. "Zeb stole some of Lucy Ann's jewelry while he was staying in the house. We found it in his room under his mattress. We think he was planning on escaping and using the jewelry to pay his way."

"Oh, is that right?" Cat looked at Lucy Ann in contempt. "Figured all that out did you, Lucy Ann?"

"Yes, I did." Lucy Ann's eyes glittered in the light from the torches. "Not only that, but he struck me when he saw that I had found the jewelry in his room." There was a collective gasp from the circle of slaves. "Everyone knows what happens to a slave when he lays a hand on a white woman." Her voice rose so everyone could hear.

Caleb breathlessly made his way into the circle with a crutch under one arm and his revolver in his other hand. Cat felt her courage go up a notch as he stood beside her. "So you went to Zeb's room by yourself, in the middle of the night?"

"Please don't, Miz Catherine," Zeb groaned from the posts.

"What are you saying?" Lucy Ann raised her chin and looked down her nose at Cat.

"You know what I'm saying. Do I need to say it out loud for everyone here?"

"Miz Catherine, please . . ."

"Caleb, can you cut Zeb down?" Cat kept her gun leveled on Thompson, who looked as if he were about to explode.

"I'd be glad to." Caleb stuck his gun in his belt and picked up Ty's sword.

"What are you talking about, Cat?" Parker's face was pale in the flickering firelight.

"Look in her pocket and see if she has a knife," Cat said to Parker. Lucy Ann sidled away but Parker grabbed her arm and patted the side of her dress. He stuck his hand in one of her pockets and pulled out a long knife.

"You don't think I would go into a darkie's room without a weapon, do you?" Lucy Ann jerked her arm away from Parker's grasp.

"Why did you go into his room at all, Lucy Ann? Why didn't you tell Parker your suspicions and let him handle it?"

Parker looked between his wife and his sister-in-law.

"Cat?" Parker's face had turned white as a sheet. "You need to leave this be."

"Caleb? How's Zeb?"

"He's free."

"Zeb, go hitch up the wagon. Portia, you and Silas run upstairs and go pack some of my things into that small trunk I have up there. Get Caleb's things, too."

"What are you doing, Cat?" Parker took a step toward her and Thompson eagerly followed.

"Caleb and I are leaving and we're taking Zeb with us." Cat brought the rifle up and aimed it straight at them.

"You can't do that."

"If she takes Zeb out of here, we won't be able to get no work out of any of them," Thompson said into

Parker's ear. "There will be an open rebellion."

"I don't want to hurt you, Parker, but it wouldn't bother me a bit to put a bullet through Thompson's skull."

"Cat, put the gun down and we'll go inside and talk," Parker urged.

"And what will Thompson be doing while we're talking?" Thompson swung away and pounded his hand with his fist.

"Parker, you can't let her get away with this." Lucy Ann's voice was brittle. "That darkie needs to be punished or they'll all be swarming through the house taking whatever they want."

"The way you've been taking whatever you wanted all these years, Lucy Ann?"

"I'm afraid I don't know what you're talking about, Cat." Lucy Ann sniffed.

"Tell me, Parker, is this the first time this has happened?"

"First time what has happened?"

"Is this the first time one of your slaves has been caught with a piece of Lucy Ann's jewelry?"

Realization swept over Parker's face like a cold bucket of water. His head flew up and his eyes narrowed. "Thompson, get these people out of here."

"What?"

"You heard me." Parker looked at the gathered slaves in the dim light from the torches. "All of you go on back to your cabins. Nothing else is going to happen tonight. Go on."

"Parker, what are you doing?"

Parker grabbed his wife's arm and squeezed it. She

tried to jerk away, but instead was jerked forward and she stumbled into Parker. "You need to go to your room and wait for me." Parker shoved her away. "*Now!*" He roared the word and Lucy Ann looked at him in shock.

She turned to Cat. "*You*—this is all your fault." She lunged toward Cat with her perfectly manicured fingers curled into claws. Cat stepped out of the way as she flew by. Lucy Ann pulled up and turned with a snarl.

"Hold this." Cat handed the rifle to Caleb. Lucy Ann lunged again and Cat met her with a firm right to her porcelain-skinned jaw. Lucy Ann sank into the dirt, landing in a puddle of her own skirts and petticoats.

"The wagon's ready, Miz Catherine." Zeb's face was stern but his eyes danced as he stood in the doorway of the barn.

Cat shook her fist and rubbed it with her hand. Caleb rolled his eyes and sucked on the inside of his cheeks to keep from bursting into laughter. "Help Mr. Caleb onto the seat, Zeb, then move the wagon around front so we can get our things."

"Where we going, Miz Catherine?"

"We're going to Wyoming, Zeb. We're going home."

Chapter Twenty-five

There were worse places he could be, Ty thought as he watched the water lap against the western shore of Nutten Island. Nutten was what the locals called it due to the large grove of nut trees that grew on the island. At least he got to walk around at times and enjoy the fact that he was outside, even though he was a prisoner. The guards mounted on the walls of the star-shaped fort made sure that he wouldn't forget it. The enlisted men were not so lucky. They were locked inside the fort called Castle William on the southern end of the island. Stuck inside the cheese box, as it was referred to. Ty had never been close enough to see what it looked like. It didn't really make much difference. No matter what it looked like, it was still a prison.

His hands tugged on both ends of his blue muffler as he dragged his foot over the tips of the long grass that had blown flat from the stiff breeze coming in off the water. Ty didn't see the grass beneath his feet, however; his mind was on rolling pastures that were guarded by majestic mountains whose tips disappeared into the clouds. Instead of smelling salty breezes that did little to disguise the stench of the nearby city, he imagined the clean smells of fresh wind and soft grass, intermingled with the faint smell of cow. Back home they'd be getting ready to drive the herd to market. He hoped that Cat and Caleb were there by now. He prayed that Caleb was well enough to help. He knew he was hoping for a lot, but that was all he had to do, so he might as well make the best of it.

Ty looked over the collection of men who were either standing by themselves or gathered in small groups. Each one had his own story; each one had been fighting for his own reasons. And there they all were, destined to sit out the remaining days of the war together.

Bishop. Why had he been sent there? He should have been hanged as a traitor, but which side had he betrayed? The man always made sure he kept a safe distance between himself and Ty. He knew Ty blamed him for Jake's death, along with the others in his troop. Only Bishop and Ty had come to New York; the other surviving men had been sent west to Elmira. Ty didn't know if that camp was better or worse than Castle William, which was full of disease according to the young doctor who visited the officers from time to time. It was no wonder the men were sick. Their conditions were no doubt worse than the ones the officers were enduring. And the officers barely got enough rations to survive. The sanitation was horrible, with nearly a thousand men crammed into quarters that should hold only half that number. But at least they could enjoy the fresh air.

Bishop. Just the sight of him made Ty's hand curl with the urge to choke the very life out of him. The man had started working the guards the day he arrived, and he was already benefiting from having some items smuggled in. How was he paying them? Who was helping him? Ty knew he had ties to the North because the man had obviously been spying for the union, but he also had ties to the South. Ty knew he had made several trips in and out of New Orleans, which had been occupied since the early years of the war. Was that how Bishop had gotten in and out so easily? The Northern blockades must have let him pass in order to receive information that only a true Southerner could have access to.

Jake had died because of Bishop's treachery. Jake had never trusted the man. And Ty had received him into his home. He had invited the traitor to eat with him at his mother's table. His frustration threatened to boil out of him, but there was no place for it to go. He locked it up in a corner of his mind. He had learned quickly in this place that acting rashly only got you into serious trouble. He might as well beat his hands against the stone walls surrounding the lonely cell that now housed him and several other officers of the Confederate States of America's army. Ty turned away from the prison and the men gathered on the shores of the island and looked out over the water, past the city stretched out along the distant shore. He didn't see any of it. His blue eyes were looking inside at the memories that filled his mind. Home. Wyoming. Cat . . .

Caleb kept his eyes down as he fidgeted with the lone crutch that was his constant companion. He was able to function on his own performing most tasks, and Zeb made sure he stayed close to help with the others. Caleb's main problems had been navigating the high steps of the stage they had ridden across the plains.

Cat watched as he placed the crutch up against the side of the coach again after a particularly nasty bump had dislodged it. She knew he hated it, that it was a nuisance for him, but she was also proud at how much he had accomplished in the few short weeks since he had lost his leg. If only he would return to his drawing. She had tried to encourage him many times to take up the sketchbook she had purchased for him in St. Louis, but he had declined, even going so far as to pack it into the valise that carried his change of clothes. The talented hand fingered the collar of his shirt while the other flew out to catch the crutch that had once again gone sailing across the coach.

Zeb hung out the window, soaking up the wide plains that stretched behind them. Since it was only the three of them traveling, he was allowed to ride inside with them. Before he had been forced to ride on top so as not to offend the delicate nature of the other passengers. Zeb had not minded a bit except for the fact that his new clothes got dusty during the ride. It gave him the opportunity to see country that he had never thought to set eyes on. He had relaxed after they crossed the Mississippi. During the first part of their trip Cat had to assure him many times that the slave catchers were not coming after him. She knew he wouldn't believe he was free until he heard it from Ty's own lips. She hoped he would have that taken care of before Christmas.

"I see a town." Zeb was watching the trail before them. Cat joined him at the window.

"That's Laramie," she informed him. Cat slipped back into her seat. Caleb, sitting across from her, had turned pale against the dark fabric that covered the bench behind him. "We're almost home, Caleb."

He nodded and swallowed the huge lump that had gathered in his throat since they had begun the last leg of their journey.

Cat laid a gloved hand on his arm. "It will be all right, I promise you."

"How will we get to the ranch?"

"I'll hire a wagon."

"This town is big, Miz Catherine." Zeb settled back into his seat only to be replaced at the window by Cat.

"Caleb, just look at how much it's grown since we've been gone." Cat turned and smiled when she saw Caleb show some interest in the new buildings that had sprung up on the outskirts of town. "Oh, my gosh. It's Zane!" Cat leaned farther out the window, slapping a hand on top of her head to keep her hat from flying off. *"Zane!"*

The cowboy looked up from the wagon he was loading and his hazel eyes widened as he recognized the trim young woman hanging from the window of the coach. He dropped the sack of flour he was holding into the wagon bed and ran after the coach. Cat jumped from the stage before the attendant had a chance to set up the small set of stairs outside the door and went flying up the street toward the cowboy who was rushing her way.

"Oh, Zane, you don't know how much we missed you," she cried as she flung herself into his arms.

"Dang, Cat, why didn't you let us know you were coming home? I know your daddy would have killed the fatted calf and had us a big party."

"I didn't have time to write and when I tried to telegraph, they said the lines were down."

"Where's the rest of you?" Zane dropped an arm around Cat's shoulders as they made their way back to the stage. Zeb was standing outside the door, waiting to give Caleb a hand. "Dang, Caleb." Zane looked at his friend with sympathy when he saw the extent of his wound, then crossed the few steps that remained between them. "Glad to see you're home safe and sound, well . . . almost sound. Dang." He threw his arms around Caleb and hugged him, then quickly adjusted the hat on his head. Caleb teetered for a moment, then found his footing.

Zane looked expectantly into the coach and then turned to Cat and Caleb. "Where's Ty and Jake?"

"Ty was captured in the same battle that Caleb lost his leg." Zane's mouth dropped open at the news. "Jake didn't make it." Cat hated to tell him about his friend in the middle of the street.

"Dang." Zane looked at the two of them, hoping they were playing a joke on him, but the set of their faces quickly told him the truth of it. "Jake . . ." He dashed at the moisture that had gathered unbidden at the corners of his eyes.

"Zane, will you take us home?" Cat took his arm. "I want to go home."

"Soon as I get those supplies in the wagon. Dang, everyone is going to be beside themselves when I show up with you two in the wagon. Who is this?" Zeb stood towering beside him with Cat's small trunk casually tucked under his arm.

"This is Zeb. He grew up with Ty. I brought him home to help with the horses."

"You mean he's a slave?"

"I ain't no slave no more. Miz Catherine says I'm a free man." Zeb stood proudly before them.

"Well, dang it, you *are* free." Zane grinned and held out a hand toward Zeb. "Pleased to meet you, Zeb." Zeb looked at Cat for approval and then timidly took Zane's proffered hand. Zane quickly pumped it up and down as if he were priming for water. "I'm sure you'll be a big help. Dang, he's bigger than Jamie," he said to Cat and Caleb.

Their few remaining bags landed in the dirt beside them and Zane and Zeb carried them to the wagon. "Just wait until you see the new girls at Maybelle's," Zane said to Caleb. "She's got a little China girl now that is . . ."

"Zane!"

"Oops. Sorry, Cat, just trying to get Caleb caught up on things."

"Don't worry about it, Zane. I don't think I'll be visiting Maybelle's anymore."

"Why? You didn't lose anything else while you were off fighting in the war, did you?"

Zane cast a suspicious eye over the front of Caleb's pants.

"No. I can assure you that everything else is still attached." Caleb braced himself against the back of the wagon.

"Then what's the problem? Maybelle would love to give you a big homecoming party. Those whores up there will be waiting on you hand and foot, er . . . sorry."

"Zane, can we go home now?" Zeb handed Cat up onto the wagon bench and she turned to give him an exasperated look.

Zane laughed and with the help of Zeb soon had the supplies loaded. He chattered the entire way home about recent doings and newcomers to the area. When they reached the crossroads that was a halfway point between town and the ranch, he pointed out an area that had been put aside to build a school for the children who lived in the surrounding area. Jason and a few of the other ranchers had taken on the project since there seemed to be a growing need for a schoolhouse in their outlying community.

"So a lot of new people are settling around here?" Cat asked as Zane talked of the school project.

"Yep, and it might get to be a problem."

"Why is that?" Cat held on to the bench as the front right wheel dipped into a rut left from a recent thunderstorm.

"Some of them are settling on the range and putting up fences to keep the cattle away from their crops."

"It's free range. How can they fence it?" Caleb asked from his seat in the wagon bed.

"Don't know. Jason owns most of his range, but some of the other ranchers just let their cattle graze on government land. Then some farmer comes in and plows a garden and fences off a waterhole and it causes all kinds of problems. Jason is hoping that building this school will bring the community together and solve some of these problems before somebody does something drastic."

"Like shooting cattle or cutting fence?" Cat could see the issues from both sides and wondered at the problems that could arise from the situation.

"Oh, that's already happened." Zane urged the team up a small rise. "Things could start getting interesting around here, that's for sure."

Cat pondered what Zane had told them as they continued on their way toward home. So much had happened in the three years since they had been gone. Two precious lives had come to them with the births of Chance and Fox. Two precious lives had been lost with the death of Jake and her miscarriage. She refused to even think of the possibility of Ty not surviving the war. Soon he would be making this trip with her. She vowed once again to have him home by Christmas. Surely the others would help her. If not, then she would just have to find a way to do it herself. The road, once again so familiar, faded from her sight as her mind wandered to the east and to an island off the tip of Manhattan. *Is he safe?*

Chapter Twenty-six

Jenny wondered briefly who was riding in the wagon with Zane as she put Storm Cloud through his paces in the corral off the new barn that now was home to Storm and his harem of mares. The colt had just recently become used to the weight of her on his back but still wasn't sure if he liked it. He trusted her completely, however, since she had handled him every day since his birth. It was just a strange feeling to have her sitting astride instead of being at his side. The blackened tips of his ears swiveled as they passed the barrel outside the corral where Chance and Fox sat watching his movements, adding some applause with pudgy hands as he pranced about the ring. From an adjoining corral his sire, Storm, watched with cloudy eyes as the colt's black tail flew out behind him like a banner. The older horse returned to his bucket of mashed oats, slowly chewing with teeth that were worn with age.

"Momma, Zane's here."

"Yes, Chance, I know." Storm Cloud whirled in the

opposite direction with the gentle direction of Jenny's knee pressed into his side.

"Can we go see if he brought us something from town?"

The colt became confused and tossed his head, now not sure of what his mistress required of him. Jenny pulled him to a stop and rubbed the finely arched neck while gently voicing her approval of the progress he had made so far.

"Momma?" Fox stood on the barrel and with a small hand shading his eyes looked toward the yard in front of Grace's cabin. "Who are those people with Zane?"

Jenny urged Storm Cloud nearer to the rail and looked over toward Grace's cabin, where the wagon had stopped. Her forehead puckered as she considered the huge dark man who was helping a petite woman from the wagon. The pert angle of a stylish hat instantly registered in her mind and she was off the colt in a flash and climbing through the fence.

"Who is it, Momma?" Jenny swung the boys down from their perch.

"It's your aunt Cat." The boys took off running on little legs and then suddenly became shy as they got closer. Jenny flew past them and arrived by the wagon just as Cat stepped onto the porch of Grace's cabin. She came face-to-face with Caleb, who had just slid from the wagon bed and propped his crutch under his arm.

"Look at what I found," Zane announced as Jenny flung her arms around Caleb's neck and began to cry. The boys were curious but shy and wrapped themselves around Zane's legs as they considered the new people who had come into their world. Zane promptly lifted them onto the wagon bench, where they could watch the proceedings. They both looked in awe at Zeb, who shyly smiled at them from the side of the wagon.

Cat waited until Jenny released Caleb and then took her turn. The two women both started talking at once.

"Why don't you wait until everyone is here so you don't have to tell it a hundred times?" Zane suggested.

"Just tell me where Ty and Jake are." Jenny wiped her nose with her sleeve while the boys watched the reunion with wide blue eyes.

"Jake didn't make it," Caleb volunteered. "Ty's been captured."

"Jake is gone?" Jenny asked as the words sank in. "He's dead?"

Cat and Caleb both nodded as the horror of that day threatened to overcome them again.

"And Ty?"

"Zane's right. We'll tell you about it when everyone is here." It was still too fresh in their minds to have to talk about it more than once. At least Caleb knew it was for him. "Speaking of that, where is everyone?"

"Grace is up at the main house with Jason. Chase and Cole are out looking for whoever shot one of the cattle last night."

"I told them about some of the stuff that's been going on," Zane put in.

"It's nothing compared to what they've been

through." Jenny looked down at Caleb's leg. "I'm so sorry, Caleb."

"Don't worry about it, Jenny. I'm lucky to be alive, thanks to Cat." Jenny looked between the two of them and wondered what had happened. She would hear the story soon enough. Cat was smiling wistfully at the boys, who seemed to be fascinated with the huge colored man who stood patiently waiting at the side of the wagon.

"Should I start the introductions?" Jenny asked.

"I think I've got them figured out." Cat moved around to the wagon seat. "You must be Chance." The dark-headed child with the startling blue eyes nodded and then looked toward his mother. "And you're Fox. You are the image of your father."

Fox looked at Jenny in confusion.

"Your father that's in heaven," Jenny explained to the boy.

"My Jamie father?" Fox pointed to the grave on the ridge.

"Yes, your Jamie father." Jenny came around next to Cat and held out her arms for Fox. "This is your aunt Cat. Her father is your grandfather Jason." She lowered Fox to the ground and took Chance into her arms. "And this is Caleb. He's your friend just like Zane is." Caleb swung around the back of the wagon.

"What happened to his leg?" Chance asked. Fox walked up and squatted before Caleb. He waved his hand below the pinned-up leg of his pants.

"It's gone," Fox announced in awe. "Where is it?" He looked up at Caleb with wide blue eyes.

"Aunt Cat buried it in a hole." Caleb grinned at

Cat, who promptly rolled her eyes. "But first she whacked it off with that sword that's lying in the back of the wagon."

The boys looked up at Cat with trepidation and then toward the evil sword that had done the whacking. Chance slid behind his mother's leg.

"Caleb, don't tell them stuff like that. Now they're scared of me."

Caleb laughed and made his way toward the porch. Fox was on his heels, watching Caleb's use of the crutch with fascination written on his sweet face. "Aunt Cat did a good thing. She saved my life. Come sit with me on the swing and I'll tell you about it." Chance started to follow and then turned and pointed to Zeb.

"Who is that?"

"Oh my goodness. I'm sorry." Cat held out her hand to the huge man who was still waiting patiently on the other side of the wagon. "This is Zeb."

Zeb walked around and ducked his head at Jenny. "Miz Catherine says you have some fine horses here, ma'am." He kept his head bowed as was his habit and looked at the ground as he talked to her.

"Yes I do, Zeb. The best you're ever going to see." Jenny held out her hand to him, noting the way he once again looked to Cat for permission. "I have a feeling that you're a fair hand with horses yourself."

"Yes, ma'am, I took care of all Mister Ty's and Mister Parker's horses."

"Then I'm sure we can use someone like you."

The dark head flew up and a wide smile covered his face. "Yes, ma'am, I can help. Yes, I can."

"Zane, why don't you show Zeb the bunkhouse and then he can go look at the barn." Jenny smiled up at the dark face and for a fleeting moment thought of Jamie. They were of the same height, but Zeb was much broader.

"Momma?" Chance was standing with her pants leg grasped in his hand as he looked up at Zeb. "Does he need a bath?"

Jenny blushed as she heard Cat giggling behind her. Zane buried his face in the sack of potatoes that he had flung over his shoulder as he unloaded the wagon. Zeb threw back his head and laughed out loud and then lowered his great height down to squat in front of Chance, who was looking between the giant and his mother in confusion. Zeb held out his hand to Chance.

"Why don't you rub it and see." He smiled at Chance.

Chance timidly touched the back of the hand that was placed before him. He licked his finger and rubbed the skin. Zeb flipped his palm over to show him the pale coloring there. "Looks like it washed off this side." Fox jumped off the step and came over to see what was happening.

"Does it stay that way?" he asked.

"All the time," Zeb answered. Fox rubbed the dark skin and then tried the skin on the massive forearm as Jenny knelt beside them.

"It's just like you and Chance have different color skin," she pointed out as she stretched Chance's darker arm out next to Fox's pale one. "And see, mine is different from yours." She showed them her tanned arm and then took Zeb's hand into hers and pulled him closer. "There's lots of different colored people in the world. Some of them are white, some are red, and some are yellow, or brown, or even black like Zeb. None of that matters. It's what's inside of your skin that counts. What's important is whether you're a good person."

Two sets of wide blue eyes looked adoringly at the beautiful blond woman who knelt in the dust beside them. It seemed she had all the answers. "Do you understand?" she asked them.

"Yes . . ." two small voices replied.

"Now, go sit with Caleb and let him tell you what happened to his leg." They scampered to the porch. "And Caleb, make sure they don't have nightmares over it."

"Yes, ma'am." Caleb lifted the two boys into the swing on either side of him.

"And don't let them play with that sword either." Two tiny faces were mirrors of disappointment.

"Zeb, have you noticed that some people will go to any lengths to get out of work?" Zane grinned at Caleb as he passed him with a carton full of supplies for the kitchen.

"Yes, sir, I sure has, sir." Zeb smiled from ear to ear as he followed Zane into the cabin.

Jenny held out her hand to Cat, who was dabbing at tears that had formed at the corners of her up-tilted eyes. "I'm so glad you're home."

"Me, too." Cat looked at the two little boys who were listening with open-mouthed fascination to Caleb's tale of battle and bravery. "Jenny, they are so beautiful. I just can't get over how much Fox looks like Jamie."

"I know. Sometimes it breaks my heart because he reminds me so much of him, and yet he will never know how wonderful Jamie was. But I am so grateful to have him and know that Jamie will live through his son."

Cat placed a gloved hand over her now empty womb. "Life goes on," she murmured, more to herself than to Jenny.

"Cat, it will happen for you. You just have to give it time."

"It did, Jenny." Cat looked past the cluster of buildings toward the east. She wondered about Ty, what he was doing, what he was feeling, how he would react when he found out that she had lost their baby. "I lost it."

"I'm so sorry."

Cat held up her hand as if to ward off the flood of tears that would come unbidden with the smallest reminder. "I don't want to talk about it. It's over and there's no going back."

Jenny squeezed Cat's hand. "Let's go find your father."

Cat's gold-green eyes scanned the surrounding buildings, taking in the new barn and corral that had been added since she had last seen the place. "It's good to be home . . . finally."

Cat had finally broken down upon seeing her father. She fell into his arms as soon as she walked into his study, where he was talking with Grace, and cried until she could cry no more. Questions were asked and answers given as best as they could but once again, Cat delayed the complete telling until everyone was together. Jenny left her there and went back down to the barn to take care of Storm Cloud. She had left the colt saddled in the corral with the distraction of the homecoming.

Jenny found the three-year-old back in his stall enjoying a good rubdown under the large gentle hands of Zeb. "I see it didn't take you long to find your way around the stable," she commented as she stroked the dark forehead of the young stallion over the door of his stall.

"Yes, ma'am. I hopes you don't mind, ma'am, but this here colt was a bit unhappy all by his lonesome out there."

"That's fine with me, Zeb. I ran off and forgot all about him when I saw the three of you."

"His pappy was having a word with him about learnin' a bit of patience hisself."

Jenny looked over at Storm, who had come back into his box from his private entrance into his own corral. "He could teach him a lot about life, if Storm Cloud will just listen," she observed. She walked the few steps down to the elderly stallion's stall and gazed into his soft dark eyes.

"That's mostly how it is with children and their folks. The old folks learn the lessons; children don' listen and have to learn the same lessons again."

Jenny laughed. "You're absolutely right, Zeb. It's the same whether you're a horse or a human being."

"This ol' feller looks like he's got a lot to tell."

Zeb stopped his brushing and looked over the high wall between the stalls.

"He does. He's seen a lot in his lifetime." Jenny went into the stall and stroked the still-proud arch of Storm's neck. "He belonged to my father. . . ."

"He musta been a fine judge of horseflesh."

"Oh, he was. We raised the finest horses in Iowa Territory for a while, until he died. . . ." Jenny wrapped her arms around the stallion's neck and rested her cheek against his silky mane. "He's all I have left of my father." Jenny was surprised to find tears gathering in her eyes. "I have some of my mother's things," she went on hastily to combat the tide of emotion. "Her Bible, a beautiful carved box and a quilt, but Storm was my father's." The horse tossed his head as if in agreement. "They had a bond between them."

"It takes a special man to earn the respect of a horse like this," Zeb observed.

"Yes, it does." Jenny blinked back tears. "He was." She wiped her nose on her sleeve. "I'm sorry, Zeb; I didn't mean to get so emotional."

"Ain't nothin' wrong with showin' your love for someone."

"What about you? Did you leave anyone behind when you came here?"

"Jus' my momma. She's back on Mister Ty's plantation. Don't know my daddy."

"I'm sorry, Zeb. I should have known better. It must have been hell, living that kind of life."

"It weren't your fault, Miz Jenny. It's jus' the way

things be. Miz Catherine says I'm free now, so it don't matter no more anyhow."

"Yes, you are," Jenny said. "I hope you'll be happy here, Zeb."

"I got all I needs right here."

The group that was considered family, consisting of Jason, Cat, Grace, Cole, Jenny, Chase, Zane and Caleb gathered around Grace's table after the evening meal. The two little boys were asleep in Grace's bed with the door left slightly ajar so their parents could keep an eye on them. Zeb had shyly eaten at the end of the table and then gone back to the barn, already infatuated with the fine mares and the two breathtaking stallions that resided within. The other hands, Dan and Randy, had gone on to the bunkhouse, confident that they would hear the tale from Zane once the gathering was over.

Caleb filled them in on the part of the war that he had seen, while Cat offered the perspective of the landowner who had seen generations of hard work lost due to the blockades and the failure of Confederate funds. They had soon reached the day when their lives fell apart and suddenly Cat found it difficult to admit to her reasons for taking off after Ty. She exchanged a look with Caleb that left the others knowing that a lot had passed between them. Caleb placed a talented hand over her delicate fingers and gave her a reassuring squeeze.

"I was foolish to follow Ty. He had stopped by the plantation before they went up the mountain and I missed him because I was in town."

"And you all know how stubborn she is," Caleb added, which brought smiles from the group. "Cat was with us as we were coming back down the mountain. We had just crossed a meadow and had gone back into the deep woods. The mules were contrary and making quite a racket. It was early afternoon and we were all grateful to be back in the shade again. We hadn't gone too far when all hell broke loose. One minute I was riding along with Jake behind me, and Bishop in front of me, and the next . . ."

"Bishop? Bishop who?" Cole's hand hit the table with a thump.

Caleb's forehead wrinkled and his eyebrows came together as he looked at Cole. "Wade Bishop. He's the smuggler who was taking the powder through the blockade."

"Son of a . . ." Cole exclaimed.

"Surely it couldn't be." Grace turned very pale in the evening light.

Cole's chair hit the floor and he leaned across the table toward Caleb with both hands planted palm down on the worn wooden planks. "What happened to Bishop?"

Caleb and Cat exchanged glances, extremely confused by Cole's evident hatred of the smuggler.

"I don't know, I was knocked from my horse and landed in the brush. That's when I lost my foot."

Cat closed her eyes to summon back the memories of that horrendous day. She heard the explosion again, she watched in her mind as Ty turned and took inventory of his fallen men. She once again saw Jake and Willie charge the enemy and then the moment when they were blown to bits. She heard the screams of the horses and then saw the look on Ty's face when he realized that Jake was gone. "He ran."

"Ran?" Cole's face was livid.

"He was fighting to control his horse and I remember him saying something about fools or idiots and then he ran."

"What do you think the chances are that he was captured?"

Cat and Caleb exchanged glances again, too overwhelmed by Cole's anger to do anything but answer. Jenny, across the table, had turned white as a sheet and Chase's eyes had narrowed and darkened. Grace had a trembling hand held to her mouth as Cole's anger bubbled and simmered beneath his usual calm demeanor.

"It would have been protocol for the patrol to have someone stationed on either end of the trail to box us in," Caleb informed him as he looked with confusion at the faces of his friends.

"So he could have been captured with Ty?"

"We never saw him again. I haven't even given him a thought." Caleb looked at Cat, who seemed dumbfounded by the entire line of questioning. "Why?"

"Wade Bishop kidnapped my niece several years ago."

"He took me, too, after I escaped from the people who stole me from the mission," Jenny added in a quiet voice. "He wanted to make me into a whore."

"He's the one who scarred me." Grace wiped the tears that had gathered in the corners of her eyes. "I knew him when I was just a girl in New Orleans."

"I had dreams about him. Dreams about all of you, and he was in them." Jenny looked at Chase as he took her hand in his. "I dreamed that all of you died and it was because of him."

"Now it all makes sense." Chase looked at Jenny with eyes of flint. Bishop had threatened all of them. The man must die.

"We didn't know," Cat whispered in amazement. "We had dinner with him at Ty's home and we didn't know."

"You had no way of knowing, Cat," her father reassured her. "I didn't know until a few years ago when Cole got a letter from Amanda saying that she had been taken to New Orleans."

"I went there looking for her, but I was too late. The trail ended there and with the war and blockade going on, there was no way for me to look for her."

"Do you think he sold your niece into prostitution?" Caleb asked.

"There's only one way to find out." Cole's voice was grim. "Ask Wade Bishop."

"If he was captured, then I know where he is," Cat announced.

All eyes in the room focused on Cat as she took Ty's letter from her pocket. "Remember Captain Myers from the dance?"

"The one we got in a fight with along with those soldier boys?" Zane asked, eyes glowing at the memory.

"Yes," Cat continued. "He was in command of the troop that ambushed us on the trail. He remembered

Ty and he let him write a letter to tell me where he was going. He's on Governor's Island in the harbor in New York. And if Wade Bishop was captured, then that's where he'll be, too."

"But what if he was a spy for the North? Wouldn't they just let him go?" Zane asked.

"I bet he was working for both sides," Grace said quietly. "It would be just like him."

"Jake never did trust him; Ty didn't either, come to think of it. It was amazing how he managed to slip in and out of port so easily," Caleb said. "I'm betting he was using both sides."

"So what are the chances that he's in the prison camp with Ty?" Chase asked the group.

"He's either there or he's not," Cole announced grimly. "And there's only one way to find out."

"You aren't seriously considering walking into a Union prison camp to talk to Wade Bishop?" Jason asked.

"Oh, I plan on doing more than that."

"Good," Cat said. "You can help me bust Ty out while you're there."

"Catherine!" Jason exclaimed.

"We can't leave him there." Cat's eyes were bright with excitement as she considered the possibility of Cole's help. She walked around the table to stand next to the former Ranger. "We don't know how much longer this war is going to last. What if he's wounded or he gets sick?"

"He's a prisoner of war. They are obligated to take care of him." Jason was astounded that Cat would actually consider doing such a thing.

"I'm sorry, Jason, but Cat's right. The stories we've heard coming from the prison camps on both sides are horrendous." Caleb knew that if not for Ty's sacrifice, he would be in a prison camp or even worse, dead from his wound. "If there's a chance we can get him out, we've got to take it."

"Then I'm going, too," Chase said as he stood to join Cole and Cat. "If not for Ty, you would have found what was left of me out in the north pasture when the snow melted. I owe him my life." He looked at Jenny. "If Wade Bishop is there, we'll deal with him for what he did to Amanda and Grace. And for what he tried to do to Jenny."

"I'm going with you." Jenny went to Chase's side.

"Jenny," Chase said firmly. "You can't be serious."

"Yes, I am. I know what it's like to sit here for weeks on end and wonder and worry. I'm not sure if I can survive that again."

"You men think you have it so bad out fighting the battles," Cat added. "It's the not knowing that's the hardest part. I've been through the waiting, too, and I'd much rather be where the action is."

Chase gently touched Jenny's cheek as she looked up at him with wide blue eyes full of confidence and hope. "What about the boys?"

"Grace will take care of them. They'll be all right for a while without me."

"Grace?" Chase turned to the woman who was still sitting in shock at the table.

"Yes . . . I will . . ."

"I'm going too," Zane announced.

"No, someone has to stay here and take care of

things," Jason declared. "And it looks like this group is going, whether I approve or not."

"We are," the four responded as one.

"I'm sorry, Jason," Cole said. "I know things are tense around here at the moment . . ."

"I understand, Cole. This man has gotten away with too much. If there's a chance for you to find Amanda, then you need to take it. And if you can get my son-in-law back in the bargain, then that's fine, too." Jason looked at Cat, who was grinning from ear to ear. "Lord knows life will be miserable enough for us around here until he's back."

"When do I get to have an adventure?" Zane grumbled. "All I ever do is work, work, work."

"Jenny, are you sure about this?" Chase asked her once again.

Jenny looked through the half-opened door at the two little boys, who were sound asleep on Grace's bed. Her heart ached at the thought of leaving them, but the memory of the months when Chase had been gone were still fresh, even after all these years. She would go with him and face whatever he faced at his side. She would help free Ty from his prison and then she would help them vanquish the specter of Wade Bishop that haunted her dreams. No longer would she be frightened of what fate was going to deal her. She would go out and meet it head-on.

"I'm sure. I'm going with you."

"We'd better start making plans," Cole said.

Chapter Twenty-seven

"Jenny, are you sure about this?"

Jenny made certain the door between the two rooms was closed firmly so as not to disturb the boys, who had not stirred from their sleep, even after being carried across the small valley by their parents.

"You sound as if you don't want me to go." Jenny folded a tiny shirt that she had been mending earlier that day and laid it on the table. "Will I be in your way if I do go?" She turned to look at him. She had seen the look that had entered his dark eyes when Bishop's treachery to their friends had been revealed. It was the same look that had come over him the day Jamie died. Wade Bishop had threatened all of them at one time or another and he needed to be stopped before he hurt them again. Jenny knew Chase wouldn't quit until he was sure the man was no longer a threat to her or their friends. The thought that she could have experienced the same fate as Amanda and missed the love that she shared with Chase, along with the wonderful gifts of her children, still scared her at times. But she had decided to meet her fear head-on, and that fear was Wade Bishop.

"It's not that I don't want you to go. It's just that I'm afraid of what might happen to you in New York."

"What do you think will happen?"

"New York is a big city, and it's not exactly the type of place that I'm used to. What if I can't protect you?"

"I can protect myself, Chase. As long as I can see what's coming, I'll be all right. Like I said, it's the not knowing that terrifies me."

Chase gathered her into his arms and stroked the long blond braid that hung down her back. "I'm sorry for what I put you through."

"Don't be sorry. You did what you had to do to protect us, to protect all of us." Jenny wrapped her arms around his wide chest and gripped the strong muscles of his back. "Now you're going to pay back a debt to Ty and help our friend find his niece. I'm going for the same reason." She leaned back against his arms to look into his dark eyes. "Don't you think that together we can accomplish more?"

"I think that as long as I have you by my side, anything is possible." His lips lowered to hers, and once again she felt the familiar thrill of being swept away on the tide of his love for her. Their bodies molded together in the dance that was as much a part of them as breathing, but yet still felt new, exciting and perfect. Each touch, each sigh became an extension of each other as they melded into one being with one spirit and one purpose. The big bed in the small cabin was the center of their universe, and they were the moon and the stars all coming together in one special moment that would last for all eternity. And when they were spent, Jenny cried and Chase held her tenderly to his chest because he knew that he, too, would miss the boys.

"But what if you don't come back?" Fox's chin quivered as he held his spoon halfway between bowl and mouth.

"We'll only be gone for a little while, Fox. We're coming back, I promise." Jenny cast a worried eye at Chase, who was pouring a cup of milk for Chance.

"But my Jamie daddy and my Sarah mommy went away and didn't come back."

Jenny smiled as she always did when he pronounced his mother's name as *Sawah* but she quickly hid it when she saw the fear showing in his big blue eyes.

"Your Jamie daddy and Sarah mommy are in heaven and even though you can't see them, they are still here with you." Jenny laid her hand over the heart that beat in his tiny chest. "We're not going away like that. We're taking a trip, like the trips that we take to town sometimes to get supplies. Only this time we're going to a bigger town and it's far away, so it will take a long time to get there. We're going to get Uncle Ty and someone who is special to Cole, and bring them back here to live with us."

"Zane says you're going to have a venture," Chance declared.

Chase laughed. "Zane thinks everyone is having an adventure except for him."

"Why can't we go have a venture, too?" Chance asked.

"Yeah, we want a venture," Fox added, now distracted from his worries.

"I promise when we get back, we'll go have an adventure." Chase helped the boys from their chairs and squeezed both of them to his sides. "Just as long as you promise to mind Grace and Grandfather and help Caleb and Zeb when they need it."

"What about Zane?" Fox asked.

"Mind him, too." Chase flashed Jenny a wide grin over the tousled heads of his sons.

"Just mind everyone else first," Jenny added. She was already dreading the day when Zane would take it upon himself to introduce her boys to the finer things of life. In the same way that she was dreading this day. How could she be both excited and sad at the same time? Her mind looked forward with anticipation to the adventure of going off with Chase to experience new things and see new sights, along with the danger that might present itself as they tried to free Ty from prison camp. But her heart was aching at the thought of leaving her children. They were at the age when they were learning so much, becoming more independent. What if they decided that they didn't need her anymore, or worse, forgot about her altogether?

Jenny immediately dismissed her thoughts as foolish as she recalled the times when she was a small girl and her father had gone off to hunt horses for weeks at a time with his friend Gray Horse. She had not forgotten about him; she had anxiously looked forward to his return. Grace would make sure the boys remembered them, just as she was now making sure that Jamie's memory would never die with his son.

Still, her heart was heavy and there were tears in her eyes as they rode away the next morning from the group gathered on Grace's porch. Chance waved from his perch on Zane's shoulders while Fox looked out from his great-grandfather's arms. Grace looked pale and Jenny felt a pang of guilt for burdening her with the care of her two precocious boys for the weeks to come. But she also knew that Caleb, Zane and Zeb would help all they could and she turned her mind from the ranch to the adventure before her. Chase reached over and took her hand, giving it a reassuring squeeze. His eyes beneath the brim of his hat were dark and determined, but the slight smile on his lips brightened her mood. They were together, and as long as they were together, everything would be all right.

Chapter Twenty-eight

Ty wrapped the bright blue muffler tighter around his neck and rubbed his upper arms through the thin fabric of his shirt. What he wouldn't give to have the thick winter coat that had been strapped to the back of his saddle the last time he had seen it. It was only early fall and already he was freezing from the damp breeze that flowed through his shoulder-length hair, bringing with it the promise of another damp, cold rain. Heavy clouds blotted out the warmth of the sun and cast a dismal gray light that blended into the greenish-gray cast of the water. Ty's body shuddered with the thick cough that beat against his rib cage without mercy. There were those who were in worse shape, he told himself in consolation as he looked out over the whitecaps that danced beyond the breakers against the shoreline. At least he got to come outside and walk around and enjoy the fresh air, even if it was unbearably cold. And there were also those who were faring pretty well despite their imprisonment, he observed as Wade Bishop sauntered by, wearing a thick coat, and followed by his usual entourage comprised of a few rebel officers and a few deserters from the Union army who had been incarcerated with the Confederate prisoners. It was amazing how the man had landed on his feet so many miles away from home and in the middle of enemy territory.

A small skiff appeared from the gray mist that had been churned up by the stiff breeze assaulting the island. Ty hoped it was the young doctor making his weekly visit to the prison. Though the tall medical student had not been much help in treating the diseases that ran rampant through the camp due to lack of medical supplies, he did bring news of the outside world, and Ty found himself looking forward to his visits. Perhaps he could even talk him into smuggling out a letter for him. Providing, of course, that he could come up with some paper and something with which to write. What he wouldn't give for some news from home. Just knowing that Cat and Caleb were safely back in Wyoming would be enough to get him through the cold winter that loomed ahead for the lonely men imprisoned on Governor's Island.

With the war going on, it would take forever for a letter to reach Wyoming. Ty hoped Cat was there. He hoped she was growing big with their child and patiently waiting for the war to be over. A smile flitted at the corner of his mouth and stretched across his lower lip at the thought of Cat waiting patiently for anything. Knowing her the way he did, he was sure that she had already convinced their child there was no need to take the traditional nine months to arrive. His smile faded. If only he could be there for the birth and the days before it. Ty's mind saw the soft rounding of Cat's belly and his hand ached to touch it, to feel the life growing beneath her heart.

The boat came closer and Ty recognized the sandy-brown hair of the young doctor sitting in the rear behind the man who worked the sails. The racking cough worked its way through his body again and he felt the searing pain in his lungs. At least he wouldn't need an excuse to have the doctor see him. Ty turned to make his way back toward the high brick walls of the star-shaped prison and saw Bishop and his men watching the skiff as it made its way toward the small wharf that jutted out into the water. Whatever he was planning would bode ill for the young doctor, Ty was sure of it. He should warn the fellow about Bishop. He wished once again that someone had warned him about the man when he had been following orders for the Confederate Army. Jake had tried to, but Jake had not trusted anyone, except for him and Caleb and their friends back home in Wyoming. The only thing that trust had gotten him was blown to bits. Jake would have chosen that over this prison, but still. . . .

A fat raindrop hit Ty's forehead and trickled down his cheek into the thick beard that grew there. The wind stiffened and tore at the end of the bright blue muffler where the yarn had snagged and become torn. Ty picked up the straggling ends and tied them together to keep the yarn from unraveling further. Perhaps Cat was knitting little caps and booties, surrounded by her family as she waited for the birth, for the war to be over, for his homecoming.

Another raindrop landed on the sand in front of

him, then another. The wall of rain swept across the water and landed on the shore, driving the imprisoned officers of the Confederate Army before it as they ran toward the doubtful shelter of their prison where they would at least be dry. Ty had learned lately to be grateful for the little things. He would be dry inside the prison and he had the blue muffler. He even had a chance for some decent conversation with the young doctor. And most important of all, he was another day closer to the end of the war and to the freedom that would come with it.

His ribs burned as he tried to outrun the rain and the never-ending cough stopped him in his tracks. He doubled over with hands on his knees. The cold rain trickled down his neck, and through the blowing mist he saw one of the guards impatiently waving him on. Ty wondered how long it would take the chill to wear off his bones once he was inside the damp walls of the prison. Maybe the young doctor would start a fire in the small stove that stood in the infirmary. Another little thing for which to be grateful. Ty gathered enough strength to sprint the last few steps to the prison and tried not to shiver as he heard the heavy gate swing shut behind him.

"You're sure it's out there?" Cole was half joking but Cat missed the humor as she gazed out over the fog-shrouded harbor.

"I'm sure." The wind whipped at the wool skirts of her stylish green suit and jerked the wide umbrella that Cole held over their heads. Chase placed a protective arm around Jenny's shoulder as the wind threatened to pitch all of them into the dark cold water that licked at the pilings of the wharf on which they were standing.

"Guess all we have to do now is figure out a way to get over there," Cole mused as he fought to keep the umbrella safely stationed over their heads.

Around them the hustle and bustle of life on the waterfront continued as the four stood in their new city clothes looking out over the water. A few of the workers glanced surreptitiously toward Chase, who stood out more in his new suit than he would have wearing his usual gear. With his close-cropped dark hair, dark eyes and regal stare, he looked more like a foreign prince from one of the desert countries than a native of the land on which he was standing. He ignored the curious looks as he had for years, which only added to the air of mystery surrounding him.

He also made sure that he kept a possessive hand on Jenny, who was catching quite a few admiring looks of her own. Chase scowled at the braver of her admirers as they looked at her slim form, which was set off by the stylish cut of the bluish gray suit Cat had insisted on getting her before they boarded the trains to come east. Her wide blue eyes were sparkling with excitement as she took in all the sights and sounds, and the cold rain had tinged her cheeks a becoming shade of pink. The graceful curve of her neck beneath the upswept hair and pert hat that Cat had added begged for his attention, but there was nothing he could do about it while they were standing on the busy wharf.

Chase was getting tired of the looks, tired of the

crowd and tired of the smells, and they had just come to the great city that held his friend captive. He felt naked without his gun but comfortable with the presence of his knife securely held in place against his spine. He promised himself that the next man who looked Jenny's way would be meeting his knife up close or taking a cold swim. He set his lips into a thin, grim line.

Cole glanced at him over Cat's shoulder and drew his eyebrows down sternly. He didn't like the odds.

Chase didn't have any trouble understanding his look, but then again, it wasn't Grace who was being leered at. She was safe at home in Wyoming taking care of his children. Where Jenny should be.

Jenny leaned back against his chest as the wind picked up. He bent his head until his cheek brushed against the side of her upswept hair in a subtle touch of intimacy. She placed a gloved hand on top of her head to protect the hat that still felt foreign pinned into her hair and sent him a sideways smile. Chase decided once again that he was glad she was here beside him.

"Chances are pretty good there won't be anyone going over there today," Cole added. "I've never seen fog that thick."

"Get used to it," Cat said as she turned away from the water. "It's fairly common around here."

"Must not bother some people. Here comes a boat now." Chase pointed toward a fog-shrouded dock that jutted out into the water. Halloos were called and soon a ghostlike skiff appeared out of the fog.

"Do you think they were at the island?" Jenny asked.

Cole shrugged. "They were somewhere. There has to be a boat that carries supplies and such, and the guards would have to get leave sometime or other."

"That boat doesn't look big enough to do more than carry a few people," Chase observed as a tall, thin young man scrambled up the ladder to the main wharf with a small leather bag tucked under his arm.

"Looks big enough to carry a doctor." Cole and Chase exchanged glances, and the plans turning in their heads were evident to Jenny and Cat.

"He looks mighty young to be a doctor," Cat observed as he came closer to them.

"Might be that most of the older ones are off at the front." Cole's eyes took on a flinty stare as he considered the boat and the fog. The young man came within a few feet of them, and his soft brown eyes looked appreciatively at the women standing before him. Jenny felt the tightening of Chase's hand on her waist as the young man's brown eyes trailed up over her breasts and lighted on her face. A fleeting look of recognition, followed by one of surprise and then shock, flashed across the boyishly handsome features. The young man stopped in his tracks with his mouth agape.

"Excuse me, ma'am." He took a step closer and peered up under the dripping umbrella. Chase pulled Jenny back and started to step in front of her, but a well-placed elbow in his rock-hard abdomen stopped him.

"Marcus?" Jenny's mouth widened into the Duncan

grin as the young man displayed perfect white teeth in a broad smile of his own.

"Jenny?"

"What are you doing here?" they both exclaimed at once and then laughed. Chase's eyes narrowed as he looked down at the young fool who seemed to know his wife. At least he had better know her, because he now had both of her hands grasped in his own. Cole and Cat were both speechless while Jenny and Marcus continued laughing at each other.

Jenny looked at Chase with joy shining from her eyes. "Chase, this is Marcus. He's my oldest friend." Jenny dropped one of Marcus's hands and reached for her husband's. "Marcus, this is my husband, Chase. He came to the mission shortly after you left us."

Marcus extended his hand to Chase. "You are a very lucky man. Jenny was the first girl I ever fell in love with."

"But surely not the last." Jenny blushed. Chase suppressed the green monster that had risen up with Marcus's words about Jenny being his first love and graciously shook the younger man's hand.

"And where is your brother? I know wherever you are, Jamie can't be far behind." Marcus made a show of peering about the wharf, looking for the tall form of his old friend.

"Oh, Marcus—" Jenny was surprised at how her voice choked on the words and she suddenly couldn't speak. She dashed at her eyes with a gloved finger.

"He was killed a few years ago," Chase explained, coming to her rescue.

"Oh." The soft brown eyes welled with tears of their own. "I'm . . . so . . . sorry."

Jenny laid a hand on his arm. "You didn't know, you couldn't know." Jenny smiled confidently at Chase and then at Marcus. "Now tell me, what are you doing here?"

"I'm a doctor for the prison camp. I treat the prisoners that are held out there on Governor's Island."

"The prisoners are sick? How about the officers, are they treated well? Are any of them sick? Do you have medicine for them? Have any of them died?"

Cat's questions tumbled out one after the other before Marcus had time to respond to any of them. He looked at her in shock and disbelief as she grabbed his arm in a firm grip.

"Cat, please." Jenny gently removed her friend's hand from Marcus's arm. "We have a friend on the island," she explained. "Perhaps you can help us."

Marcus looked at the four faces before him. "I can try."

"His name is Ty Kincaid. Major Tyler Kincaid." Cat waited breathlessly for any sign of recognition on the kind face of the young doctor.

Marcus smiled. "I know him. I know him quite well. As a matter of fact, I just saw him."

Cat's knees went weak as relief washed over her body. Cole held her up with a steadying arm as she dissolved into tears while shaking her head at the offered help.

"How is he?" Jenny asked.

"Considering where he is, he's all right. He has a bad cough that might turn into pneumonia . . ."

"Pneumonia!" Cat exclaimed with a look of horror on her face.

"It's not the best place to be." Marcus's eyes were kind as he explained the circumstances to Cat. "This camp has been shut down once before because of the diseases that run through it. It's overcrowded, cold and damp. There are not enough blankets, food or medicine to go around."

"We could help with that," Jenny offered.

"It would be appreciated," Marcus replied. "I just can't get over your being here."

"When are you going back?" Cat was desperate for information about Ty.

"Why don't we all go someplace out of the rain where we can talk?" Cole suggested.

Jenny blushed when she realized she hadn't introduced Marcus to her friends. After she had rectified the situation, he rode with them in their rented carriage to a nearby restaurant. As soon as they were seated, Cat began firing another barrage of questions at the young doctor.

"How is Ty? Is he eating? Has he lost weight? Was he wounded when he was captured? Does he have a coat? Does he need shoes?" Her chin quivered as the questions tumbled out.

Marcus threw up his hands in surrender. "Slow down, Mrs. Kincaid, please, and I'll tell you all I know." Cat bit her lip and blushed. "He's thin, as is to be expected. As far as I know, he wasn't wounded when he was captured although he does have a scar over his brow." Cat nodded; she knew about the scar. "He's just developed the cough in the past month, probably because he doesn't have a coat. The only thing he has to keep him warm is some silly blue scarf that he wears around his neck."

Cat dissolved into tears while Jenny and Cole did their best to comfort her.

"I knitted it for him," she said, sobbing. "I can't believe he still has it."

"I'm sorry," Marcus apologized. "I can take him a coat and supplies next time I go if you want. You'll just have to provide some money for the guards with whatever you send."

"I want to see him." Cat dried her eyes and regained her dignity. "How much money would it take for that to happen?"

Marcus chewed on his lip as he considered the faces around him. Jenny smiled at him encouragingly. "You want me to help you break him out of there."

Cole shifted uncomfortably in his seat while Chase's regal face remained impassive.

"Before I answer that, let me ask you a question," Jenny replied. "Is there a prisoner on the island named Wade Bishop?"

Marcus looked in amazement at the faces around him. He had just had a conversation with Major Kincaid about Wade Bishop. Not much of a conversation really, just a kind warning from the officer to be wary of the man and his cronies.

"Yes, there is, although I don't know him."

Cole's eyes turned to ice and Jenny exchanged glances with Chase. "A lot has happened since the last time I saw you, Marcus. Maybe I should start at the beginning . . ."

Chapter Twenty-nine

"Is that better?" Jenny turned, placed her hands on her hips and looked at Cat with eyes full of laughter.

"I didn't see any difference at all. Watch me again." Cat once again took off across the salon of her aunt's town house with her hips twitching in a slow, sensuous motion. Chase, who was sprawled across a dainty settee with his legs spread wide, covered his face with one hand to hold back the laughter that threatened to erupt at Cat's lesson to Jenny in being flirtatious.

"So what did you do that I didn't?"

"I don't know, maybe it's something that you have to be taught from childhood. You're just not walking swishy enough."

"You want me to walk swishier?" Jenny asked incredulously.

"Yes," Cat answered as if it were the most logical thing in the world.

"I really don't see what difference it makes how I walk."

"But it does." Cat took off across the room again, using small mincing steps that set her skirts swaying like a bell. "We need the guards to be watching your backside so they won't pay attention to your face, or rather Ty's face."

"So you're going to give Ty swishy lessons also?" Jenny grinned widely at her friend.

"Yes, I am." Cat turned and looked at her. "I'm serious, Jenny; this will work if you will just try it."

"I don't see anything wrong with the way she walks now." Chase's dark eyes glowed as he admired Jenny's graceful strides.

"You're just blinded by love." Cat took the time to throw a heavily embroidered pillow in his direction. "We want the guards to be blinded by lust."

"I'm absolutely sure I don't like that idea," Chase said as he ducked the pillow.

After hearing Jenny's story and realizing the treachery of Wade Bishop, Marcus had agreed to help them with their two-part plan. Cole had been out for most of the day using some of Jason's contacts to get permission from the government to question Wade Bishop while the rest of them worked on a scheme for getting Ty off the island.

Marcus had suggested having Cat and Jenny visit the prison with him as part of a ladies' aid society that wanted to help the prisoners. He would call Ty in as a typical medical case for the ladies to question. On a return trip, while they carried in much needed supplies, they would bring Ty a duplicate of Jenny's clothes. He would disguise himself and leave with Cat, pretending to be Jenny, overcome with a sudden faintness due to the condition of the prisoners. A large handkerchief placed over Ty's face to cover the smells would help disguise him. Cole, also in disguise, would be waiting in the boat to help with the getaway. Jenny would return later on with Marcus after Ty and Cat were safely away from the island. Marcus felt sure the plan would work if they timed it around the shift changes of the guards so they wouldn't see Jenny leave twice.

Chase was not happy about Jenny's involvement in the plan, especially the part about leaving her within the prison walls, but also could see no way around it. Cat's idea had been to have the guards so bewitched by Jenny's backside that they wouldn't notice anything else and had proceeded to give her lessons in the proper walk for the task.

"Well, as ridiculous as I feel doing this, it's going to be a lot worse for Ty," Jenny stated as she once again tried to walk swishy.

"And that's if you even get him to agree to go through with the plan," Chase added.

"Well, why wouldn't he do it?" Cat asked indignantly.

"He might have foresworn himself not to escape." Chase leaned forward on the settee. "Sometimes the officers are asked to do that."

"He also might not want to put you in danger," Jenny added.

"It might go against his sense of honor," Chase observed.

"Men and their stupid code of honor." Cat stalked across the room toward the set of windows that faced the street, this time without the swishing. "His sense of honor is what got him in this mess to begin with."

"Now, you know you don't mean that, Cat," Jenny said as she sat down next to Chase. "Ty didn't choose the circumstances; he just did what he had to do."

"I know." Cat sighed as she looked through the window onto the busy street below. "He didn't choose for the war to last this long, and he didn't choose to be captured. But he did choose to fight and if any good has come out of that, or any part of this war, it's a mystery to me."

Jenny joined her at the window. "It will be over soon, Cat. The war can't go on much longer." She slid her arm around the petite frame of her friend. "And with luck you will get to see Ty tomorrow."

Cat laid her head against Jenny's shoulder as they looked out the window. "He doesn't know that I lost the baby. What if he's angry with me?"

"Why would he be angry with you?" Jenny turned Cat's shoulders so she could look into the green-gold eyes that were suddenly full of tears.

"If I had stayed home and taken care of myself, then maybe it wouldn't have happened."

"Or you could have stayed home and Caleb and Ty both would have died and you might have lost the baby anyway." Jenny smoothed a golden-brown curl that bounced beside Cat's shell-like ear. "These are things that you have no control over, and Ty will not blame you for losing the baby."

"No, he won't. He will be grateful to know you're alive and that Caleb is alive," Chase added as he slipped up behind Jenny. "He will be sad about the baby, but he won't blame you."

"Knowing Ty, he will probably blame himself." Cat sniffed and dashed away the tears as Chase and Jenny grinned in agreement.

The sound of the door in the hallway alerted them to Cole's return. "I still think you ought to give the sneaking-him-out-under-a-hoop-skirt idea a try. Might be a bit easier than getting him to walk swishy," Chase suggested as he went to meet their friend.

Jenny rolled her eyes at his remark as she took a moment to comfort Cat. "By this time tomorrow you will know that he's fine, and it won't be too long after that before we have him out of that horrible place."

"Jenny?" Chase called from the hall. Jenny gave Cat another squeeze and went to see what her husband wanted.

"Jenny, I think you got it!" Cat exclaimed as she watched Jenny walk away. Jenny looked over her shoulder and stuck out her tongue at Cat, who couldn't help giggling.

Cat felt a shiver dance down her spine as the heavy door was barred behind them. How could Ty survive in a place like this? How could any of the men imprisoned there survive? Losing one's freedom had to be one of the worst things imaginable. The knowledge that it had happened to someone like her husband was almost more than she could bear.

Marcus had arranged for them to have passes under the guise of a ladies' aid society known for its work improving the conditions for the prisoners. A donation to the warden's retirement fund had also helped clear the way for their entry into the thick walls of the fort. The warden had also insisted on having them up to his office for tea, which had taken every bit of Cat's patience as she made polite chitchat about local society while Jenny pretended that she knew the people they were talking about. Fortunately the warden was not a local, and Cat had played the name-dropping game many times before. She had managed to bluff her way though the afternoon, remembering acquaintances from the seasons she had spent in the city with her aunt. Now they were being escorted to the camp hospital to see for themselves the conditions and what medical supplies could be provided for the poor prisoners of war. Marcus had provided a guard with a list of patients that he wished to see that day, a Major Tyler Kincaid being one of the names included.

The men who came before Ty to be seen by the doctor were overwhelmed by the presence of the two beautiful women in the infirmary. Jenny helped when she could while Cat tried desperately not to climb the walls as patient after patient came in, was treated with what little supplies were available, and then sent out. She was anxious to see Ty, but also fearful, as she viewed the pitiable condition of the prisoners.

Finally he was there, standing in the doorway. His blue eyes grew wide above his scraggly beard and jutting cheekbones. Marcus gently pulled him through the door and shut it firmly behind him.

"Why am I not surprised to see you here?" Ty smiled as Cat flew into his arms with a sob. "Watch out. I'm filthy and covered with living crawling things."

"I don't care," Cat cried. "I don't care. You're alive and that's all that matters."

Ty placed a finger under her chin and lifted it to look into her eyes. "And I see that you survived also, but . . ." His eyes dipped to her belly, still flat beneath the gown.

"I lost it, Ty. I'm so sorry," Cat whispered, her eyes wide with fear.

"Caleb?"

"He's alive, but he lost the leg."

Ty pulled her against his chest again and wrapped a hand in her hair. "I'm sorry you had to go through all that. I should have known, I should have kept better watch, I . . ."

"Stop it, Ty. Stop blaming yourself for what happened that day. It just happened."

"No, it didn't. We were betrayed."

"By Wade Bishop?"

"How did you know that?" Ty leaned back and looked down into his wife's face, then at Jenny and Marcus, who were trying to give them the privacy they needed by staying in the corner. "How did you two get in here anyway? Jenny, what are you even doing here?"

"Chase and Cole are here, too," Cat explained.

"On the island?"

"Waiting for us in the boat," Jenny answered. "It turns out that Marcus is an old friend of mine."

Ty looked in confusion at the three faces before

him and then was overcome with a fit of coughing. "I think I need to sit down."

Marcus pulled out a chair from the table. "That's a good idea. Sit down and let me check that cough while the women tell you about the plan."

"Plan?" Ty's eyes narrowed at Cat. "What are you up to now?"

"Ty, you are not going to believe this when I tell you but . . ." Jenny filled Ty in on the history of Wade Bishop.

"I'll kill him!" Ty exclaimed as he heard the story.

"Typical." Cat snorted in response.

"You can't, Ty. We don't know where Amanda is," Jenny explained. "And we want to get you out of here before Cole comes in to question him. We don't need to give him a reason to hurt anyone else."

"We've kept our distance from each other so far."

"But you've been watching him, and I'm sure he's been watching you," Marcus said.

"Well, you are right about that. He's planning something, and somehow or another he's got a connection on the outside."

"As you do." Cat slipped her hand into Ty's.

"How exactly were you planning to get me out of here? It's not like I can just walk out as an escort for you two."

"Well, maybe you can for one of us anyway." Jenny's blue eyes sparkled as they explained the plan.

"I can't pass for you, Jenny. Look at me."

"You'd have to shave," Marcus said.

"I'd love to."

"And then you have to learn how to walk swishy," Jenny added.

Ty and Marcus looked at her as if she had lost her mind while the women dissolved into giggles.

"No, really, Ty, I think you could pass for me. You've lost so much weight that you could wear my clothes and you're only a few inches taller than I am. I'll wear a bonnet that covers my face and hair and you'll have to pretend to be sick so you can cover your face with a handkerchief."

"And how will you get out?" Ty asked as he considered their plan.

"She'll come out later with me," Marcus answered. "We'll wait until the guard change. There should be enough confusion that we can get by. If not, we'll just tell them that you overpowered us."

"Look at me; do you think they'd believe that?"

"Desperate times call for desperate measures," Marcus replied.

"What does Chase think about this?"

"He agrees that it's the safest way to get you out," Jenny informed him.

"But he's not happy about your role in it." Ty knew his friend well.

"He owes you his life."

"Please, Ty. Let us get you out of this place." Cat squeezed his hand. "Then maybe Cole can find Amanda and Wade Bishop will get what he deserves." Ty looked at his beautiful wife standing beside him. How lucky he was to have such a woman to stand by his side, one who loved him even when he was covered with dirt and fleas. She had supported him and his decisions, even the foolish ones, through all the years he had known her. He caressed a curl that dangled over her shoulder and then kissed her hand, which was tightly clutched in his own.

"When is this great escape supposed to happen?" He wanted to get out of there as much as she wanted him out. He also knew that the only way to take care of Wade Bishop was on the outside. And he did want to take care of Wade Bishop.

"In three days?" Cat said hopefully as she smoothed the ragged ends of the now-faded blue muffler. "I can't believe you still have this."

"I wouldn't give it up for anything." Ty grinned through his beard. "Not even when I was offered the prime piece of a roasted rat."

"Ty," Cat cried in horror. "We have to get you out of here!"

"All right, but first tell me about this walking swishy thing."

Chapter Thirty

Fog shrouded the city again. The weight of it on the small boat distorted the sounds that drifted across the water. The four occupants were already nervous and each creak of the oars brought their heads about as they searched the mists for anyone who was on to their plot. Jenny, leaving a grim-faced Chase behind to follow in another boat, had thought to add a shawl to the bonnet that covered her hair and shielded her face from unwanted attention. She hoped that the fog would stay with them all day. It would help to aid Ty's escape better than a bright and cheerful fall day that would put the guards in a mood to flirt. Of course, no guard would want to flirt with a woman who was feeling under the weather; at least she hoped not.

Cat had attached a bag beneath her skirts. Inside was a bar of soap, a razor and a pair of scissors. Jenny was wearing two identical dresses, one on top of the other. Cat had paid the dressmaker dearly for the job, and to keep it secret.

They pulled up to the pier in silence that was as

oppressive as the fog. Marcus greeted the guards as he usually did while Cole, with a hat pulled low over his face, helped the women from the boat.

"At least I don't have to worry about walking swishy today," Jenny whispered to Cat as they followed Marcus off the dock and up the long path toward the prison gates.

"Why is that?"

"They can't see us."

Cat looked over her shoulder and saw that the guards, dock and boat had all disappeared into the thick fog.

"Do you think it's God's way of saying He approves of our plan?" Cat whispered back.

"I sure hope so."

Jenny pulled an embroidered handkerchief from her sleeve and held it to her nose as they exchanged opinions about the weather with the guard at the door. There were already a few men waiting at the infirmary and Marcus gave the guard the list of patients who needed follow-up care. Soon it was Ty's turn and he quickly shaved and washed off as much of the months of grime as he could with the small bucket of water that had been provided for the doctor's use.

Jenny took off her outer layer but stopped cold when Ty took off his tattered shirt. She wondered if it would even fit him. His frame was gaunt and each rib showed severely through his skin.

"Oh, Ty," Cat said, sobbing as she wrapped her arms around his narrow waist.

"Don't worry, sweetheart. Some of Grace's good home cooking will have me back to normal in no time." He shivered against her as the cold, damp air caressed the bare skin of his back and another coughing spell overcame him. "Got to make sure that doesn't happen or they'll find us out for sure."

Marcus produced a small bottle of whiskey from his bag. "See if this helps." Ty looked at the bottle dubiously, but then took a swig.

"It will either help, or I won't care one way or the other," Ty exclaimed as the fiery liquid burned down his throat and erupted in his stomach. "Better leave it at that. In my condition any more will put me under."

Cat grabbed the bottle from his outstretched hand and raised it to her own lips.

"What are you doing?"

"Joining you," she said with a gasp as she wiped her mouth on the back of her hand. Jenny rolled her eyes and handed Ty the dress.

He looked at it in confusion and then back at Jenny. "You two had better help me. I only have experience taking them off."

"Tyler Kincaid!" Cat exclaimed. His grin was foolish as they helped him into the dress, directing him where to place what and to hold still while they worked buttons and tied ribbons. The shawl was arranged and the huge bonnet was placed on his head, leading to another near outburst of laughter. Jenny handed him the handkerchief as Marcus urged them to hurry.

"Are you ready?" he asked.

Ty looked at Cat, who nodded in agreement.

"Let's do this," Ty said. "Wait." He picked up the

muffler and stuffed it down his bodice, which brought smiles from all of them.

"Not as good as the actual woman, but at least you're trying," Marcus observed.

"Good luck," Jenny whispered as the door opened and the production began.

Marcus hurried the two women out of the prison, explaining all the while that one of them had been overcome by the conditions within. He would see them down the long path to the docks and return to finish up with his patients. They were waved through by the guards while the tall woman kept her face covered with the handkerchief. The smaller one comforted her friend and helped her make her way down the fog-shrouded path to the dock. The story was told once again to the guards on the dock and the boatman quickly jumped out to help the women in.

"Make sure you come back for me," Marcus instructed the man as he pulled away from the dock.

"Yes, sir, I'll make sure somebody does," Cole replied, disguising his voice since he was hoping to come back on a different mission.

The boat pulled away and the occupants watched with wide eyes and stiff spines until the island disappeared into the mist. A collective sigh was released as the distance grew and finally Cat launched herself into Ty's arms.

"We're not out of the woods yet," he said into her hair.

"Best leave your bonnet on, ma'am. I'd hate for someone to get a real good look at you," Cole drawled.

"Cole, if I weren't so happy to see you right now, I'd throw you overboard."

"Then who would do your rowing?"

A sound on the water brought their heads up, and the call of a bird brought a smile to their lips. Cole answered with one of his own and with a few quiet directions, Chase soon pulled up beside them.

"It's good to see you in one piece." Chase grabbed Ty's hand over the side of the boats.

"I guess I'm the only one who made it through in one piece," Ty returned. "Thank you, all of you."

"Let's wait until we get Jenny out before we celebrate. There's a warm bath and a hot meal waiting for you. I'm going to get my wife."

"Give it another few minutes to be sure the guards have changed," Cole instructed him as he pulled away.

Chase waited until he could no longer hear the sounds of their boat in the distance. The thought of Jenny still being on the island was driving him crazy. His mind knew that she would be fine, that the worst that could happen was that she might be detained for a while if they discovered that Ty was missing right away. But his heart and his gut were telling him otherwise. Jenny trusted Marcus, he reminded himself. What else could possibly go wrong?

Bishop. What if Bishop picked today of all days to pay a visit to the infirmary? What if he happened to come in while Jenny was in the room by herself? Would he recognize her after all these years? Chase knew the answer to that question as soon as it formed in his mind. Marcus had told them that Ty had some concerns about Bishop watching the young doctor's boat. Was Bishop planning his own escape and perhaps hoping to use Marcus as an unwilling aid? Chase knew that Marcus would do whatever the man asked to protect Jenny, but would he be strong enough to stop him from taking her?

A shiver ran down his spine as he stared straight into the fog in the direction where he knew the island lay. Jenny was in danger and he was sitting in the middle of New York Harbor in a boat. Chase pulled out his revolver and checked the load, which he knew was fine. The hilt of his knife was comfortably within reach and the weapon would easily slide out of his boot. He put his back to the oars and began rowing, hoping and praying that Jenny and Marcus would be on the dock waiting for him.

Cole scanned the wharf as they drifted toward the pier. The skyline of the city looked brighter as the sun began its descent into the western sky. For the most part the area where they were docking looked deserted, but Cole still searched the area, his gray eyes shifting from one end to the other. A feeling in his gut told him that something wasn't right. Would Federal soldiers be waiting to take all of them into custody for aiding in the escape of a prisoner of war? Had something gone wrong on the island? Had Marcus and Jenny been captured? The boat butted up against the dock and Cole quickly jumped out to secure the lines. Ty gathered his skirts and jumped onto the wooden surface, then turned to give Cat a hand.

The sound of an explosion echoing across the water

turned all three of their heads to scan the fog.

"Could that have been a cannon shot sounding the alarm?" Cat asked.

"No, it was too big. It sounded more like something blowing up," Ty replied. "Maybe a building."

"Or a boat," Cole added.

"Do you think it came from the island?" Cat was worried, as they all were, about Jenny.

"It's hard to say with the fog and the water." Cole scanned the wharf above once again. A few of the workers' heads had come up at the sound, but then they had gone back about their business. The three of them scrambled up the ladder and found the hired carriage waiting.

Money can buy all kinds of loyalty, Cole mused as they climbed in. He just hoped it would continue to buy silence. As they drove away they heard another explosion echoing across the water.

Jenny and Marcus had just passed through the prison gate when the explosion rocked the island. Soldiers started running in different directions while questions were shouted and orders given. Their first guess was that they were under attack by a Confederate gunboat. The fog added to the confusion and Jenny and Marcus realized that it would aid in their escape. Before they could get to the path to the dock, there was another explosion, this one seeming to come from the prison walls. The force of it sent them flying to the ground, where they both lay stunned, trying to catch their breath.

Jenny shook her head as she rocked up onto her

hands and knees. Her ears were ringing and the breath had been knocked from her.

"Marcus?" she finally managed to gasp as she blinked against the fog. She felt rather than heard the footsteps behind her and turned right into a group of men.

"Well, what do we have here?" a familiar voice drawled over the ringing in her ears.

Jenny drew back her arm and punched Wade Bishop in the jaw. The impact of the blow knocked him to his knees as two men grabbed her from either side. He worked his jaw for a second before rising again.

"It looks like you're in need of my services again, Jenny." His evil smile flashed beneath the dark beard that was a result of his incarceration. "I wonder how you've survived this long without me."

An impact from behind sent Jenny and her captors flying into Bishop. Jenny took advantage of the distraction and raked her nails down the side of Bishop's face as she fell into him. He grabbed her arms and tried to hold them away but she was strong from years of hard work and he was weak from prison fare. Marcus, meanwhile, was struggling with the two who had held her. They rolled against her legs and she lost her balance, which gave Bishop the advantage he needed. Another group of three men arrived and they soon had Jenny subdued and gagged and Marcus lying unconscious on the ground.

"Let's go before the guards find us," Bishop commanded, and they took off with Jenny dragging her heels.

Chase will be waiting at the dock. Her mind was whirling as she fought against the hands that held her. Jenny knew her husband well enough to know that he would be alert and definitely armed. But she also wondered what Bishop's escape plan was. Had they arranged this around Marcus's visit to the island? Were they planning on using his boat to escape? The explosions had been too well timed to be a coincidence, and since Bishop was running free, she knew that it had been planned with help from the outside.

They turned away from the path and cut through the grove of nut trees that grew on the island. *They have a boat waiting,* Jenny realized and her heart sank. There was no way Chase would find her if they took her off the island. New York was a big city. How would he know where to look for her, even if they stayed in the city? Bishop had a base in Nassau; he had regularly run the blockade. Her fight became more desperate as she struggled against the hands that held her.

"Wait!" Bishop shouted as his men attempted to subdue her. They managed to turn her toward him and he backhanded her, but to his surprise she took the punch and her wide blue eyes glared at him over the gag. Another one of the men solved the problem by picking up a sturdy tree branch and hitting her in the back of the head. She sank like a stone between the arms that held her and never knew it when she was dumped into the bottom of a boat that had been dragged up on the sand.

The cold brackish water in the bottom revived her, but the rocking of the boat and the fact that her hands and feet were tied made her heart sink. *Chase, Chance, Fox*... She blinked back the tears. *Will I ever see you again?*

The first explosion occurred while he was still on the water. The second came as he pulled up to the pier. Chase snagged the line over a post as he jumped from the boat. With gun in one hand and knife in the other, he ran up the path toward the prison. He found Marcus unconscious on the ground but before he could revive him, he was surrounded by soldiers, all of whom were pointing guns at him.

"Drop your weapons! Place your hands on your head! Step away from the body!" Orders were shouted at him and his temper boiled but he remained calm because calm was the only way he could find Jenny.

"He's not dead," he assured them as he calmly stepped back. "I'm here to take him back, along with the women."

"The women have already left, sir," a soldier informed the officer in charge. "One of them got sick and they left earlier today."

Where is Jenny? Chase's mind whirled as his dark, hawk-like eyes scanned the area. Marcus would not have left her and yet here he lay, obviously beaten and unconscious.

"Do you know anything about the explosions?" the officer was asking him.

"No. I heard them as I was coming in to pick up the doctor." *Where is Jenny? Why are these idiots asking me about explosions when my wife is missing?*

Chase fought the urge to throttle the officer along with the men who surrounded him.

One of them had the presence of mind to check on Marcus, who moaned as he was helped to a sitting position.

"Doctor Brown, can you tell me what happened?" the officer asked.

"Some men escaped." His warm brown eyes focused on Chase. "They hit me."

"Do you know this man?"

"Yes. His friend sent him to take me back. He was going to make sure the women got home safely after Mrs. Duncan got sick."

Marcus had made sure that they would not be implicated in Ty's escape. He had also made it clear that Chase was not part of the group that had just attacked him. But that still didn't answer the question boiling in his mind. *Where is Jenny?*

"Release him and return his weapons." the officer barked. "You say you came up from the dock?"

"Yes. No one came that way." Chase stuck his gun in his belt and returned his knife to his boot.

"Okay, men, spread out and check the beaches. Maybe they're stupid enough to try to swim to shore." The soldiers took off.

"Marcus, where is she?"

"Bishop has her." A chill went up the young doctor's spine as he saw the change that came over Chase. The dark eyes flashed death as a steely resolve settled onto his regal face.

"Let's go."

Chapter Thirty-one

Ty could not ever remember a bath feeling as good as the one in which he was soaking. The bowl of hot stew sitting on the table beside him was an added bonus. He was taking it slow where that was concerned. He knew it would take a while for his stomach to readjust to having normal food again instead of the short rations he had survived on for so many months. The sound of the rain pounding on the roof made him realize how lucky he was to be away from the island. He would almost think he was dreaming if not for the way his stomach growled in response to the delicious smells of the stew.

Cat had taken what remained of the clothes he had been wearing and thrown them into the stove. She had brought him clothes from home, which now lay on a chair beside the bed but he was dubious of their fit. He looked down at the hip bones that jutted out and the row of ribs above his hollow stomach. *Not much to look at.* Cat returned from her errand with a smile on her face. *God, please let everything be in working order*, Ty thought as he watched her come toward the tub.

"Would you like some more hot water?"

"No. I think I've had just about enough." Ty took her hand as she tested the water. "I'm so weak now, I don't know if I'll be able to stand up."

"Maybe there's something I can do about that," she purred as she crouched next to the tub. Ty laid his head back against the side and drank in the sight of her. The fire lit her face and cast a gold light into her eyes.

"I'm sorry I wasn't there when you lost the baby."

"I'm sorry I lost it."

"It wasn't your fault."

"If I had stayed put . . ."

"Shhh." Ty placed a finger against her lips. "No more ifs. No more reliving the past and trying to make it right. It's done and it's gone and we can't change it. From now on let's think about the future and live in the present. I want to be with you, Cat, right now, and tomorrow and for the rest of my days. When I die, I want to be buried next to you and I want our children, if we are so blessed, to come visit us and lay flowers on our grave. But for now, I just want to be."

"Be Ty, married to Cat, being together?"

"Be a part of each other. Because that's the way it's supposed to be."

"Because you are Ty and I am Cat and we belong together."

"Yes."

"You finally figured it out, did you?"

Ty snaked his arm out and wrapped it around her waist, pulling her into the tub. Cat giggled as water splashed onto the floor around them and her skirts floated around her. His lips soon silenced her laughter as the months of wanting added urgency to their need.

"Take this thing off," Ty commanded as he tugged at her skirts.

"I can't. There's no room to move," she said, gasping as he attacked her throat. "The water's cold. You'll get sick."

His hand found its way inside her undergarments and her eyes widened, then darkened with passion. She squirmed around in the tub and found what she was looking for. Ty threw his head back as she settled around him, encasing him in a warmth that he thought he would never feel again.

"I love you."

"I love you."

He couldn't wait for her. It had been so long, but she didn't mind because he was there. She watched the wonder of his fulfillment run across his face and then he shuddered beneath her.

"I'm sorry, I'm sorry."

"Shhh. It's all right. We have time now." She kissed his forehead and cheeks as he came back to himself but the sounds of boots pounding on the stairs brought her head up.

"Jenny and Chase must be back." Cat stepped out of the tub and dropped her dress into the puddle of water they had left on the floor. She removed her undergarments and was reaching for a towel when a fist pounded on the door.

"Cat! Ty!" They recognized Chase's voice and heard the desperation in it. Cat pulled on a robe and opened the door as Ty stood and wrapped a towel around his waist. "Bishop has Jenny." Marcus and Cole stood behind him, but Cat could not take her eyes from Chase's face. She had seen that look before. She had seen it the day Jamie died.

"Do you know how many times I have thought about you in the past ten years?" Bishop drew a line down Jenny's cheek with his finger while she shot daggers at him with her eyes. She was soaking wet and shivering from the boat ride and bruised and battered from being thrown on the floor of a carriage. She had been dumped into a chair with her hands still tied behind her back and her feet tied at the ankles. The gag that had been stuffed into her mouth had come from one of the unwashed prisoners and tasted of things she would rather not think about. And now Bishop was talking about old times as if they had been classmates.

"You're the only one who ever got away." He sat down at the table and a scantily dressed woman put a plate of food down in front of him. "And not only that, you've grown more beautiful through the years. I knew you would." He picked up the knife and fork and began on his meal as if he were attending a dinner party. "Do you remember the first time I saw you, Jenny? You were taking a bath and that big dummy was guarding you." Bishop laughed as he deposited a portion of roast beef in his mouth. "I could have taken him right then if I had wanted to but I decided to wait, and sure enough, you fell right into my arms.

Remember that?" Jenny watched as he next went after a bite of potato. "I'm a very patient man, Jenny. I have learned through the years that if you wait long enough, things will come to you." He graced her with a smile. "And see, here you are."

Jenny rolled her eyes.

"There's only one thing that bothers me." He looked steadily at her over his upraised fork. "How did you escape that night? The door was locked and there was no way you could have climbed out of the window. Monette figured that someone must have helped you and we questioned every girl that was working there." Jenny knew in her heart that the "questioning" had probably come with a good beating also and hated to think she had been responsible for that, but then again, where would she be if she hadn't escaped? "But no one knew, or if they did, they didn't say." He shrugged. "It was a shame really. We lost some good workers, but they were easily replaced."

Jenny willed her face above the gag to remain impassive as she considered the horror behind his words. He had to be insane to talk so casually about the things he had done.

"I bet you didn't know I had another sister." He swung his hand out to encompass their surroundings. "This place belongs to Roxanne. Monette is the oldest and Roxanne is the youngest. And me, I'm right in the middle."

"Where you should be, darling."

Jenny couldn't believe it. Except for the color of her hair, the woman standing with her hands on Bishop's shoulders was the image of Monette. Of course, Jenny had only seen her once, and it had been ten years ago, but the picture had remained clear in her mind.

"Glad to see you finally made it ashore, big brother."

"Like I said, I'm a patient man."

"And who is this?"

"This is an old friend of mine, Jenny. Jenny, this is my sister Roxanne."

Roxanne smiled at her as if they were meeting in the park.

"You won't believe this, but I bumped into Jenny over on Governor's Island."

"Well imagine that!" Roxanne flicked her fingers through her brother's untidy hair.

"She must have been bringing comfort to the prisoners."

"Well then, she'll fit right in here."

"That's what I was thinking."

Jenny worked the ropes that held her wrists. The water had just made them tighter and the skin beneath was raw. If they didn't remove the gag soon, she would probably throw up. *Oh, Chase, please find me.* How could he find her? How would he know where to look for her in this horrible city? *God, please . . .*

"I don't have any empty rooms right now, but I can put her in with Amanda. She won't even know she's there." Roxanne giggled.

Amanda. Could it possibly be the same Amanda? Jenny's mind raced at the possibility.

"Just make sure the door is locked. And put a guard outside."

"Okay, darling, just leave it to me." Roxanne gave her brother a peck on the cheek.

Jenny was hauled out of the chair by a huge man and carried up three flights of stairs, which she saw upside down as she had been unceremoniously thrown over his shoulder. Her hands and feet were untied and she was shoved through a door into a dark room. She heard the sound of the lock as she spit out the gag. A screech from the hall told her ears that a chair had been dragged up to the door and she realized that Roxanne had been as good as her word.

Jenny willed herself to be calm as her eyes adjusted to the darkness of the room. The rain beating on the roof above gave her assurance that she was on the top floor, but she also knew that it would wash away any signs of her passage.

The hysterical laughter that followed that thought nearly overwhelmed her. *Signs of her passage.* If only she were in Wyoming or somewhere out in the country, Chase would find her trail in no time. But she was in the city and she had come there after traveling over a small piece of the ocean. There was no way he would be able to find her. She would have to find him. Jenny went to the window. It was nailed shut.

There was a movement followed by a murmur, and Jenny turned to the bed. Someone was there. She focused on the bed in the darkness and finally was able to discern a dark head of hair against the gray cast of the sheets.

"Hello?" Jenny called out.

"No." It was a woman's voice, but it was soft and far away. Jenny stepped closer to the bed.

"Amanda?"

"Leave . . . me . . . alone. Leave . . . me . . . in . . . peace." The words were slurred, as if the woman had to think about them.

There was a dresser by the door and Jenny fumbled around the top of it, hoping to find a lamp. She finally knocked over a candle, and some more groping on a shelf above led her to some matches. The candle flamed into life and revealed a sparse room containing nothing but the dresser and the bed. Jenny carried the light over to the bed.

The woman threw her arm over her face to shield her eyes and turned away from the light. "Please . . ."

"Amanda?"

"What?" The face seemed pained. Jenny reached out and pulled the arm away. Cole had shown her the miniature of Amanda that he carried in his watch. This woman had the same dark hair and her face was the right shape, but her eyes were squeezed tightly shut. When opened, would they be the same light gray as Cole's?

"Are you Amanda from Texas? Is Cole Larrimore your uncle?"

"What. . . ." The dark head tossed as if trying to escape the questions. "Un . . . cle . . . Cole . . . find me . . . lost."

Jenny sat down on the bed. This had to be Amanda. Was she sick? She didn't feel feverish, yet she was fighting the sheets as if she were. Jenny looked around the room again and went back to the dresser. She set the candle down on top and opened the first drawer. Nothing there, just a few scanty night things, similar to those the girl below had been wearing.

They made Amanda whore for them. Jenny looked back at the woman on the bed. They must have drugged her. She turned back to the dresser and went through the rest of the drawers. Nothing. Jenny dropped her head on her arms on the top of the dresser. *Please God, get me out of here.*

A reflection of the candle caught her eye and she lifted the light to the shelf above. There was a bottle on it and she picked it up to read the label. "Laudanum." Opium. This was how they controlled Amanda and probably the other girls, too. They were addicted to opium and would do whatever it took to get it. Even whore for it. She raised the candle to the shelf again and found a spoon.

Jenny went back to the window and found nails in both corners. She used the spoon to dig at them and the soft wood soon gave way. Her fingers bled as she gouged them with splinters and she felt her nails chip and break, but she kept at it, frantically digging and praying that they would leave her alone for this one night. Surely Bishop would take time to enjoy himself after being in prison all those long months. There was a guard posted outside her door and he was, after all, a patient man. *Please God, let Bishop wait until tomorrow. Please God, help me get this window open.* The second nail landed on the floor with a plink and she was able to raise the window.

The rain was steady and the air was cold, so she took the time to throw the bedspread over Amanda so she wouldn't come out of her dreamlike state. Jenny surveyed the area below. There were four stories between her and the alley below and not a soul in sight. There was a huge stone wall around the grounds of the building across from the one in which she was imprisoned and the sight of a bell tower made Jenny realize that it was a church. Only Wade Bishop and his sisters would have the audacity to put a whore house next to a church. Jenny leaned out and realized that she could probably reach the gutter that ran down the corner of the building. But first she would have to hang onto the roof above, and it was slick with rain. And she was no longer a foolish girl of fifteen but a grown woman with children. If she ever wanted to see her children again, then she had to go, and she had to go now.

She turned and sat backward on the window ledge. The rain drenched her face as she looked up at the roof. At least there were some benefits to being so tall. She reached up and grabbed the top sill of the window with one hand and pulled herself up to reach the roof with the other. With her feet planted on the ledge, she pulled the other hand up and swung free, praying for strength.

There was no doubt in her mind that the fall would kill her. Bishop would find her body and dump it in the harbor and her family would never know what had happened to her. She braced the toes of her shoes against the wood siding and slid her hands down the roofline, one slide, two, three, until she could grab the gutter pipe that ran down the side. Her knuckles scraped against the siding as she braced her feet against a joint in the pipes and held on for dear life.

She took a moment to look down, hoping there

would be something soft below for her to land on, but the only thing she saw was the rain barrel, which was full to overflowing. She took another breath and moved her feet below the joint. She started to slide but the next joint stopped her. She looked at the side of the house and realized she had made it down to the next floor. That wasn't so bad—only three stories to fall instead of four. Maybe she'd survive with nothing more that a broken back and broken legs. That would make it easy for Bishop. She wouldn't be able to move. She could just lie on her back all day and do his business.

"Come on, Jenny, you can do this," she mumbled to herself as the rain continued to beat down on her head. Only the strength of her grip on the pipe kept her from falling, along with the fact that the toes of her shoes were standing on a joint in the pipe that was less that an inch in width.

"Going somewhere, Jenny?" She looked up and saw Bishop, now cleanly shaven except for his thin mustache, leering at her from the open window. Jenny lifted her toes and came to another jarring halt after sliding down the next story. "Why don't you just stay where you are and we'll help you down?"

How could the bastard sound so reasonable? Jenny looked back up, blinking against the rain. How long would it be before he had someone outside? She lifted her toes again and slid again. She was some ten feet off the ground with the yawning width of the rain barrel below her. She let go again and landed with her feet on the edge of the barrel. The door opened and the huge form of the man who had carried her up the stairs came spilling out with the light. Jenny hiked up her skirt and landed a kick under his chin as he came running toward her. She was rewarded for her efforts by the sight of him landing flat on his back in a puddle. She jumped down from the barrel and took off down the alley just as two more men came running out.

"You're just going to make it harder on yourself!" Bishop yelled from the window as she sprinted down the stone wall with her skirt held up around her waist. The wall turned and she followed it, hoping for an opening of some kind. She found a gate made of tall iron bars but it was locked. The two men rounded the corner as she grabbed the bars and walked her way up far enough to grab the top of the wall with her hand. She felt hands reaching for her ankles as she kicked her way over and fell into the shrubbery below. She knew it wouldn't take them more than a minute to get over the wall, so she took off again across a rain-soaked garden toward a small door in the back of the church.

"Please, God," she prayed as her hand touched the knob. It was unlocked and she slammed it behind her and slung the bolt home just as the two men reached the door. She heard them beating on the door and she took off down the hallway toward a light coming from a room.

"Somebody help me!" Jenny yelled as she ran into the room. An older woman with shorn gray hair knelt at a small altar with her beads in hand, saying her prayers.

"Saints preserve us!" she cried as Jenny came barreling into her room.

Jenny heard the splintering of the door behind her and realized she was trapped in the room.

"Sister—" She grabbed the woman and spun her around. "Sister, please, get word to my husband. His name is Chase Duncan and he is at the Manchester Townhouse on Fifth Avenue." She heard the footsteps pounding down the hall. "Tell him I'm in the house behind the church. Now hide, please . . ."

Jenny ran out of the room and took off down the long hallway. She heard the men gaining on her. A hand reached out and grabbed the skirt that she held bunched around her waist. She felt the fabric give and hoped it would tear but it was wet and stretched instead. She tried to wrench herself away but went down as one of the men tackled her from behind.

"Check that room she was in and see if there's anybody there!" the henchman yelled as he clamped his hand over Jenny's mouth and wrapped his legs around her to keep her from kicking and clawing.

The other man stuck his head in the room, looked under the narrow cot and opened the wardrobe. "Nobody in here," he announced.

"Help me get her out of here," the first one said as he threw his coat over Jenny's shoulders and tied her arms down with the sleeves. One grabbed her upper body and the other her legs, and they carried her bucking and kicking from the church.

The elderly nun crept from the back of the wardrobe where she had hidden in the darkness behind the black habit of her order. She still held the smoking candle in her hand as she looked down the hall to where the men and their burden had disappeared through the door that hung splintered from its hinges.

"Jenny? Jenny Duncan? Was that you?" Sister Mary Frances asked the hallway. Doors along the way opened and nuns in various stages of dress poked their heads out to see if it was safe. Sister Mary Frances ignored most of the questions as she quickly dressed in her habit. Chase Duncan. Surely it had to be Chase the Wind, the young half breed who had been taken in by the orphanage all those years ago. Which meant that Chase and Jamie had found Jenny after she had been carried away. But that was more than ten years ago. What was Jenny doing in New York City? And why were those men chasing her? The sister crossed herself as she recalled the stories going around about the house located behind the walls of the church grounds. *Oh Jenny, what kind of trouble have you gotten into now?* Sister Mary Frances grabbed a cloak to protect her clothing from the rain and went to inform one of the younger sisters of her plans before she slipped out into the night.

Chapter Thirty-two

"What am I going to do with you, Jenny?"

Jenny looked at the ropes that held her spread eagle on the bed. Her hands were already growing numb from the tightness of the bonds. Bishop had learned his lesson after two escapes on her part. She was not to be left alone and she was to be kept tied up until he said otherwise.

"You could let me go," Jenny suggested as she dropped her head back on the pillow.

Bishop threw his head back and laughed. "One thing I can say about you, my dear, sweet Jenny. You sure do make life interesting."

"Why? Why are you so interested in me?"

He reached a hand out and trailed it down her cheek. "Like I said, you're the only one who ever got away." His perfect teeth flashed beneath the thin mustache. "And I love a challenge."

"But I'm worthless to you now. I'm married . . ."

"A woman of experience."

"I have children . . ."

"A mature woman." He fingered a damp blond curl that had fallen from its pins in her escape attempt.

"I'm scarred."

"What? Where?"

"None of your business."

His face, usually pleasant, suddenly turned evil as his hand grasped the collar of her dress and ripped it down the front to the waist. Jenny coughed and gagged as the pressure of the dress on her neck choked her before it gave way. The ridged scar over her left breast made a sharp contrast against the fine lace trim of her camisole. Bishop's index finger traced the outline above her breast as Jenny strained against the ropes to escape his touch.

"And how did this come to be?"

Jenny's eyes narrowed as the finger remained. "A man tried to mark me as his." She looked at Bishop in contempt. "I burned off his mark and my husband took care of the man who put it there."

Bishop laughed again. "And what did your dear husband do to the poor unfortunate fool?"

"He castrated him."

Bishop flinched as if he were suddenly burned. Jenny felt immediate satisfaction at knowing that she had roused some fear in him even though he was hiding it well. His finger trailed down between her breasts and stopped at the torn waist of her dress. "Quite an impressive threat, my dear. But of course that all depends on him finding you . . . and me, which is not likely."

"Oh, but you don't know him. He'll find me."

Bishop opened the door of the room and motioned

to one of his men. The burly man appeared with a nun before him and thrust her into the room. "Was the sister supposed to tell him where you are?" The nun stood with head downcast and hands gracefully folded before her.

Jenny swallowed hard as she realized her last chance of rescue was gone. *Chase, Chance, Fox . . . Oh, God, please tell them how sorry I am . . . Please take care of them . . .* "Let her go, Bishop. She's not a part of this."

"Oh, but she is, Jenny. Just like before in Texas. We punished the ones who helped you escape. Of course I realize now after watching you shimmy down that drain pipe that you didn't have any help, but it's too late to worry about that now." Bishop placed his hands on the shoulders of the nun, who had remained silently looking at the floor during the discussion. "But hey, at least she'll have a chance to hear your confession before you go to hell. And believe me, Jenny, you are going to hell." The look in his eyes was enough to confirm it.

Jenny squeezed her eyes shut against the tears that threatened. *Don't let him see you cry.* The door shut firmly behind him.

"Jenny?"

Jenny opened her eyes to look at the nun who had approached the bed.

"Jenny Duncan from St. Jo, Missouri?"

"Sister? Sister Mary Frances?"

"Yes, child." The nun untied the ropes holding her hands.

"Don't. You'll only make it worse on yourself."

"Hush. Don't think for a minute that I would leave you like this." Sister Mary Frances pulled the torn edges of Jenny's dress together.

"I can't believe I didn't recognize you." Jenny felt as if she were dreaming. Maybe Bishop had given her some of the opium already and she *was* dreaming.

"I was probably the last person you were expecting to see." One hand was freed and Sister Mary Frances began on the other one.

"I'm so sorry I got you into this mess."

"Don't worry, dear. Help will be here soon."

"But they captured you."

"I know, I expected it. Another of the sisters went out after me to find your husband. Am I correct in my guess that you married the young man from the orphanage?"

"You sent someone to get Chase?"

The nun patted her hand and smiled. "Yes. I knew that you would need me and I knew they would be watching. I was a decoy. Your husband is probably on his way right now."

"Oh, sister." Jenny threw her arms around the nun's neck. "I can't believe you're here. I thought you were in Boston."

"I was, for a short while, but then God called me here." The nun smiled sweetly. "Do you think it was just for this purpose?"

"I don't know. I'm just so glad He did."

"The strange thing is I was just dreaming about you, or rather I was dreaming about your brother."

"You were dreaming of Jamie?"

"Yes. It was the strangest thing. He was very handsome and grown, and there were no scars. He was just sitting on the edge of my bed talking to me. He told me to get up and open the door to my room. And the strange thing is, I did, and since I didn't know what else to do, I lit a candle and started praying . . ."

"And I saw the light and went straight to your room." Jenny burst into tears.

"What is it, child?" Sister Mary Frances looked up as she untied Jenny's feet.

"Jamie was protecting me."

"I don't understand how . . ."

"He's dead but he still . . . He was killed a few years ago by Logan."

"The bully from the orphanage?" the nun asked in shock and crossed herself. "I have not gone a day without praying for you and your brother since you disappeared. Tell me what has happened to you since the day you were taken away."

"Oh sister, you just might not believe it all." Jenny wiped a tear as the nun took her hand.

The pounding on the door surprised them. Of course, it was the wee hours of the morning but the house was ablaze with light as Chase, Cole, Marcus and Ty pored over a map of the city, trying to find a clue as to where Bishop could have holed up with Jenny, if he was still in the city at all. The possibility of his wife being taken away in a ship was something that Chase didn't want to consider. Cat went to open the door and found a young nun shivering on the stoop. Once again she gave thanks that her aunt was out of the city.

"Is this the Manchester house ma'am?"

"Yes." Cat was puzzled. What was a nun of all people doing, standing on her aunt's porch dripping wet in the middle of the night?

"I'm looking for Chase Duncan."

Chase's sharp ears had picked up the mention of his name and he was in the foyer before Cat had a chance to invite the woman in.

"Mr. Duncan?"

"Yes."

"Sister Mary Frances sent me with word of your wife," the young nun began.

"Sister Mary Frances?" Marcus asked from behind a stone-faced Chase.

"Yes."

Chase pulled the young woman into the foyer. She looked at him in trepidation, not sure if he was a man or the devil himself incarnate. "Where is she? Have you seen her? Is she all right?" His eyes flashed with a strange silver light as he questioned the trembling young woman.

"No . . . I mean . . . no, I haven't seen her. The sister said for me to bring you to the church. She said she's being held in the house behind the grounds." Sister Mary Frances had been firm in her instructions. She had also told the young woman there was nothing to fear, but the nun wasn't so sure about that. The man she was seeking looked as though he was ready to kill someone. But then again, maybe he had a reason to kill someone if his wife was being held against her will. The sister shivered, but whether it was from fear or from the cold rain that soaked her bones, she wasn't sure.

"Do you know who she's talking about?" Cole asked.

"Sister Mary Frances was the nun who took care of us at the orphanage," Marcus explained.

Ty handed Chase his coat and then swung on his own.

"Where are you going?" Cat asked, knowing the answer.

Ty pulled her into his arms. "You know where I'm going. And you know I have to go." Chase was already down the steps and helping the nun into the carriage. Cole and Marcus were behind him. "Just stay here, Cat. Promise me you won't follow."

"Just let me go to the church. I'll stay put once we get there. I promise." She couldn't let him leave her. Not when she had just got him back. Cat looked at the young nun who was nervously wringing her hands as Chase mounted the carriage. "Besides, I have to keep our young sister from sending for the authorities. I didn't go to all this trouble to bust you out just to have you recaptured again."

"Get your coat." Ty knew better than to argue with her. And he didn't want to leave her behind.

The ride through the rain-soaked streets was quiet except for the noise of the carriage. The young sister sat up front next to Chase, who firmly guided the horses on their mission. *How did Sister Mary Frances know where to find her? How did Jenny find the sister? What was Bishop doing to her? Was she still in the house? Was she still alive?* His mind raced with plans to get her back and his will beat down the doubts that threatened his sanity. He refused to consider the possibility that she would not be there. Her rescue was necessary for his life to continue. Without Jenny there was nothing. He couldn't bring himself to think about the boys waiting back home for their mother and father to return. He concentrated on Jenny and the enemy whom he had never seen but ached to kill.

After what seemed to be an eternity of riding through the streets, the young nun beside him breathed a sigh of relief as they came into sight of the church. Chase stopped the carriage before they turned the corner that would bring them to the front of the building.

Cat tearfully kissed Ty good-bye and went with the sister to the church while the men waited in the shadows to see if anyone was watching. Chase, Cole and Ty checked their weapons while Marcus watched them doubtfully. Cole looked at the young doctor and then handed him the extra revolver that he had stuck underneath the back of his coat. Marcus tested the weight of the weapon and then shrugged.

"I usually take bullets out instead of putting them in."

"To each his own," Cole said, sighing.

"Just try not to hit one of us when the shooting starts," Ty told him. Chase wasn't listening to the exchange. His dark eyes were focused on the building behind the church grounds.

They split into two groups. Cole and Ty took one alley while Chase and Marcus followed the other.

They saw one another again when they came to the lane between the church grounds and the building where Jenny was being held. A few lights shone in some of the upstairs windows. The ground floor was dark. Chase motioned for Cole and Ty to go around to the front while he and Marcus approached the back door.

"Sister, we have to get out of here," Jenny whispered. She knew the door was well guarded as she could hear the occasional creak of the chair that was placed against it.

"How?"

Jenny shook her head and checked the window. It was nailed shut as expected, only this time there were no tools to help her dig the nails out. And the room was located in the middle of the house, so there would be no drain pipe handy, just a straight fall down three stories.

Jenny picked up the rope that was still lying on the bed and then looked toward the door. "We need a distraction," she whispered to Sister Mary Frances. "Can you break the window?"

The nun looked confused for a moment but then understood as Jenny took a place behind the door with the rope held taut in her hands. Sister Mary Frances looked around the room for a moment and then took off her shoes. She dropped them into a pillowcase from the bed and then took a position by the window. She nodded at Jenny and then swung the sack at the window with all her might. They were rewarded by the sound of breaking glass.

"Jenny, don't!" the nun yelled.

The sound of a chair screeching was followed by the doorknob being turned. Jenny jumped on the back of the guard as he came through the door and wrapped the piece of rope around his neck. The man clawed at the rope and slammed Jenny against the wall. Sister Mary Frances came at the man, swinging the pillowcase with the shoes inside at his head. Jenny held on for dear life as the man clawed at the rope while trying to block the blows that were raining about his face and shoulders. His breath finally gave out and he sank to the floor, landing with a thump. Jenny was off him in a second and grabbed the nun's hand.

"We've got to get out of here now . . ." She poked her head out in the hall and found it clear. "Let's go!"

They ran to the back staircase and were greeted by the sounds of someone running below them. Jenny looked down and then looked up. "Come on." She pulled the sister up the stairs.

"Why are we going up?"

"Because there's someone else we have to get out of here."

"What?"

A shot was fired below and Jenny stopped in her tracks. "He's here." She grinned at Sister Mary Frances. "Chase is here." She jerked on the nun's hand. "Let's go."

He had hoped to make a silent entrance but Marcus had put a quick end to that. The young doctor looked sheepishly at Chase with the gun still smoking in his hand. He was obviously proud of himself for saving Chase's life. He hadn't seen the knife that Chase held in his hand, ready to do its silent work. The sounds of running feet on the floors above gave notice that the alarm had sounded. Chase ducked his head toward the darkened hallway and stepped over the body with Marcus on his heels.

They heard shouts, heard the creak of both sets of stairs. Chase tried to count the number by listening to the footsteps but he knew there were too many of them to tell. Doors slammed in the hallways above and he wondered if Cole and Ty had made it through the front successfully. Surely they would meet up somewhere on the ground floor.

Several men charged down both the front and back sets of stairs, carrying lamps and weapons. One group found the body lying on the kitchen floor in a pool of blood and immediately fanned out. Chase watched from the shadows and wondered which one of them was Bishop.

"Here!" someone shouted and the men all converged toward the front. Cole and Ty had been discovered and immediately shots were fired. Chase made his way toward the back staircase and took the steps two at a time with Marcus breathing down his back the entire flight. Chase briefly wondered if he should leave the young doctor behind before he wound up getting himself killed. The chances of him staying put were probably slim, however, and he would only get into more trouble without him.

Chase reached the second floor and looked down the dimly lit hall and then up the next flight of stairs. All was quiet, but the soft glow of a lamp alerted him to the fact that someone was above him. The sounds coming from below were not encouraging.

"Go see if they need help," he mouthed to Marcus.

Marcus looked down the stairs with wide eyes, swallowed the lump in his throat, and with gun cocked, crept down the hallway toward the front staircase. Chase watched him for a moment and then silently tackled the next flight.

Marcus crept down the stairs with his gun pointed straight ahead. He heard shouts and the grunts and crashing of a scuffle. He cautiously looked through the banister. Flickering light from a lamp on a table in front of the window cast long shadows across the men who struggled on the floor, tangled together in a fight to the death. Marcus recognized the lean features of Cole as he raised his fist to strike the man who was lying prone beneath him. Ty, weakened from his time in the prison camp, was having his own problems as he struggled to reach a gun that lay just beyond his reach while strong fingers tightened around his throat. Cole finished his opponent and threw a shoulder into the man holding Ty, knocking him to the floor as Ty gasped for air. Another man, apparently forgotten in the corner, raised his gun.

Marcus caught the reflection of the lamplight on the gun barrel. He stood and fired. The impact of the bullet hitting the man's chest sent his own shot astray and the globe from the lamp burst, showering the heavy drapes with oil and flame.

Cole finished off his opponent and hauled Ty to his feet. "Good shootin' there, Doc." He grinned at Marcus.

"Where's Chase?" Ty croaked.

"Somewhere up there." Marcus pointed. The drapes flared as the fire consumed them and the flames started licking at the ceiling.

"Think we oughta do something about this fire?" Cole asked as the three of them watched the deadly dance of the flames. A scream was heard from the floor above and then a woman's voice shouted in alarm. The three men dashed towards the kitchen as doors above slammed and the house's occupants came streaming down the stairs. The whores were leaving and their madam with them.

"Who is she?" Sister Mary Frances asked as Jenny tried to rouse the young woman from her dreams. The nun was trembling at the sounds of gunshots ringing from below accompanied by shouts and flying furniture.

"A friend of a friend," Jenny answered. "Amanda, wake up." Jenny shook the young woman's shoulders.

"Leave me in peace . . ." The words were slurred. Jenny pulled her to a sitting position as Sister Mary Frances kept an eye on the hallway through the crack left open in the door. "Please."

"*Amanda! Wake up!*" Jenny shook her again.

"Who are you?" The eyes blinked and tried to focus on the unfamiliar face before her.

"A friend of your uncle." Jenny smiled confidently at the young woman. "We're here to get you out."

"Uncle . . . Cole?"

"Yes."

The young woman looked doubtfully at Jenny and

then in bewilderment at the nun who watched from the doorway.

"Leave me please."

"I can't."

"I don't want him to see me like this; I don't want him to know. Please don't tell him you found me, please . . ."

Jenny was aghast as the young woman dissolved into tears before her.

"Someone's coming!" Sister Mary Frances whispered.

"Amanda!" Jenny shook her.

"It's Bishop!"

Jenny grabbed Sister Mary Frances and the two of them took their places behind the door.

"You're running out of places to hide, Jenny," Bishop called out as he came down the hall.

Jenny knew he was right. There was no place to go and it was just a matter of time before he opened the door. She shoved Sister Mary Frances behind her and braced herself.

The door gave way and came slowly swinging toward them. Jenny shoved back with all her might and was rewarded with the impact of the wood against a body. The door came flying back at her in the next instant and she fell backward on top of Sister Mary Frances as she tried to escape its impact. Bishop grabbed her and pulled her to her feet and then she felt the cool barrel of a revolver against her temple.

"Jenny," he said, sighing. "It looks like I'm going to have the pleasure of making you a widow today."

Jenny bit the arm that was placed under her neck

and was immediately flung across the room, only to be hauled up again. "Do that again and I'll be sending the sister on to her own sweet reward." She heard the sound of a bullet sliding into a chamber. "Do you understand?"

Jenny nodded and went willingly with Bishop as he pulled her toward the hall with his arm once again wrapped around her shoulders and under her chin. Her back was pinned tightly against his chest so that she could be used as a shield.

"Let her go!"

Jenny saw the form of her husband take shape out of the shadows down the hallway and felt a surge of relief course through her body. She caught the flash of silver in his eyes as he stared down his nose at Bishop in that contemptuous way that he had. She felt the rage boiling up in the body that was pressed intimately against her own and was glad for it. His anger would lead him to make a mistake.

"I take it this is your husband." Bishop casually rubbed his cheek against her ear and lowered his arm. His hand dipped inside the torn halves of her dress, and he squeezed her breast. Chase's head jerked at the insult to the love of his life. "My compliments on your choice of a wife," Bishop shouted down the hall. "Too bad you won't be keeping her." He leveled his gun and sighted down its barrel. "But you won't miss her for long."

"*No*!" Jenny screamed and threw her arm up just as the shot was fired. She saw Chase twist and dive but then watched in horror as his body jerked with the impact of a bullet. "*Chase!*"

"Time to go, Jenny." Bishop pulled her toward the front staircase.

"No . . ." Jenny screamed as she fought against the arms that held her. The impact of the gun butt against her temple silenced her and Bishop dragged her toward the stairs. Jenny saw stars exploding in her head as she sagged against the hated body. The hallway became a swirl of darkness and light and Sister Mary Frances's horrified face drifted slowly away as they moved down the hall.

The impact took her breath away. One moment she felt as if she were floating, the next she was tumbling against a wall. Jenny landed halfway slumped against a doorway as two bodies rolled over her in a ferocious fight. She gasped for breath as she dimly became aware that Chase was still alive and wrestling with Bishop. A trail of blood dripped down his arm from his shoulder and Chase howled as Bishop buried his finger in the wound.

Jenny felt a tug on her arm and found Sister Mary Frances pulling her away from the vicious struggle.

Chase ducked his head and charged into Bishop's chest. They crashed through the doorway into Amanda's room and fell onto the floor. Jenny found her feet and scrambled after them with Sister Mary Frances clinging to her arm. It was hard to tell in the darkness who was who. Both men had dark hair and flashing white teeth. Both had long, lean frames, although Chase's was wider and stronger. Bishop had to be weak from his imprisonment but Ty had said that he had managed fairly well by getting food and clothing smuggled in. Chase was also at a disadvantage due to the bullet wound in his shoulder, which spouted blood steadily as the men wrestled. The floor became slick with it as each grappled for the upper hand in what both knew was a fight to the death.

Amanda watched wide eyed as the men wrestled and rained blows on each other. They found their feet and then crashed into the bed. She stumbled off the bed and fell into Jenny and Sister Mary Frances, who threw her arms around her as she collapsed against them.

Chase and Bishop gripped each other by the lapels and swung into the wall. Bishop pinned Chase against the wall and pulled him back, only to slam him into it again. Jenny watched in horror as Chase's head snapped against the wood and his eyes glazed over. How much more could he take?

"Just remember as you're dying," Bishop hissed in his face as he slammed him again, "that I will take very good care of your wife."

"That's my job." Chase gathered himself and with a surge of energy spun Bishop around. His back crashed through the window and Bishop grabbed in surprise at the frame as the upper half of his body leaned precariously through the broken glass. All he got for his efforts was deep cuts from the jagged pieces that filled the frame. Chase still held him by the lapels of his coat and Bishop stared at him in wide-eyed disbelief as he dangled over the alley. "I just have one question for you before you go."

Bishop looked down at the ground, four stories below and then back at Chase, whose eyes held the promise of his death. "What?" Bishop snarled.

"Whatever happened to a young girl named Amanda who you took off the streets of Laredo several years ago?"

Bishop looked at Chase as if he were insane, then his eyes flicked over the three women who were watching.

"Amanda?" Chase asked Jenny.

"It's her."

Chase released his hold on Bishop.

Sister Mary Frances crossed herself as Jenny ran to her husband.

"Chase! Jenny!" Cole and Ty called as they ran through the hall.

"Jenny?" Chase gasped as he turned to her.

"Chase."

"Do you have any more enemies?" he asked.

She grabbed his arms as his body wavered. "None that I know of."

"Good." His dark eyes rolled up in his head and he collapsed on the floor.

"*Chase!*" Jenny fell to her knees beside him just as Cole, Ty and Marcus came crashing through the door.

"Where's Bishop?" Cole demanded. Sister Mary Frances pointed to the broken window.

"Chase?" Jenny stroked the regal face of her husband, which showed pale in the dim light. Marcus knelt beside her as Cole and Ty rushed to the window.

"He's lost a lot of blood." He pulled Chase's clothes away to examine the wound.

"We need to get out of here," Ty said as he turned away from the broken body that lay on the ground below.

"Amanda?" Cole caught a glimpse of the quivering young woman who had crouched in the corner. Beside her, Sister Mary Frances knelt, trying to give her comfort.

"Did any of you forget that the house is on fire?" Ty asked.

The women looked up in horror at the men.

"Help me get him up," Marcus commanded. He quickly tied Chase's shirt sleeve around his shoulder and then with Ty's help hauled him to his feet. Cole ripped a sheet from the bed and wrapped it around his scantily clad niece before he gathered her into his arms.

"Let's go." Smoke was filtering up the front staircase, so they turned toward the back. As they clattered down the stairs, they could feel the heat from the fire that had gathered around the front of the house.

"Is there anyone else in here?" Sister Mary Frances asked in horror.

"We passed most of them on our way up looking for you." Cole tossed over his shoulder as he led the way down the stairs. He casually stepped over the body that was still lying on the kitchen floor. The nun stopped in her tracks, then lifted her skirts and hopped over it. The rain that greeted them as they tumbled out the back door was welcome after the burning heat from the fire. Chase moaned as it hit his face and partially revived him.

"Ty!" Cat waved from the carriage that was parked at the corner of the wall in the alley. The group ran as best as they could with their burdens and piled in. Cat popped the reins and the team took off.

"Will he live?" Jenny placed her hands on the sides of Chase's face as Marcus lowered him into her lap.

"He's lost a lot of blood. We need to get that bullet out of him."

"I hope he stays unconscious for that," Ty commented from the front beside Cat.

"Voice of experience?" she asked.

"Unfortunately."

Chapter Thirty-three

Marcus kept pressure on the wound as the carriage bounced and careened through the wet streets. Cole kept a firm hold on Amanda who burrowed her head into his shoulder after pulling the sheet over her head.

Soon they were pulling up before the town house and hastily they carried Chase inside. A floral centerpiece crashed to the floor and a fine linen table cloth became blood splattered as they lay him on the dining room table.

"Get me some light!" Marcus commanded. Ty gathered lamps while Cat fetched the young doctor's bag that had been left in the salon earlier that evening. Cole left Amanda in the care of Sister Mary Frances and joined the others in the dining room.

Each face was grim as Marcus silently went to work. Ty held the lamp over his shoulder and Cat wiped the blood that continued to pour forth. Jenny held on to Chase's hand and prayed while Cole watched beside her. Marcus finally held up the slug and flung it on the oriental carpet beneath him. He stuck his finger back into the wound and felt around until he found the source of the blood.

"Jenny, hand me a needle and thread from my bag." Jenny dropped Chase's hand and quickly did as he asked. She found a case inside that contained an assortment of needles already threaded with the narrowest thread she had ever seen. "The smallest one."

The group watched in wide-eyed wonder as Marcus worked with the needle using only the sense of touch.

"Will he lose his arm?" Ty had seen it happen hundreds of times in the war.

"Not if this works," Marcus assured them. He handed the needle to Cat and then requested a larger one from Jenny. He continued to sew until the last layer of skin was tightly closed up. "Find me something to use as a bandage."

Cat immediately went to the linen drawer in the huge hutch that dominated one wall of the dining room. What had once been a stately white tablecloth, with the aid of Chase's knife soon became padding, bandage and sling for Chase's left arm.

"What happens now?" Jenny asked as the group let out a joint sigh of relief.

"We wait." Marcus wiped his forehead and backed away from the table. "Leave him here. I don't want to take a chance on opening up that wound. Just get some pillows and blankets and make him as comfortable as possible."

Jenny looked at the pale face of her husband and smoothed the dark hair back from his forehead. "Thank you, Marcus." She looked at her friend with blue eyes full of gratitude. "For everything you've done."

Marcus suddenly became shy as the group looked at him. "Why don't you get cleaned up? You look like a wreck."

"Thanks a lot." Jenny looked down at her torn damp dress and then ran a hand through the tangled mess of her hair. "I guess you're right."

"Come on, Jenny." Cat took her hand. "Let's get you cleaned up." Jenny looked at Chase lying so still on the table.

"Go. I'll stay with him," Marcus assured her.

"We sure could have used someone like you in the field hospitals," Ty said when the women had left.

"From what I hear there are more wounded than the doctors can keep up with."

"It just makes me realize how lucky I was." Ty looked at his friend lying so silently on the table. "Others weren't." Jake hadn't been, but at least he hadn't suffered.

"Have you told her yet that you're going back?" Cole asked.

Ty looked up in surprise at the older man's comment. "No," he said, shrugging. "She'll just have to understand that I'm honor bound to do it."

Cole nodded in agreement and left to check on Amanda.

He found his niece curled up on the sofa with a shawl thrown over her for warmth. Sister Mary Frances sat in a chair beside her and bestowed a beautiful smile on Cole when he entered the room.

"How is she?"

"Sleeping now, but she has a long road ahead of her."

"What do you mean?" Cole asked. "She's free now."

"Free from the house of evil and the people who held her there, but she's in another kind of prison that doesn't allow for escape."

"What are you talking about?"

"Opium. They fed her opium to control her."

Cole felt the joy that had consumed him at Amanda's rescue drain from his body as the words sank into his consciousness. *Opium.* He ran a hand through his damp, graying curls and looked at the beautiful face that held the innocence of sleep. She didn't even know about her mother's death. How would she ever escape the power than opium held on her body?

"What should I do?"

"Pray, talk to Marcus and pray." Cole was amazed at how serene the sister seemed after the adventures of the night. "There are places that treat these addictions. She can be helped."

"But will she want help?" Cole felt helpless as he looked at Amanda. She had been Bishop's captive for close to four years. How many of those had she spent under the influence of opium?

"She's the only one who can answer that question."

Cole nodded and sank into a chair before the fire.

Jenny, Marcus and Sister Mary Frances talked until the first light of morning brightened the dining room where they sat, waiting for Chase to awaken. Ty and

Cat had gone to their room. The escapades of the night had worn Ty out after his months of imprisonment. Cole watched over Amanda who still slept peacefully on the sofa.

Marcus caught Sister Mary Frances up on his life since leaving the orphanage. It had been a happy one, and his little sister Mary had remained in Denver with their aunt and uncle after he had come east to be a doctor like his father. He had still been in training when the war broke out and with most of the licensed doctors serving with the army had found ways to make himself useful and learned a tremendous amount on his own. He planned on going back to the West when his training was over and starting his own practice in one of the small towns that were constantly opening up in the wild.

Jenny told them of her life since Jamie's death and talked about her children. She missed them dreadfully and couldn't wait to get back to them. She felt as if she had been gone for years instead of just the few weeks it had actually been.

When the full light of morning came through the window facing the street, Chase turned his head as if to escape the light. Jenny and Marcus were at his side in an instant.

"Chase?" Jenny leaned over his chest. Her blond braid slid over her shoulder and swept against the broad expanse of skin. "Can you hear me?"

His lips moved slightly and his head turned.

"Chase?"

The dark lashes fluttered against purplish bruises

the lay beneath his eyes. He blinked and then her face swam into focus as it hovered over his.

"Where are we?"

"Safe. We're safe. All of us."

A quick smile flitted across his regal face. "It's about time." Jenny dropped her head on his chest and wrapped her arms around his head. "Can we go home now?" she heard him ask.

"Just as soon as you're able to travel," Marcus said as he and Sister Mary Frances left the room. Cole met them in the hallway and sheepishly held up the morning newspaper: CONFEDERATE PLOT TO BURN NEW YORK CITY FAILS!

"Apparently we were all part of a Confederate plot to burn down the city," Cole informed them.

"And to think I've never been south of the Mason-Dixon Line," Marcus replied.

Chapter Thirty-four

"Tell Grace I love her and I'll be home as soon as I can."

They were standing on the platform of the train station. Chase's arm was still in a sling but his color had returned to its normal hue, and the arm, while weak, was functioning as it should thanks to the remarkable talents of young Doctor Brown. He had also found a hospital to take Amanda and with Sister Mary Frances's gentle care there was high hopes that the young woman would recover from her addiction. Cole planned on staying until she was able to make the trip with him back to Wyoming.

"Tell Daddy the same," Cat added. She was going with Ty back to the lines to wait out the end of the war.

"Are you sure you want to do this?" Jenny asked them for what seemed like the hundredth time.

"It's what we have to do," Ty assured her.

"We'll be fine as long as we stay together." Cat

linked her hand in her husband's. "We'll be home before the spring roundup."

The all-aboard sounded and hugs were quickly exchanged. "Let's go home," Chase said to Jenny as she clung to Cat. She nodded tearfully and let him guide her onto the train.

Snow was falling as the stage pulled into the town of Laramie. They had telegraphed ahead to tell the ranch of their arrival. Jason was waiting for them with the buggy and soon they were on their way to the ranch. Jason chatted about the escapades that the boys had had while they were gone. They had attached themselves to Zeb and followed him everywhere. Caleb was wearing a wooden leg and had learned to walk on it without crutches. Jason was concerned about him, however, because he was not drawing and no amount of encouragement could get him to pick up a pencil. They had even returned his old sketchbook to him in hopes that it would inspire him but he would have nothing to do with it.

There had been a few raids on the cattle while they were gone. Nothing serious had come of it and since the incidents had stopped with the advent of winter, it was the consensus that whoever was responsible had moved on.

"When do you expect Cole to be back?" Jason asked again as they turned down the drive toward the ranch.

Chase and Jenny exchanged looks from their seat behind Jason. Why was Jason so concerned about Cole's absence? They both sensed that there were things that he wasn't telling them but he had assured them repeatedly that the boys were fine. They would find out soon enough and Jenny felt her heart rise up in her throat as they pulled up in the small valley in front of Grace's cabin just as night was falling.

"Momma! Daddy!" Fox flew out the door and wrapped himself in Jenny's skirts as soon as she alighted from the buggy. She knelt in the snow and wrapped her arms around the small body, burying her nose into the soft swirls of his russet hair.

"Oh my little Fox I missed you so much." She looked up at the porch where Chance peered at her with his startling blue eyes from his hiding place behind Caleb. "Chance?"

Chase knelt beside her and pulled Fox into a hug.

"Go on, go see your momma," Caleb encouraged.

Chance drug his feet but finally came down the steps and let Jenny hug him. She looked tearfully at Chase over the dark head that was held against her shoulder. Chase shrugged. "Just give him some time," he mouthed.

"Momma, Grace is sick but she's getting fat and Storm is sick too. Zeb sleeps with him in the barn but he won't let us." Fox started chattering as he examined the buttons on Chase's coat.

"What?" Jenny looked up at Caleb who shrugged and took a hobbling step away from the door. Grace stepped out onto the porch and Jenny's mouth dropped open.

"Grace?"

"Dang!" Chase remarked as he took in the swelling belly beneath her apron.

"You don't have an idea as to when Cole will be back, do you?" Grace asked sheepishly.

"Better be quick if you want my opinion." Chase flinched as Fox tugged on his arm. Both boys wrapped their arms around his legs and his hands swept through their hair.

Jenny ran up the steps and threw her arms around Grace. "I thought you couldn't!"

"So did I! All these years and it's never happened. And now I'm too old!" Grace dabbed at her eye with her apron. "Damn Cole Larrimore anyway."

"He'll be back soon. And we found Amanda."

"I know. It's so wonderful."

"Wait, what about Storm?" Jenny turned and looked toward the barn.

"He's sick, Jenny," Caleb informed her. "He went down a few days ago. Zeb hasn't left his side and Zane's stayed with him, too."

Jenny took off at a run for the barn with Chase and the boys following her. The familiar smells assaulted her senses as soon as she passed through the wide doors into the warmth.

A few of the mares nickered as she passed their stalls and she unconsciously reached out to stroke soft muzzles that reached toward her in recognition. She walked slowly, her heart racing, her mind dreading the inevitable. Storm Cloud snorted as she went by, tossing his head at her, then looking back through the high bars at the stall next to his.

"Welcome back, Jenny." Zane opened the door of the stall for her. She squeezed his hand as she went by.

Storm lay on his side taking in short bursts of air. The sound of his labored breathing reminded Jenny of the steam engine that had carried them west from the city. Zeb sat beside him, stroking the arch of the stallion's neck.

"He's been waitin' for you, Miz Jenny."

"Thank you, Zeb."

Jenny knelt in the straw beside the noble animal. He recognized her and moved his head as if to rise but then dropped it again. She gathered his head in her lap and stroked his forehead. "I'm here, Storm. I'm here."

"He wants to let go; he just can't for some reason." Zeb stood with head bowed beside the animal.

"He's a fighter." Jenny dropped a kiss between Storm's ears. "It's all right now. I'm here. You can go."

"Daddy, is Storm going to die?" Chance asked.

"It's his time to go." Chase knelt and wrapped his arms around the boys who stood on either side of him. "He's waiting for your mother to help him."

Jenny bit her lip and looked at Chase with blue eyes full of tears. "He needs help, Jenny."

Zeb and Zane nodded in agreement.

"Take them away."

"Come on, boys. Let's go." Chase turned the boys toward the door. "It's the right thing."

"I know."

Zane laid his gun in the straw next to Jenny and followed Zeb and Chase who were trying to quiet the boys who wanted to see and wanted to know what was happening. The sound of the door closing behind them sounded so final to Jenny.

"Thank you, Storm." Jenny willed back the sobs that threatened to erupt as her mind raced back to a day from long ago. "You saved my life, remember? You found me out on the plains and took me to Gray Horse. Dad would have been so proud of you." The dark eyes of the stallion were glazed and distant. "He was proud of you. So proud. I remember how he used to ride you, how you would strut when he was on your back, the both of you just showing off for each other and Momma and whoever else happened to be around." The tears were streaming and she didn't care. "I know you've missed him. I miss him. Oh, how I miss him, and Momma and Jamie . . ." Jenny looked up at the ceiling. "He's waiting on you, Storm. I bet if you close your eyes you can see him." Jenny eased out from beneath the noble head and picked up the gun. "Can you see him?" She cocked the gun and flinched as the bullet slid into the chamber. "Storm, go to Dad."

Zane and Zeb picked up the boys as the shot echoed through the night and carried them into Grace's cabin. They remained amazingly quiet although Chance's eyes over Zeb's shoulders were wide and tearful. Chase smiled reassuringly at his son until he disappeared into the cabin then he looked up into the night sky at the gentle flakes that swirled around in the darkness before falling gently to the ground. He closed his eyes and remained with his face uplifted sensing rather than feeling the soft impact of the snow as it landed on his face and melted against the warmth of his skin.

Arms wrapped around his waist and a blond head buried itself under his shoulder. "He was all I had left." Jenny's voice vibrated against his Adam's apple.

"I know." His arms wrapped around her and held her tightly against his chest. "But we have each other, and the boys."

"I love you, Chase." Her hand found the opening between the buttons on his shirt and crept inside to rest against his chest where his heart beat firmly against the palm of her hand.

"I love you, Jenny."

They carried Storm's body on the back of an old wagon to the lake where Chase and Jenny had spent many an afternoon. The day was crisp and clear without a cloud in the sky. The men solemnly gathered wood and placed it reverently beneath the bed of the wagon after unhitching the horses that had pulled it there through the light dusting of snow. Chase lit a torch and joined Jenny and the boys as the flames flared into life. Behind them stood Jason, Grace, Caleb, Zane and Zeb with heads bowed in respect for the great stallion.

"Why are we burning Storm?" Chance asked.

"Why?" Fox added.

"It's not Storm anymore. It's just his body." Chase knelt beside his sons as the flames licked up around the wagon. "We're setting his spirit free so he can run like he used to before he got sick."

The dry wood of the wagon caught and the gray coat of the horse's body became lost in the towering inferno of flame and smoke. The wind caught the smoke as it rose into the sky and bent it to its will, taking it toward the east.

"Go, Storm. He's waiting for you," Jenny said to the smoke as it spiraled away with the spirit of the great horse riding the crest of the wind toward the plains of Iowa. Where her father was waiting.